Beyond The Horizon

Beyond The Horizon

Short Stories From Contemporary Indonesia

edited and introduced by
David T. Hill

Published by

MONASH ASIA INSTITUTE

First published 1998 by
Monash Asia Institute
Monash University
Clayton, Victoria 3168
Australia

National Library of Australia Cataloguing-in-Publication Data:

Beyond the horizon: short stories from contemporary Indonesia

Bibliography
ISBN 0 7326 1164 4.
ISSN 0727 6680

1. Short stories, Indonesian - Translations into English. I. Hill, David T. II. Monash University. Monash Asia Institute. (Series: Monash papers on Southeast Asia; 46).

899.2213010802

Printed by Waterwheel Press Pty Ltd
139 Chetwynd Street, North Melbourne

For more information about this and other publications, write to:
The Publications Officer
Monash Asia Institute
Monash University
Clayton, VIC 3168, Australia

This book is dedicated to Dr Soebardi, Dr Soepomo, Dr Soewito-Santoso, and Mrs Yohanni Johns, whose commitment as language teachers and guides to what lay beyond the horizon has had such a lasting influence upon so many of us.

David T. Hill is a Senior Lecturer in Southeast Asian Studies, and a Research Fellow in the Asia Research Centre on Social, Economic and Political Change, Murdoch University, Perth, where he teaches courses on Indonesian language, Southeast Asian Literature, and Indonesian Culture and Politics. He is author of *The Press in New Order Indonesia* and editor of Ruth Havelaar's *Quartering: A Story of a Marraige in Indonesia During the Eighties.* Together with Krishna Sen, he is currently writing a book on culture, media and politics in Indonesia.

Contents

Acknowledgments

The genesis of this anthology lies in a series of workshops held by three friends and colleagues in the Department of Indonesian Languages and Literatures at the Australian National University, Canberra, during 1979–80. Dubbing ourselves 'Rats' (for reasons best not dwelt upon!) Jan Lingard, Marian May and I worked through a selection of short stories, as an exercise in sharpening our language and translation skills.

In December 1980 I left for two years doctoral fieldwork in Indonesia, during which time I met many of the authors whose works we had translated and got a strong sense of their support for a larger project. After fieldwork, however, the demands of thesis writing and teaching at Monash University left little time to continue the translation project. Marian began teaching in the Centre for Development Studies at the ANU; Jan continued her interest in translation, initially at ANU and now at the University of Sydney, producing three impressive publications.

In 1990 I commenced teaching a course on Southeast Asian Literature at Murdoch University, which made me acutely aware of the paucity of suitable material in English. The original translations produced by Jan, Marian and I remained largely untouched until in 1992 when I introduced a new advanced Indonesian course at Murdoch designed to develop interpreting and translating skills. This provided an ideal opportunity for me, with the assistance of the students in this course, to review contemporary translation theories, reconsider the practical problems posed by literary translation, while surveying the range of short fiction produced in Indonesia. All of the students in this course, in their own ways, have helped me work through some of the problems of translating Indonesian literature. This current volume is one practical outcome of that advanced Indonesian course and it is with pride that I include here translations by Kenneth Eu, Bishi Leathem, Amanda Miller, Meta Mulia, Sam Nunn, Tom Plummer, and Simone Robinson, all former students, whose translations were produced as a direct result of course seminars.

Thus this anthology represents the culmination of endeavours, of both learning and teaching, a collaboration between colleagues, teachers and students. Commenced more than 15 years ago, it involves contributions from a range of translators, with differing approaches and diverse experience. As editor, I have generally attempted to respect the interpretations made by the original translators, although in some cases I have intervened more directly to revise early drafts.

Yet in approaching this task, I have been conscious of the interpretive role of the author, translator, editor and reader, each of whom embarks upon their task from differing departure points if moving towards a common goal. It is not always a harmonious labour, as they re-plough the same furrow made more complex by each re-working. It was not uncommon for our Murdoch translation workshops to spend an hour debating only a handful of key paragraphs, in a passionate but productive clash of principles, with each participant confident of their own reading of the original and rendering of the translation. It was a recognition of the complexities of the process of reading and translating, where respect was earned by, and given to, the arguments and analyses presented as much as to the end result achieved. Such clashes of contrasting approaches may be evident in the collection which follows but should not, I hope, detract from its cohesion and value.

An anthology of translations is a work of considerable collaboration. Each of the authors has entrusted their original Indonesian-language story to a translator, often personally unknown to them, for rendering into English. It is a delicate and difficult process, with both the author and translator often judged (sometimes blamed!) for what is a shared product. It is made more complex by the further intervention of an editor. I thank sincerely all authors and translators for their willingness to contribute to this venture, and apologise to all should they feel unfairly represented by any violence done to their work, either by translator or editor.

The editors and staff of *Horison* magazine, in which most of the Indonesian material translated here first appeared, deserve my deep appreciation. But more than that, I want to acknowledge my respect for their commitment over three decades to the production of the country's longest-running literary magazine, a significant feat, as anyone who has tried to publish a 'little magazine', fraught with the constant threat of financial insolvency, will appreciate. It has not been a journey without controversy, but *Horison* deserves to be valued as a rare achievement in the history of Indonesian publishing and Indonesian literature.

At various times John McGregor and Mandy Miller helped me considerably with this, as with several other projects, lightening the load and making it more pleasurable. Thanks too to Irene Finlay for help with typing and word processing problems. The staff at the H.B. Jassin Literary Documentation Centre, Jakarta, particularly Dr Jassin himself and Mr Oyon Sofyan, have encouraged me in this as in other ventures, and provided a variety of information and materials over many years, for which I thank them.

I particularly wish to acknowledge my considerable debt to Ruth Stone who has laboured long and hard on this project. Her suggestions with translations, attention to detail in text-editing, and precision in research (particularly on the authors' biographical notes), have all been executed competently and efficiently, and offered with cheerful good humour, making her not only indispensable, but a genuine delight to work with.

It is with gratitude that I acknowledge the crucial financial support of the Australia-Indonesia Institute, under its programs to promote closer bilateral relations by, among other ways, making the literatures of each more accessible to the other. The School of Humanities at Murdoch University, too, helped me conclude the project by providing resources and financial support. Considerable work on the project in Indonesia was conducted during research leave, for which I thank my colleagues upon whose shoulders extra responsibilities invariably fall at such times.

Appreciation too is due to the publishers of the various magazines and journals in which some of these translations have previously appeared: *Review of Indonesian and Malaysian Affairs,* ('Jakarta', 'The General Smiles on 17th August'), *Indonesia* ('The Factory'), *Span* ('Matias Akankari') and *Tenggara* ('Generals', 'The critic'). I thank various anonymous 'readers' from these publications for their comments, and acknowledge particularly Mansur Medeiros' wise advice on parts of 'Jakarta'.

Finally, as with everything in life, my time on this project has been immeasurably enriched by the pleasures of sharing with Krishna and Su-mita, for whom no 'thank you' would be adequate.

David T. Hill

Notes on Authors

A. A. Navis. Born in Padangpanjang, West Sumatra, on 17 November 1924, Haji Ali Akbar Navis was the eldest of 12 siblings. He was educated at the progressive nationalist secondary college, INS Kayutanam, Sumatra, which has produced a string of social and political leaders since its founding in the 1930s. Since 1969 he has been head of the school foundation board. In addition, Navis has been editor-in-chief of the local Padang paper *Semangat* (1971–72), and a member of the West Sumatra Regional Assembly (1971–82).

As the author of a dozen books and recipient of the Minister for Education and Culture's Arts Award (1979), he is perhaps best known for his 1956 award-wining short story 'Robohnya Surau Kami' (The Decline of our Local Mosque). His more recent works have won short story competitions sponsored by Radio Nederland Wereldomroep (1975) and *Femina* (*Feminine*) entertainment magazine (1979).

Amri Marzali. Amri Marzali received an anthropology degree from Gadjah Mada University (UGM) in 1973, and then studied for a Masters degree at the Australian National University (ANU) (1981–83). In 1992 he completed a PhD in anthropology at Boston University.

Amri Marzali now teaches Anthropology at the University of Indonesia (UI) and the Bogor Institute of Agriculture, and has a special interest in forest conservation.

He explained his writing of 'Support Our Troops' as follows: 'I wrote the story when I was in the USA in 1990–92, in the midst of writing my PhD in Anthropology. At that time there were lots of Americans, including me too, who did not agree with Iraq's impropriety against Kuwait—a sovereign nation recognised by the UN. I certainly respected the right of Americans to feel proud of their victory against Iraq.

'Nonetheless, in that pride I sensed an attitude of excess amongst Americans. Iraq was not an equal foe for the Americans and their allies. Also, I felt something which I could not express objectively, that is, a racialist and anti-Arab attitude which was bound up in that pride. Yet, in my heart, I could sense such an attitude.

'So my short story could possibly be regarded as a cynical response to the attitude of Americans in celebrating their victory over Iraq'.

Chairul Harun. Born in August 1940 in Kayutanam, West Sumatra, Chairul Harun was educated in the Faculty of Social and Political Sciences and Mass Communications at Ibnu Chaldun University in Jakarta.

During his career he has served as a transmigration officer in Palu, Central Sulawesi (1961–63), been a journalist with the daily *Aman Makmur*, Pekanbaru (1963–65), and *Angkatan Bersenjata*, Padang (1967–70), correspondent for Central Sumatra with the magazine *Tempo* (1971–79), and member of the editorial board of the daily Padang newspaper, *Singgalang*.

Chairul Harun has also taught theatre studies at the Padang Panjang Art Academy and has been active generally in promoting traditional arts in Western Sumatra. In addition to serving as head of the Indonesian National Arts Coordination Body for West Sumatra, he has also led the Padang Culture and Literature Committee.

Many of his articles and essays have been published in daily newspapers. His novel *Warisan* (*The Inheritance*) was commended in the Jakarta Arts Council Novel Composition in 1976 and subsequently received an award from the Education and Culture Department Book Award Committee in 1979. Chairul Harun's poems have appeared in an anthology entitled *Monumen Safari* (1966), and he has written numerous children's stories.

Gerson Poyk. Born on 16 June 1931 at Namodale-Baa, Rote, in the Lesser Sunda (Nusa Tenggara) island chain linking Java to Papua, Gerson Poyk was schooled in the neighbouring islands of Flores, Alor, Timor and finally in Surabaya, East Java, before teaching on other outer islands of Indonesia, on Ternate and Sumbawa, till 1958. Since then he has mostly lived on Java and Bali, though his work as a peripatetic journalist has involved long and frequent travels throughout Indonesia and abroad.

A highly-regarded feature writer, he has won a major national award, the Adinegoro Prize for Best Journalist, in both 1985 and 1986. His no-less-significant achievements as a writer of fiction have been acknowledged with several national plaudits, such as the annual award offered by the literary magazine *Sastra* (Literature) in 1961, and the prestigious ASEAN literary prize in 1989.

In the early 1980s Gerson was involved in establishing a small National Studies Institute (*Institut Studi Nasional*) to foster research into social and political issues. More recently, he has been attempting to establish a private college for the training of film workers, to stimulate a critical tradition independent of state-sponsored cinematography colleges.

Three of his stories are included in this anthology. In them, his concerns are for those without power in his society, the minority groups—sexual, ethnic, social, political, economic—whose voices are rarely heard. 'Matias Akankari' particularly, highlights the cultural and political ravine that separates ethnic minorities from the metropolitan superculture of Jakarta. In much of his writing the style is 'naturalistic', often heavily sarcastic, sharpened by pathos. One of only a handful of authors from Eastern Indonesia, it may be that his sympathies for the underdog have been sharpened by his own experience as an outsider in a Javanese-dominated society.

Hamsad Rangkuti. Born on 7 May 1943 in Titikuning, Medan, North Sumatra, Hasyim Rangkuti (as he was originally named) was the fourth of six children in a struggling working class family. His mother was a labourer on a tobacco plantation and his father a nightwatchman.

As a young writer, Hamsad (as he became known) aligned himself with those writers critical of the Indonesian Communist Party and the cultural organisation, the Institute of People's Culture (*Lekra*), which had the support of the Left. In 1964, he moved to Jakarta, working with the literary magazine *Sastra* (*Literature*) in 1968, before moving to *Horison* in 1969. He has remained with *Horison* ever since, and is currently the editor-in-chief.

In 1980 his first novel, *Ketika Lampu Berwarna Merah* (*When the Light Turns Red*), was runner-up in the Jakarta Arts Council novel-writing competition. It was published in 1988 with the revised title *Lampu Merah* (*Red Light*). In 1982 his first two collections of short stories appeared, *Lukisan Perkawinan* (*Pictures of Marriage*) and *Cemara* (*Pine tree*), followed in 1985 by a novella, *Klamono*, set in Irian Jaya.

Another story by Hamsad Rangkuti, 'The General Smiles on 17th August' follows 'Long life for Mr Joyokoyoroyo and his Cronies'.

Jasso Winarto. Born 23 August 1942 in Sragen, Central Java, Jasso Winarto completed an economics degree at Gadjah Mada University (1968) and was later appointed editor of the magazine *Eksekutif*, and editor of the daily newspaper *Media Indonesia* (1989–90).

His drama, *Mimi Pelacurku* (*My Whore, Mimi*) (1972), won an encouragment award at the Jakarta Arts Council Drama composition contest in 1972. A film script by him (*Wasdri*) and another film which he directed (*Bandot*), have both been banned by the Indonesian Department of Information.

He was removed as executive editor of *Media Indonesia* in 1990 after the Department of Information issued the paper with a 'stern warning' over a controversial report comparing President Suharto with Pharoah. He is currently Executive Director of Sigma Research Institute Inc., an market research and investment advisory service in Jakarta.

M. Fudoli Zaini/ Mohamad Fudoli. (Since 1980 Mohamad Fudoli has used the name M. Fudoli Zaini) Born 8 July 1942 in

Sumenup, Madura, he attended high school in Pamekasan, Madura and graduated from the Sunan Ampel IAIN (State Institute for Islamic Studies) in Surabaya in 1966. In 1968 he continued his education abroad at Al-Azhar University in Cairo in the Institute of Islamic Studies (studying history) and the Institute of Arabic Studies (studying literature), gaining a Masters Degree and then PhD. He previously worked in the Indonesian Embassy in Cairo, and now teaches at the Sunan Ampel IAIN in Surabaya.

His short story 'Kemarau' (Drought) won a consolation prize from the Radio Nederland Wereldomroep Golden Windmill Literary Contest in 1975. It has been translated into Dutch. Other stories have won various prizes in *Horison*. He received the Department of Education and Culture's Book Award for 1985 for his collection of short stories, *Kota Kelahiran* (*Town of my Birth*).

When asked about his motivation for writing 'Drought', he replied, 'I wanted to say that spiritual drought is far more concerning that the kind of physical drought we normally experience. Overcoming physical drought is easier and more straightforward than overcoming spiritual drought. The tragedies in our life are more likely to be caused by being overwhelmed by spiritual drought' (Pers. comm, 26 December 1995)

Another of his stories 'Cancer' appears later in this anthology, under the name M. Fudoli Zaini.

Moes Loindong. Born in Tataaran village (Minahasa) on 9 May 1941, Moes Loindong completed senior high school and spent two years at the University of Central Sulawesi (UNSULTENG) in Manado.

Moes Loindong participated in the Sulawesi uprising known as *Permesta* in the late 1950s serving in the rebel forces from 1957 until the end of the uprising in 1961. At present he has his own small business in Surabaya.

Having begun writing fiction and poetry as a young schoolboy, he continued until the mid 1970s, when for a decade he found himself too busy. But after suffering health problems, his doctor recommended he return to his hobby for therapeutic reasons. And it worked!

M. Shoim Anwar. Born 16 May 1963 in Jombang, East Java, M. Shoim Anwar completed studies at the Surabaya State Teachers' Training College in Indonesian Literature and Language. He has been active in local literary activities in his home town and has been editor of the cultural magazine *Kalimas*. At present he is concentrating on writing and has appeared at various events to read his short stories and at seminars as a speaker.

M. Shoim Anwar's short stories have been published in various campus magazines, newspapers and magazines. In three consecutive years (1988, 1989, 1990) he won the Surabaya Arts Council short story competition. His short stories have also appeared in the collection *Cerita Pendek dari Surabaya* (*Short Stories from Surabaya*). He has published several novels and short story collections.

Nh. Dini. Born Nurhayati \Srihardini in Semarang on 29 February 1936, Dini is arguably Indonesia's leading woman author. Her works have been translated into Japanese, Dutch, German, French, English and Russian.

She established her national reputation as a competent writer of short fiction at the age of 20 with her first published collection *Dua Dunia* (*Two worlds*) (1956), reinforcing this with the serialisation of her short novel *Hati yang damai* (*Peaceful Heart*) four years later.

Married to a French diplomat, Yves Coffin, in 1960, she lived abroad for two decades in Japan, Cambodia, the Philippines, the USA and France, until her divorce and return to Indonesia in 1980.

Her publications include the best-seller, *Pada Sebuah Kapal* (*On a Boat*) (1973), *La Barka* (1975), *Keberangkatan* (*Departure*) (1977), and *Namaku Hiroko* (*My Name is Hiroko*) (1979), and a series of autobiographical tales beginning with *Sebuah Lorong di Kotaku* (*A Laneway in my Town*) (1978). Since her return to Indonesia she has published a biography of the poet Amir Hamzah, *Amir Hamzah: Pangeran dari Seberang* (*The Prince from Across the Water*) (1981), several collections of short stories, such as *Tuileries* (1982), and major novels like *Orang-orang Tran* (*The Transmigrants*) (1985) and *Jalan Bandungan* (*Bandungan Road*) (1989).

In 1990 she received an Arts Award from the Indonesian Department of Education and Culture. She now lives in her home-town of Semarang, where she has established a children's lending library, as part of her efforts to promote the reading habit among young people.

Pamusuk Eneste. Born into the Nasution clan of the Batak ethnic group in Padang Matinggi, North Sumatra on 19 September 1951, Pamusuk has chosen not to use the clan name, adopting instead 'Eneste', derived from the Indonesian pronunciation of its major consonants, ie, NaSuTion = N.S.T.= eN-eS-Te.

The death of his school-teacher father in 1954 meant the family had to subsist on a minimal pension augmented by the modest income from his mother's petty trading ventures. As a school-child Pamusuk left Sumatra in 1968, and followed his older married sister to Jakarta where he continued his senior high school education. He studied under eminent scholar H.B. Jassin in the Department of Indonesian Literature at the University of Indonesia, Jakarta from 1971–77.

Pamusuk Eneste was editor in chief of the campus magazine *Tifa Sastra* (*Literary Beat*) (1972–78) and the cultural affairs editor of the campus newspaper *Salemba* (named after the locale of the university) (1976–78). He also taught Indonesian at the St. Carolus Nursing Academy in Jakarta during 1978, prior to taking up a position as Lecturer in Indonesia at Hamburg University, West Germany (1978–81). On his return to Indonesia in 1982 he became editor of Indonesian Language and Literature with the largest publishing house in Indonesia, P T Gramedia, as well as lecturer in the Faculty of Arts at the Pakuan University, Bogor.

During his period in Hamburg, his short stories (including the two translated here) frequently appeared in *Horison*. Many were collected in *Orang-orang Terasing* (*The Alienated*) (1984) and *Isabel Blumenkol* (a name) (1986).

He has also edited an impressive range of valuable collections on Indonesian literature, including: *Leksikon Kesusastraan Indonesia Modern* (*A Lexicon of Modern Indonesian Literature*) (1981), *Proses Kreatif* (*The Creative Process*) (Volumes 1 and 2, 1983 and 1984), *Mengapa dan Bagaimana Saya Mengarang* (*How and Why I Write*) (1986), and *Ikhtisar Kesusastraan Indonesia Modern* (*A Guide to Modern Indonesian Literature*) (1988).

Raised as a Protestant, Pamusuk is married to a Javanese Catholic graduate in Chemistry from Gadjah Mada University in Yogyakarta.

The italicised dialogue in 'The Critic' was in German when the story was published in *Horison*.

Putu Wijaya. Born in Puri Anom, Tabanan, Bali, on 11 April 1944, Putu Wijaya graduated in Law from Gadjah Mada University (UGM) in 1969, and during his studies joined Bengkel Theatre (1967), established by Indonesia's most famous playwright, Rendra. From 1971–79 he worked as an editor of the country's leading news weekly magazine *Tempo*, and then became managing editor of *Zaman* entertainment magazine (1979–85)

In Jakarta he began the drama group 'Theatre Mandiri', for which he is best known. The troupe has performed regularly at the Jakarta Arts Centre and other prestigious venues around the capital and several other Indonesian major cities, as well as touring in the USA in 1991. More recently Putu Wijaya has moved into television and film, establishing a production company, which has produced several television series. He has won three prestigious Citra Awards (the Indonesian Academy Awards) for his scenarios.

Putu Wijaya participated in the International Writing Program at Iowa University (1974–75), the World Theatre Festival in Nancy, France, and the Third Horizonte Festival in West Berlin (1985). He spent 1985–88 in America as a Fulbright Scholar, including a period as guest lecturer at the University of

Wisconsin (1985–86). He spent 1991–92 in the Centre for Southeast Asian Studies in Kyoto University on a Japan Foundation Fellowship. He has received awards in many drama, novel and short story competitions, including the ASEAN Literature prize, the SEA Write Award, and the Arts Award from the Minister for Education and Culture (1991).

He has published a long list of novels and short story collections, all to critical acclaim. His stories have been translated into Dutch, Russian, French, German, Japanese, Arabic, Thai and a collection has been translated into English as *Bomb: Indonesian Short Stories by Putu Wijaya* (1988).

'A Letter' was the first of many of his stories to be published in *Horison*.

Safron Rasyidi Sidal. Born in Yogyakarta on 8 March 1963, Safron Rasyidi Sidal began writing for local publications while in high school. He completed a degree in Theatre Studies in the Department of Dramaturgy at the Indonesian Institute of the Arts, Yogyakarta. Since 1993 he has been working in the Directorate of the Arts in the Indonesian Government's Department of Education and Culture, Jakarta.

Sides Sudyarto DS. Born on 14 July 1942 in Tegal, Central Java into an impoverished village community, Sides Sudyarto DS's formal education ceased during High School. On the back cover of his first published collection of poems, *Kebatinan* (*Spirituality*) (1975), he declared his resentment that universities and institutes of formal learning offered no opportunities to those from under-privileged backgrounds. His 'almamater' was instead *Horison* which, together with rival journals *Sastra* and *Budaya Jaya* and daily newspapers, provided outlets for his writings. He has been a journalist with Indonesia's leading daily newspaper *Kompas*, editor of the entertainment magazine *Jakarta Jakarta*, editor with *Sinar Harapan* book publishers, managing editor of the popular psychology and lifestyle magazine *Tiara*, and editor of the daily newspaper *Media Indonesia*.

Quiet, with a wry sense of humour, he is perhaps best known as a poet, with several collections published in the 1970s and 1980s, together with a novel, *Rona Hati Kekasih* (*The Colour of a Lover's Heart*) (1986). Much of his poetry has been informed by religious, particularly Islamic, themes, and his long interest in Western philosophy.

When asked why wrote of 'The Lebaran Prayers', he responded 'I wrote this short story, at least in part to illustrate that such is the fate of ordinary people who are victims of ignorance and poverty'.

Totilawati Tjitrawasita. Born on 1 June 1945 in Kediri, East Java, Totilawati Tjitrawasita was the second of 13 children. In 1967 she became assistant editor of the Javanese-language weekly magazine *Jaya Baya*, co-founded by her father, and in 1970 she won the national Zakse Award for young journalists.

Her collection of short stories, *Sebuah Cinta Sekolah Rakyat* (*A School Crush*) (in which 'Jakarta' appeared) was awarded first prize for fiction by the Book of the Year Foundation in 1977. Her contribution to the Arts, including her membership of the Surabaya Arts Council, was recognised in 1979 when she was made an honorary citizen of the City of Surabaya.

'Jakarta', like many of her Indonesian-language stories, had initially appeared in Javanese (in 1972), for she wrote in both these languages with equal passion until her untimely death of cancer on 10 August 1982 at the age of 37.

Wildan Yatim. Born 11 July 1933 in Padang Sidempuan, North Sumatra, Wildan Yatim was and raised in West Sumatra. He attended senior high school in Jakarta and then studied at the Bandung Institute of Technology, graduating with a Biology degree in 1961. He was awarded a Doctorate from Padjajaran University in Bandung in 1988.

He was a member of the Muslim Students' Association (HMI), editor of the magazine *Scientiae* (1958) and the West Java edition of the influential weekly newspaper *Mahasiswa Indonesia*. During the political turbulence of 1966–68 he was active in KASI, the Indonesian Academics' Action Front in

Bandung. He later went on to become lecturer in the Medical Faculty at Andalas University and subesequently Deputy Dean of the School of Mathematics and Physical Sciences there. At present Wildan Yatim teaches in the Faculty of Medicine at Padjajaran University in Bandung.

His short story 'Surau Baru' (New Prayer House) won a *Horison* award in 1969, while another, 'Perburuan Penghabisan' (The End of Persecution) won the consolation prize in the *Horison* Short Story Contest 1977–78. His novel *Pergolakan* (*Turbulence*) (1974) won third prize in the Jakarta Arts Council International Book Year Committee Novel Contest in 1972 and in 1975 this same novel won the Education and Culture Department Book Award.

Y. B. Mangunwijaya. Born on 6 May 1929 in Ambarawa, Central Java, Y. B. Mangunwijaya completed studies at the 'Sancti Pauli' Institute for Philosophy and Theology in Yogyakarta (1959), and then took a degree in architecture in West Germany (1966). In 1978 he was awarded a fellowship at the Aspen Institute for Humanistic Studies in Colorado, United States.

His short story *Kapten Tahir* (*Captain Tahir*) won a consolation prize in the Radio Nederland Wereldomroep Golden Windmill Contest in 1975. His book *Sastra dan Religiositas* (*Literature and Religiosity*) (1982) won the Jakarta Arts Council Literature award, and his novel *Burung-burung Manyar* (*The Weaverbirds*) (1981) won the ASEAN Literature Prize in 1983, and was published in English translation in 1991. A Catholic priest and social activist who is regarded widely as an influential moral conscience in Indonesia, he has worked with street-kids in Yogyakarta, where he is currently developing a small experimental primary school for the very poor.

Notes on Translators

Kenneth Eu Tuck Wah was born in Malaysia and completed his Bachelor of Commerce degree at Murdoch University in 1995.

Bishi Leathem holds a Bachelor of Asian Studies degree (which included two semesters study in Indonesia) and is currently working for the Australian Agency for International Development.

Jan Lingard is a lecturer in Indonesian in the School of Asian Studies, University of Sydney. She has translated *The Outlaw* by Mochtar Lubis (1987), *Eyewitness* (with Bibi Langker and Suzan Piper) by Seno Gumira Ajidarma (1995) and *Diverse Lives: Contemporary Stories from Indonesia* (1995).

Marian May is Associate Lecturer (Academic Skills), Graduate Studies in Demography, in the Research School of Social Sciences, Australian National University. She has a Bachelor of Arts (Asian Studies) with Honours from ANU, a Diploma of Education from Canberra College of Advanced Education and Graduate Diploma in Applied Linguistics from the Northern Territory University.

Mandy Miller holds a Bachelor of Asian Studies degree (which included two semesters study in Indonesia) and is currently the Publications Coordinator at the Asia Research Centre, Murdoch University.

Meta Mulia is an Indonesian student completing a Bachelor's degree in Psychology and Asian Studies at Murdoch University, Western Australia.

Sam Nunn completed a Bachelor of Asian Studies degree at Murdoch University and obtained his Master of Arts in Development Studies in 1996. He has studied in both Indonesia and Malaysia and has most recently worked as a hospital interpreter in Perth.

Tom Plummer has an Honours Degree in Southeast Asian Studies from Murdoch University, having spent three semesters studying in Indonesia. He is a founder of the Perth based SamBung Foundation, a 'grass-roots' community organisation building links between cultural workers and students in Indonesia and Australia.

Simone Robinson completed a Bachelor of Asian Studies Degree (in Southeast Asian Studies) in 1993, which included a year's study in Indonesia. After gaining a Graduate Diploma in Education in 1995 specialising in languages other than English, she commenced teaching Indonesian at Perth College.

Introduction

For most Australians Indonesia lies just beyond the horizon, geographically and metaphysically: alluring, but illusively out of reach. The holiday destination for millions of foreign tourists each year proves a seductive enigma to most who are drawn by images of lazy tropical beaches, exotic temples, friendly people and natural grandeur. For Australians it seems to hold a particular fascination, our fourth most popular holiday destination, only just behind the traditional (English-speaking) favourites: New Zealand, USA and Britain. In 1995 nearly 350,000 Australian tourists were drawn to Indonesia, where they constitute the fifth largest national grouping, and the largest from outside Asia. In addition, Australian business people are increasingly looking to Indonesia as a vast and increasingly affluent market. The number of Australian students undertaking part of their university studies in Indonesia, too, is growing year by year. For young Australians particularly, the tourist centres of Bali and Yogyakarta hold an irresistible attraction, shimmering enticingly upon the horizon.

This small collection of stories attempts to take the reader beyond the horizon into a literary realm conjured up by a sample of some of Indonesia's most creative contemporary authors. Like President Suharto's New Order itself, the anthology spans the past three decades, when the short story was the most popular literary genre in Indonesia. Arranged chronologically in the order of their initial publication, the tales give an impression of both the changing styles and the enduring pre-occupations of the country's authors.

This introduction will attempt to provide a context for these stories by describing something of the history of Indonesia's most prestigious literary magazine, in which most appeared. It will then range over some of the key issues which emerge from a study of the fiction that follows.

Horison

All of the stories in this anthology have been published (and, as far as can be ascertained, written) since the assumption of power in Indonesia by Major-General Suharto and his 'New Order'. After a putsch on 1 October 1965 was blamed on the Indonesian Communist Party (PKI), the army moved in the early weeks of October 1965 to eliminate the Communist Party in what was one of the bloodiest pogroms in post-war history.[1] The events of 1965–66 irrevocably changed Indonesian political, social and cultural life, leaving an indelible mark upon the nation and the New Order state. It was a watershed in the production of literature just as much as in the conduct of politics.

Suharto's ascendancy brought with it the release from prison of several dozen anti-Sukarnoist political prisoners, many held under martial law provisions since the late 1950s. One of the most vociferous and internationally-connected was the journalist, editor and author Mochtar Lubis, who, for his criticisms of President Sukarno, had been held from 1956 under house arrest and since 1961 in prison. Lubis had become a symbol of opposition to Sukarno and the Indonesian Communist Party in the arts and the media. He was honoured and respected by the student leaders and activists whose mobilisation of tens of thousands of young people on the streets provided the images of legitimacy so essential to the New Order's claim to represent a popular movement against the Left.

Among the anti-Sukarno student leaders who approached Mochtar Lubis prior to his release in 1966 was Soe Hok Djin (later to take the name Arief Budiman), who impressed upon the detainee the need for a fresh literary magazine to demonstrate the new mood in literary circles. Lubis's release in mid-1966 provided the impetus for the establishment of a path-breaking

1 The most comprehensive review on the controversial events of 1965 is Cribb, 1990 while a useful general overview of post-war Indonesian history is Cribb and Brown, 1995.

monthly cultural and literary journal, forged by an alliance of young generation cultural activists and highly respected senior authors and literary figures, such as the literary historian, H.B. Jassin. *Horison* (*Horizon*), as the modest black-and-white publication was titled, was to set the standard against which all subsequent artistic periodicals have been measured.[2] It was no coincidence that the journal's founders sought, by the very name of their magazine, to challenge Indonesian readers to look beyond the constraints of their own intellectual and creative horizons.

In its first edition in July 1966, *Horison* defined itself a 'monthly magazine of literature in the broadest sense'. It was committed to 'stimulating ideas and experiments in the field of literature specifically, culture generally'. Apart from the works of Indonesians, it promised to 'always strive to present the works of artists and intellectuals from outside Indonesia, especially works which articulate new thoughts and experiments in the field of culture' (*Horison*, 1966:3). In his introductory editorial, editor-in-chief Mochtar Lubis defined the new course for the magazine towards 'freedom and constructive values', constituting a clear break with the 'monolithic power' of the past (a thinly-veiled criticism of the formerly influential left-wing Institute for People's Culture, *Lekra*, which had been proscribed only four months earlier).[3] He called upon readers to 'leave the narrow space which till now has imprisoned our spirit and thoughts (and) let us free ourselves from the shackles and traps of slogans of a chauvinistic and xenophobic nature' (*Horison*, 1966:3). Its stark matt black-and-white cover, clumsy typography and yellowish paper were typical of low-cost publications at a time when newsprint was rationed and of dubious quality. But its emergence was widely endorsed by those intellectuals, artists and writers who had aligned themselves with the emerging New Order.[4]

---

2 Parts of the following discussion have appeared in Hill, 1993 and 1994.
3 On *Lekra*, see Foulcher 1986.
4 For a description of *Horison* during the early years, see Chambert-Loir 1972 and Hume 1968.

As the first New Order literary magazine and the one most closely identified with the '1966 Generation' of student activists and artists, *Horison* was self-consciously secular, and almost as strong in its anti-communism as in its opposition to Sukarnoist populism. But its humanist commitment and a growing concern among staff about army-instigated human rights abuses meant that a number of stories sympathetic to the victims of the anti-communist purges were published.[5] Even such guarded criticism of the methods used to suppress political opponents of the New Order required some courage since often the barest hint of association with *Lekra*, the Indonesian Communist Party or its various organisations was enough to justify one's detention without trial.

The ruthless dismantling of *Lekra* and the execution or detention of thousands of its members had left a discernible void in critical artistic production which was to last well into the 1980s. Frank, direct criticism in the Socialist Realist tradition, of the kind employed by *Lekra*, was stigmatised. Yet, after initially supporting the political change in direction by the Suharto government many of the intellectuals, authors and artists associated with *Horison* did become increasingly critical of the government and its engineering of social change. While unwilling to embrace or defend the ideological commitment of their former *Lekra* rivals, as this anthology shows some of these artists tried to push the political limits of conservative humanistic art by focussing stories upon social inequalities, corruption, the role of women, the alienation of working people, and the stranglehold of the bureaucracy and the military over the lives of the people.

Widespread bans on left-wing publications had effectively cut by one-third the number of national daily and weekly newspapers and periodicals. But for those writers who survived the change of regime the first decade of the New Order was an expansive period. While there were other specialist 'little' magazines regularly publishing some fiction, such as *Budaya Jaya* (*Glorious*

5 eg, six of the stories in Aveling 1975 appeared initially in *Horison* (the remaining four in *Sastra*).

Culture) and *Basis,*[6] established writers inhibited by earlier political circumstances embraced *Horison* enthusiastically, and new ones sought its imprimatur. When Ajip Rosidi compiled his comprehensive, 690 page anthology, *Laut Biru Langit Biru,* in 1977 covering the first decade of 'New Order' literature, at most only ten of the 62 authors included had not published in *Horison*. For many it was their major outlet.

Statistics provided in the most comprehensive bibliography of Indonesian literature in journals indicate the unique achievements of *Horison*. Even by 1983 after its first 17 years, *Horison* had already published over 2,100 literary texts (including short stories, poems and dramas), more than any other of the 113 periodicals surveyed (Kratz, 1988:12, 889). Even by the end of the 1960s *Horison* had come to be regarded, along with the Jakarta Cultural Centre, Taman Ismail Marzuki (TIM), as one of 'the two leading institutions in Indonesian intellectual/artistic life' (*Prisma*, 1983:2). This prominence allowed *Horison's* editorial board to play an important role as 'gatekeeper' influencing literary production in New Order Indonesia.

The magazine has been dogged by financial problems since its inception. In the 1970s it was funded for several years by the International Association for Cultural Freedom[7] which assisted various comparable publications around the world. In the 1980s four major publishers, the daily newspapers *Sinar Harapan* and *Kompas*, the news weekly magazine *Tempo* and the women's entertainment magazine *Femina*, provided modest monthly

---

6 *Budaya Jaya* was a small-circulation intellectual journal produced between 1968–79 by the prestige publishers, Pustaka Jaya, with the financial backing of the Jakarta city council. It included poems, plays and artistic criticism but also essays on a range of general philosophical, intellectual and social issues. *Basis*, Indonesia's longest running cultural monthly magazine, has been published by Yogyakarta Catholics since 1950. Its role in fostering the arts in Yogyakarta is substantial but it is not primarily a magazine of fiction. On *Horison*, see Teeuw 1979:48-53

7 On the IACF and its predecessor the Congress for Cultural Freedom, an intellectuals' organisation established during the Cold War, see Coleman (1989), Marchetti & Marks (1980:43) and Berman (1983:143:143-5).

subsidies to cover running costs. But even with such sponsorship *Horison* could not compete with the increasingly sophisticated commercial press.

Daily papers, like *Kompas*, had became vehicles for more serious essays which may have formerly found their way into *Horison*, and together with an increasing number of attractively presented popular entertainment magazines, newspapers also enticed short story writers with higher honorariums (often more than three times that offered by *Horison*), more efficient management and wider circulation. *Horison* suffered from such competition.

In a major analysis of contemporary Indonesian literary culture the country's leading social science journal, *Prisma*, implied that the decline of *Horison* over this period was due partly to an absence of serious debate on such questions as literature and social change in Indonesia, alluding to the intellectual void left by the banning of *Lekra* (*Prisma*, 1983:2). The *Horison* editorial team made various attempts to broaden the content of the journal and boost its appeal. Mochtar Lubis stressed in the monthly 'Cultural Notes' column that *Horison* was widening its own horizons to 'wipe out the limits on thought or study and to abolish the boundaries on the possibilities of our creative energies in all fields of national life' (*Horison*, 1979:3). He strived to diversify the magazine's contents, to include ideas on 'urban and rural problems, education, economic development, the future, the environment, ecological protection' and other problems.

The magazine was re-vamped in 1982, yet virtually every year its special anniversary issue re-visited the ideological clashes of the 1960s. The pressure to ostracise those former leftists who had emerged from detention by 1979 was not specific to *Horison*. Periodicals generally were cautioned by the authorities against publishing material by former political prisoners and lists of black-banned authors were circulated from time to time to newspaper editors. Despite the influence on *Horison* of people like Arief Budiman, who increasingly shared a common political position with the ex-*Lekra* writers, the magazine remained steadfast against the left.

In July 1993 there was another abortive attempt to re-vitalise the magazine when an agreement with the publishers of the country's largest newsweekly magazine *Tempo* was annulled by Mochtar Lubis after only one issue of a new look *Horison* had been produced. In a very public schism a number of the original stalwart members of *Horison* resigned in protest at Lubis's actions. After a hiatus the Lubis group brought out the next issue in September (but dated July/August) which included a sombre single-page statement by Lubis thanking those who had resigned for their past contributions to the magazine. Evoking something of the grief surrounding the imbroglio, the notice was printed in white lettering on a solid black page. Undaunted, Lubis and his supporters have continued to seek additional commercial sponsorship in order to keep *Horison* alive.

In 1995 it vanished again for four months until in October a special issue appeared vehemently attacking the granting of the prestigious Ramon Magsaysay Award for 'Journalism, Literature, and Creative Communication Arts', one of Asia's most prestigious literary accolades, to former *Lekra* office-bearer Pramoedya Ananta Toer. Only one previous Indonesian author had won this particular award: Mochtar Lubis in 1958 when he was being held as a political prisoner as Pramoedya himself was for 14 years.[8] *Horison's* cover collage featured a photograph of Mochtar Lubis returning his own Magsaysay Award in public protest against the honour bestowed upon Pramoedya. That it took such a controversy to awaken the magazine from its four-month malaise suggests the periodical's relevance to national literary and cultural life in the late 1990s may be declining.

Nonetheless, in November 1996, *Horison* launched a new initiative by including a special 16-page regular insert designed to stimulate an interest in literature amongst high school students at government and religious (*pesantren*) schools. Entitled *Kaki langit* (*Horizon*), it was supported by the Ministers of Education and Culture, and Religious Affairs, who wrote forewords to the inaugural edition. It was an effort by the magazine to tap a new

8 Ramon Magsaysay Awards are given for various achievements. Fifteen Indonesians, including literary historian H.B. Jassin and Muslim leader Abdurrachman Wahid, had received them in other categories.

market amongst Indonesia's youngest generation of readers. In its plans for expansion such government support was crucial since *Horison* was costing Rp.15 million (about AUD$8,100) an issue to produce and never covering costs, despite a regular monthly subsidy from the publishing giant PT Gramedia of Rp.1.5 million (Sumbogo and Anwar, 1996). Yet, driven by the tenacity of its staff and the immovable determination of Mochtar Lubis, Indonesia's archetypal 'little literary magazine' continues to appear.

Despite schisms and slumps, the vicissitudes of politics and the iron will of economics, it is indeed laudable that *Horison* has now passed its 30th birthday. Battered it may be by the constant struggle to survive from month to month, issue to issue, but it is still unrivalled as Indonesia's longest surviving literary and cultural monthly. Its contents provide valuable insights into the Indonesia that has emerged during 30 years of New Order government. The stories presented in it, and in this current anthology, are penned by those artists, nurtured during the Suharto period, who sustain a writing tradition informed by universal humanist values which form a dominant influence upon modern Indonesian literature. Despite its glossy competition from the popular press, *Horison* remains the magazine in which aspiring Indonesian short story writers seek to appear, if only once, as a measure of their achievement. Its longevity is a tribute to those that have sustained it and an indication of the determination of the ideological forces it represents.

The Stories

In fact, the stories which follow go beyond *Horison*. Included also are major but marginalised women writers, routinely excluded from serious consideration by literary magazines and critics, as well as select works appearing in other significant fora, such as the rival cultural monthly *Budaya Jaya* (Glorious Culture), or produced for national literary competitions, such as that sponsored by Radio Nederland. Ultimately, the stories were chosen (albeit somewhat arbitrarily, given the massive output) not so much because of their source, but for the light they shed on Indonesia's culture and society over the past three decades.

Like all stories, they are rich with possible interpretations. The following comments are not intended to limit interpretation; they are, inevitably and unavoidably, individual responses to the texts which no doubt offer many more fertile readings.

A 1990 survey by Tineke Hellwig of more than 800 fiction books by leading Indonesian publishers indicated that women had written almost 40% overall and 56% of those best-sellers with print runs of 10,000 or more (Hellwig, 1994:163, 231–32). Despite this numeric strength all too often women are regarded by Indonesian literary critics and editors as not worthy of serious consideration, producing 'popular' rather than 'serious' fiction, writings more suited to (women's) entertainment magazines than literary magazines. Indeed, women rarely appear as authors in *Horison*. In a listing of authors whose works appeared in *Horison* between 1966 and 1983, for example, it appears less than 10% were women.[9] Since its establishment there has never been a female member of either the *Horison* editorial board nor its advisory board.

Even Indonesia's most highly regarded woman writer, Nh. Dini, is an infrequent contributor (whose omission from an anthology such as this would have left an unacceptable void). Dini's works have been translated into Japanese, Dutch, German, French, Russian and English. She spent two decades abroad living in Japan, Cambodia, the Philippines, the USA and France while married to a French diplomat. Yet when she returned to Indonesia in 1980 after the end of her marriage she chose to settle again in her Central Java home-town of Semarang rather than be drawn to the nation's centre stage in Jakarta. In her short story 'The Factory' Dini is sharply critical of the irresistible pull of the city, of its wealth and lifestyle, and of the acquisition of productive farm land by foreign industrialists. The wise earth-mother of Dini's story is unimpressed by the tacky veneer of affluence with its sticky plastic chairs and urban drift.

---

9 Kratz, 1988:848–50 lists the names of 352 authors only 33 of which are identifiably female. This calculation does not take into account names which are not gendered (such as those using only initials), or the use of pseudonyms which disguise the author's gender.

With steely determination she cleaves to the fields and the red mud which has, and will continue, to sustain life and meaning.

Like Dini, Totilawati Tjitrawasita, the other woman included in this anthology, is an unusual exemplar of women writers in Indonesia. Totilawati, who died of cancer in 1982 aged barely 37, lived in provincial Surabaya where, in addition to editing a major Javanese-language magazine *Jaya Baya* established by her father, she wrote prolifically in the Javanese vernacular in preference to the national language of Indonesian. Her Indonesian-language fiction was eventually recognised in 1977 when her collection of short stories, *Sebuah Cinta Sekolah Rakyat* (*A School Crush*) (from which the story included in this anthology was taken), was awarded first prize for fiction by the Book of the Year Foundation. Much to her chagrin many of the stories in the award-winning collection had attracted little attention when they appeared previously in Javanese, which she attributed to the lack of serious consideration or appreciation by literary critics for literatures in regional languages.

Given her preference for writing in Javanese, it is perhaps not surprising she never appeared in *Horison*. Her story, 'Jakarta', juxtaposes the symbolic power and corruption of the nation's capital with the transparent honesty of regional life and values. It may be no coincidence that Totilawati's story traverses something of the same emotional terrain as that of Dini's 'The Factory': social and cultural change driven by political and economic power rarely benefits those on the margins. Both stories seemed fitting inclusions in this collection, as tacit criticisms of the Jakarta-centrism of much of Indonesia's public (literary?) life.

Neither of these stories by women writers conform to the stereotypical model of 'women's writing', as so often defined by (male) literary critics in Indonesia. In neither story, for example, is there flowery exaggerated emotion or the ubiquitous romance. Partly this might be because this stereotype, with all its unflattering connotations so commonly associated with the short stories published in 'women's entertainment magazines', obscures considerable evidence that such 'women's fiction' is not the exclusive preserve of women (either as authors or readers).

Many male writers, too, plumb the financial potential offered by it and undoubtedly many male readers consume it. Such 'magazine fiction' often extends beyond the constraints of the popular 'romantic' genre (Allen, 1995). Despite the financial incentive, both Dini and Totilawati, writing from the regions outside the capital, from somewhat beyond the pull of the market, chose to write against the urban current and ennoble the rural and the regional, above the metropolitan.

Writing also from the 'regions' is Gerson Poyk, the only writer included from Eastern Indonesia. Concern for the marginalised and minorities runs through many of his stories, which are peopled by the disabled, the lonely and the downtrodden: the 'crab barber' and prostitute in 'Swaying', the blind army veteran and his sex worker wife in 'Applause on a journey', and the Irianse villager regarded by all in the capital as a oddity in 'Matias Akankari'. Like the 'Honorable Minister' in 'Applause on a Journey', the state and its elevated officials are completely impervious to the poverty and pain around them. 'Matias Akankari', in the words of one Indonesian literary critic, is 'a satire against metropolitan society, the jet-set society undergoing cultural degradation' (Rampan, 1982:181). Like the protagonist in Totilawati's story, Jakarta is clearly not Matias' capital, for it offers him nothing. His Indonesian 'liberator' quickly tires and abandons him. Even when the city's inhabitants are black like him, their interests are not his. He has no space, no place of refuge in this, the nation which has claimed his homeland. Together with several other stories in this collection, there are elements in 'Matias Akankari' which may be read as questioning the extent to which the national principle, 'Bhinneka Tunggal Ika' (Unity in Diversity), the foundation of the multi-ethnic archipelagic nation-state of Indonesia, has been sustained.

While all of the stories in this collection have been published in Indonesia, and none have been banned or incurred the wrath of the authorities, there is a strong edge critical of the New Order and its bureaucracy which runs through many of them. For several authors the institutionalised power and corruption of the New Order is an emotive target, and yet their depiction of the moral conflicts and the choices made by their characters vary greatly. In Chairul Harun's 'Telephone' the protagonist is a well-meaning *bupati* (district officer), who is aware that government rural development programs have failed due to ineptitude and poor timing. Yet he is tormented by the expectation that underlings must report only favourable results to their superiors, or be removed.

Moes Loindong's protagonist in 'On the dark side of the moon' faces a similar dilemma. He returns from training abroad fired with dedication to serve his country through his job processing import applications. But it is not easy to make a clear moral choice when he detects his boss's complicity in a murky smuggling operation. While technically breaking the law the boss's collusion appears ironically to facilitate regional 'economic development'. He, like his boss, knows that 'development' has been elevated (in the story as it is in New Order rhetoric) to be the primary imperative of all government activities. The story avoids presenting glib solutions to the dilemma faced by countless government officials.

Hamsad Rangkuti's contributions deal with similar themes. 'Long Life for Mr Joyokoyoroyo and his cronies' is a cynical caricature of the corrupt business people who have sold out Indonesia's rich resources for personal profit, and the elevation to martyrdom of an insignificant driver who takes justice into his own hands. In Hamsad Rangkuti's 'The General Smiles on 17th August', too, those who wield power are again the author's target, but he is particularly damning of the falsification of history which has made military heroes out of cowards and traitors, and manipulated the sentiments of the common people.

In A.A. Navis's enigmatic 'The Governor's Cats' a plague of rats tests the patience and ingenuity of the local governor, who is endeavouring to purge the complex which houses both his administration and his residence. The tale of the battle to rid the Governor's buildings firstly of rampaging rats and then cantankerous cats is light-hearted. The problem stumps 'Professor Alatas, a scholar working on the sociology of corruption', presumably a tongue-in- check allusion to Professor Syed Hussein Alatas, the Indonesian-born author of *The*

Sociology of Corruption (1968, translated into Indonesian in 1982). It ties up substantial amounts of the regional parliament's budget and challenges the best efforts of an environmentally unfriendly private entrepreneur! But governors (and governments) have considerable difficulty in exterminating 'pests' that have adapted so successfully to survive and thrive within the structures of power. As the Governor's escapades may illustrate, it seems perhaps that, even with the best will and motivation in the world and the advice of experts of all kinds, it is often easier for those in power to come to an accommodation with 'parasites' than it is to eliminate them! Navis, who was a member of the West Sumatra Regional Assembly for more than ten years, spins a humourous Pied Piper tale, but clearly with a critical edge.

That critics have a crucial, if unappreciated, role in Indonesian society is underscored by Pamusuk Eneste's ironic snapshot, 'The critic'. Sombre and pessimistic, the yarn plays topsy-turvy with popular assumptions about the relationship between student critics and the state. Like Hamsad Rangkuti's 'The General Smiles on 17th August', the inglorious role of the military in Pamusuk Eneste's whimsical realm of 'The Republic of What's-a-Name Land' is lampooned again by his other inclusion, 'The Generals'. In it senior army officers, made militarily redundant, have taken over all manner of civilian jobs: a jibe, perhaps, at the Indonesian military's doctrine of 'dual function', used to justify officers occupying key civilian positions in the government. The dilemma in What's-a-Name Land (and critics might suggest, in Indonesia) is what to do with a surfeit of generals!

In 'Pop Dreaming', Catholic priest, social reformer and political activist Y.B. Mangunwijaya also takes a playful swipe at the military, along with another sacred cow, the academe with its pretentious intellectuals and agitating students. The familiar world of the dazed student protagonist is turned upside down as he attempts to come to terms with some surprising good fortune. Mangunwijaya's allusive prose, with its barbed word-plays and sarcastic allusions to contemporary politics, has a bizarre comical quality (and posed considerable difficulties for translation!). While the author mocks the military's confused role in keeping the peace, he seems similarly amused by student pre-occupations with romance and campus radicalism!

A brooding mystical atmosphere permeates 'Dialogue', Safron Rasyidi Sidal's eerie tale about a gravestone engraver with an awesome and terrifying power to bring his carvings to life. He is tormented by the fear of his gravestones rebelling against him, accusing him of deceit and corruption. It is an off-beat (almost hallucinogenic) story generously open to interpretation. Are the 50 'subversive' gravestones symbolic of Indonesia's demi-centenary of independence? Do they evoke the 'Petition of Fifty', an opposition group of disillusioned retired generals and politicians, academics and students, which formed in 1980 to protest against President Suharto's claim to be the embodiment of the state ideology of *Pancasila* (Five Principles)?

Slightly off-beat, too, is 'A Banana in the Corpse's Stomach', by M. Shoim Anwar, in which a tiny, otherwise insignificant incident between friends becomes the source of undying animosity. After the death of one of these men, the other, in a dialogue with another companion, explores the consequences of everyday actions and compares such quotidian values with the motivations of the great actors of history. They range over alternative interpretations of history and debate the importance of forgiveness. It all begins with a banana and becomes a debt of honour. But the fundamental argument of this slighted colleague is that honesty has to start with trivialities.

A debt and the rocky and corrupt course of Justice forms the subject of Jasso Winarto's salutary tale, 'The Debt'. It is an unembellished story of a generous and honest man, who falls foul of a policing system which often contradicts the principles of natural justice. In a country where many are suspicious of the power of the authorities and where money is assumed to oil the wheels of justice, the story's none-too-subtle moral is both a truism and a poor reflection upon the much-vaunted 'rule of law' in Indonesia.

In the face of international condemnation over widespread human rights infringements, the New Order has long stressed its claims to be a *negara hukum* (a state based on the rule of law).

Several of the stories in this anthology take task with such claims. One, Sides Sudyarto's 'The Lebaran Prayers of a Group of Political Prisoners in a Concentration Camp', does so in relation to the taboo subject of political prisoners. While no specific country or location is mentioned, when Sides Sudyarto wrote this story in 1977 tens of thousands of political prisoners were still being held without trial by the New Order. Many remained in detention for up to fourteen years. When 'The Lebaran Prayers' appeared very few short stories (and, to my knowledge, no novels) had been published which raised the politically sensitive issue of political prisoners. Those which did deal explicitly with the politics of 1965–66 tended to condemn of the leftists, who were assumed to be atheists. The protagonist in Sides Sudyarto's concentration camp is an 'ordinary run-of-the-mill bloke', trying to come to terms with his incarceration, with his poverty-stricken childhood, with his role in history, with his faith in the Almighty. A common faith brings both the guards and the guarded together in communal prayer, but religious faith and the man whose task it was to tend to the spiritual needs of the nameless 'Writer of the Diary' and his fellow detainees, were unable to temper the barbarity of the political system which incarcerated and disposed of them. It is a bitter statement about the fragility of law not only in the concentration camps.

The trauma and dislocation caused by the political upheaval of 1965–66 emerges too in Wildan Yatim's 'Coming Home', but in this case the protagonist, Piko, had incited the torture and murder of leftists in his district before disappearing into the low-life of Jakarta for several years. As in Totilawati Tjitrawasita's 'Jakarta' and Gerson Poyk's 'Matias Akankari', the national capital, where Piko has sought shelter, had provided no uplifting example, no moral insight nor even economic sustenance for the refugee from the provinces. Is it a crisis of confidence which draws Piko back to his decaying village, to try both to regenerate the communal life of its inhabitants and to re-join his relationship with his emotionally disturbed wife? The community, like their fields starved of water by the break-down of the irrigation system, had been wounded, perhaps irreparably, by the violent schisms and blind vengeance of the past.

The symbol of the primacy of water in sustaining rural life is also central to M. Fudoli Zaini's 'The Drought', in which tensions between belief systems in a small village are brought brutally to the surface by a prolonged drought. The drought threatens not only their fields but also their fellowship and sense of community. In the midst of their suffering, the village head can get no 'help from the city'. The civil authorities are helpless. It is to their spiritual leaders that the people turn. But, in their supplications for rain, the villagers are caught between the teacher at the local mosque and the guardian of the village graveyard, between prayers to the Almighty or sacrifices to the dead. There is no doubt where the author's loyalties lie, neither in this, nor his other contribution to this anthology, 'Cancer'. In 'Cancer', Fudoli Zaini depicts the moral and physical disintegration of a woman through the eyes of a distant male acquaintance. It is unquestionably a male's perspective. The woman, a former nightclub dancer, cast off by her husband and forced to leave her children, is given little authorial sympathy. Instead, her (im)moral choices are seen to call forth a physical punishment. It is a common depiction of women, particularly widows or divorcees, in Indonesian fiction (Hellwig, 1994:182–96) yet contrasts sharply with the strong, independent mother in Dini's 'The Factory', for example.

A far more sympathetic representation of the woman as mother and wife is given in Putu Wijaya's 'A Letter'. An unnamed woman, watches over her sleeping children in a pre-dawn vigil, as she drafts and re-drafts a letter to her absent husband. Since he left for studies abroad months ago he has made no contact. She is desperate with worry, tearful at being rejected, angry at being ignored, and groping constantly for some glimmer of hope which might sustain her love for her husband and the father of her children. As she pours out her sorrow in the tortured prose of her letters, she moves from initial desperation, through resignation, and finally to a self-sustaining realisation that she is capable of shouldering the responsibility for the family and had the strength to continue alone. One significance of this story is that it is the first of many by Putu Wijaya to appear in *Horison*. He developed into one of the country's most highly regarded experimental authors and dramatists.[10] While his early style, as evidenced in 'A Letter', is naturalistic and largely undifferentiated from much that appeared in the literary and entertainment magazines of the time, he was quickly to develop a strikingly powerful 'absurdist' style which came to typify his work from the mid-1970s. Since then he has stamped his mark upon prose fiction and successfully captured the imagination of his substantial theatre audiences.

Putu Wijaya has lived and worked extensively abroad, in both Japan and the United States of America. When 'A Letter' appeared in 1970 the number of Indonesians studying abroad, like the husband of the story's protagonist, was relatively small. Two decades later, by the time the Gulf War broke out in Kuwait, Indonesia was irrevocably enmeshed in the international community. It had become commonplace for middle-class professionals and academics to go abroad for postgraduate studies, most commonly to America or Europe, but also in significant numbers to Japan, Canada, Australia and elsewhere. When America led a multinational force into Kuwait in January 1991 to drive out the Iraqi army, Amri Marzali, like the central character in his story 'Support Our Troops' was completing his doctorate at Boston University. The story (which one might be forgiven for assuming was at least partly biographical?) describes an Indonesian postgraduate student's observations of America's jingoistic support for the attack on Saddam Hussein. It is a gentle, even fond, dig at the brash giant's flamboyant celebration of its victory over a far-away tiny desert country. Woven into the narrative are a variety of warm-hearted vignettes of the lives of the expatriate Indonesian community, with its students, illegal immigrants and businesspeople, some of whom have embraced wholeheartedly America's anti-Iraq rhetoric. 'Support Our Troops' is the view of America from outside, a perspective from an Indonesian looking beyond his horizon, at the experience of coming to terms with life abroad.

---

10 There have been several studies of Putu Wijaya's work including Rafferty 1988 and 1989.

It is not new for Indonesians to write of their experiences of the world abroad. It was particularly evident in the early post-independence years when a number of young writers, like Pramoedya Ananta Toer and Sitor Situmorang, travelled to Europe for extended periods. But Amri Marzali's critique of American values suggests a growing confidence by this generation of Indonesians, many of whom live and work for years away from their homeland. It is, in a way, Amri Marzali's prolonged exploration of a land beyond his horizon which gives the story its edge. While categorised as 'fiction' (partly at least because of its publication in *Horison*, a 'literary' magazine), 'Support Our Troops' shares much with a recent book of biographical 'reportage', *Australi Ya Ya Ya* by Ruhan Tagar, an illegal immigrant from Yogyakarta who lived and worked in Sydney from 1987 to 1991 (Tagar, 1996). Tagar's attempts to come to terms with Aussie life, expounded in chapters such as 'sex culture', 'fuck me I'm drunk', and the obligatory 'BBQ', seem to prove that sometimes 'fact' *is* stranger than fiction!

***

Varied though the stories in this anthology are, there is no pretension that they constitute the literary canon or occupy some objective pinnacle at the heights of Indonesian literature of this period. Such a claim would be naive, although their selection did follow a detailed study of *Horison*, together with various other key publications and sources.

The short story genre is not a traditional form of literary expression in Indonesia. Its history is brief. Pioneering steps in this (essentially European) tradition of narrative fiction may be traced from the 1920s but it was not until the 1940s that it took firm root. By the 1950s, encouraged by an upward surge in literacy levels in the national language after Independence in 1945, and a raft of little magazines publishing (and, importantly, paying for) short fiction, the genre came into its own. So popular did such magazines become that concern was expressed that Indonesian literature was becoming too dominated by the short story, that it was becoming a 'magazine literature'.

Observers feared the genre was undermining the standing of the novel, long regarded by literary historians in Indonesia as the more significant of the two forms.

For those unfamiliar with the traditions of Indonesian short story writing, the craft skills evidenced in the stories that follow may surprise or dismay. At times, the styles may seem pedestrian, the tales unvariegated and the denouement predictable. It is not for any stylistic innovation that most stories have been chosen. That is not to say Indonesian literature is without its experimentation, as earlier comments on the stories by Putu Wijaya, Mangunwijaya and Safron Rasyidi Sidal indicate. Generally however, the anthology draws from the stylistic mainstream, and illustrates with some breadth the dominant forms of such short fiction in Indonesia. These stories then should be valued as products of their own 'new' tradition, as a rich contribution to non-English world literatures, developing at arm's length from the norms so often taken for granted in the English-speaking world, but worthy of equal consideration.

The writers include some of the most highly-regarded in the country (such as Nh. Dini, Putu Wijaya, YB Mangunwijaya, AA Navis, Gerson Poyk), strong established practitioners (like Wildan Yatim, Chairul Harun, Totilawati Tjitrawasita, Hamsad Rangkuti, Pamusuk Eneste, M. Fudoli Zaini), imposing 'dabblers' (like fellow journalists Sides Sudyarto DS and Jasso Winarto) and recently emerging figures (like M. Shoim Anwar, Moes Loindong, Amri Marzali, and Safron Rasyidi Sidal).

The contents cannot claim to be comprehensive and there are several notable absences. Taking its material from *Horison* produced during a period when left-wing writers were either detained or otherwise refused avenues for publication, the anthology only includes works from that stream of politically-acceptable Indonesian literature which was permitted space by the New Order. In addition, I have tended to shy away, for example, from authors who have been more prolific before rather than after 1966, or who have been extensively translated elsewhere (such as Mochtar Lubis, Pramoedya Ananta Toer, Danarto, Seno Gumira Adjidarma and Leila Chudori).[11]

11 Details of such translations are given in 'Further Reading'.

Nonetheless, despite such limitations, the anthology aims to provide a useful introduction to contemporary short fiction in Indonesia, with works which are entertaining and insightful of social, political, and cultural change beyond our horizon.

David T. Hill
April 1997

References

Allen, Pamela (ed. and trans.) 1995, *Women's Voices: An Anthology of Short Stories by Indonesian Women Writers*, Longman, Melbourne.

Aveling, Harry (ed. & trans.) 1975, *GESTAPU: Indonesian Short Stories on the Abortive Communist Coup of 30th September 1965*, Southeast Asian Studies Working Paper, University of Hawaii.

Berman, Edward H. 1983, *The Ideology of Philanthropy: The Influence of the Carnegie, Ford and Rockefeller Foundations on American Foreign Policy*, State University of New York Press, Albany.

Chambert-Loir, Henri 1972, '*Horison*: Six Annees d'Une Revue Litteraire Indonesienne', *Archipel*, 4.

Coleman, Peter 1989, *The Liberal Conspiracy: The Congress for Cultural Freedom and the Struggle for the Mind of Postwar Europe,* The Free Press, New York.

Cribb, Robert (ed) 1990, *The Indonesian Killings 1965–66: Studies from Java and Bali*, Centre of Southeast Asian Studies, Monash University, Clayton.

Cribb, Robert and Brown, Colin 1995, *Modern Indonesia: A History Since 1945*, Longman, London.

Foulcher, Keith 1986, *Social Commitment in Literature and the Arts: The Indonesian Institute of People's Culture 1950–65*, Centre of Southeast Asian Studies, Monash University, Clayton.

Hellwig, Tineke 1994, *In the Shadow of Change: Women in Indonesian Literature*, Centre of Southeast Asian Studies, no.35, University of California at Berkley.

Hill, David T. 1993, '"The Two Leading Institutions": Taman Ismail Marzuki and *Horison*', in V. Matheson Hooker (ed), *Culture and Society in New Order Indonesia*, Oxford University Press, Kuala Lumpur.

—— 1994, '*Horison*, History and Hamsad Rangkuti: Translator's Introduction to "The General Smiles on 17th August"', *Review of Indonesian and Malaysian Affairs*, 28(2).

Horison, 1966, 1, July.

—— 1979, XIV(1), January.

Hume, E.M.J. 1968, 'The Reaction in Indonesian Literature Towards the Sukarno Regime with Particular Reference to the Literary Journal *Horison*', unpublished BA thesis, Australian National University, Canberra.

Kratz, Ernst Ulrich 1988, *A Bibliography of Indonesian Literature in Journals: Drama, Prose, Poetry*, Gadjah Mada University Press/SOAS, Yogyakarta.

Marchetti, Victor and Marks, John D. 1980, *The CIA and the Cult of Intelligence*, Dell Books, New York.

Prisma: The Indonesian Indicator, 1983, 'A Note From the Editor', 29, September.

Rafferty, Ellen & Sears, Laurie J. (eds.) 1988, *Bomb: Indonesian Short Stories by Putu Wijaya*, University of Wisconsin, Madison.

Rafferty, Ellen (ed.) 1989, *Putu Wijaya in Performance: A Script and Study of Indonesian Theatre*, University of Wisconsin, Madison.

Rampan, Korrie Layun 1982, *Cerita Pendek Indonesia Mutakir*, Nur Cahaya, Yogyakarta.

Sumbogo, Priyono B. and Mauluddin Anwar 1996, 'Majalah Horison: Kaki Langit Masuk Sekolah', *Gatra*, 9 November, posted on the internet <Indonesia-1>.

Tagar, Ruhan 1996, *Australi Ya Ya Ya*, Pustaka Utama Grafiti, Jakarta.

Teeuw, A. 1979, *Modern Indonesian Literature*, vol.2, Martinus Nijhoff, The Hague.

The Short Stories

Swaying

Gerson Poyk

---

translated by Jan Lingard

In the shade of a tree growing beside a straight road running along in front of the station, a very sunburnt white man was having a haircut.

At the time, a continuous breeze was blowing, cooling the man's skin, as well as affording the usual dry season scene of falling leaves floating along with the dust.

In front of the man having the haircut and the man doing the cutting, a small mirror hung on a rusty nail stuck in the bark of the tree. Hanging on another nail above the mirror was a square, glass-covered frame containing a military citation signed by the President of the Republic. There was another similar one below the mirror, but it was signed by the Minister for the Armed Forces.

While it was pleasant having a hair cut in the caresses of the breeze, unfortunately as the branches and leaves swayed, so did the mirror and the citations. This made it difficult for the man to focus on the citations he was trying to read because the letters on the citations were shaking like banners of war. The longer he looked at them the more blurred they became.

'Are they your awards?' asked the customer.

The barber sniggered.

It was quiet for a few minutes as the snipping of the scissors at the white man's head continued, but then came the sound of a throat being cleared, followed by;

'Those two citations were to compensate for my legs that were amputated as a result of the bullets of the Revolution'.

So! It was the story that the sunburnt European had been looking for ever since his eyes had been drawn to a legless barber cutting his customers' hair from a stand—a table modified for his physical condition. But suddenly the white man had the feeling that his throat was in the vice-like grip of a human crab who bore a grudge against the Dutch, so that he hastened to say:

'I'm not Dutch. I'm German, and now I'm an Indonesian citizen'.

'Is that so', said the barber to the clicking of his scissors. 'This is the first time I've given a white man a hair cut, and I bet it's the first time you've had your hair cut by a barber with no legs'.

'But at least you've got the citations'.

The crab man reached into the drawer of his stand and took out a photograph, the size of a postcard.

'This is what I used to look like. I was quite a handsome fellow, even though only a railway track soldier, in other words I had two stripes', he chuckled.

The customer took the photograph, so the half done haircut was held up for a while and the scene changed to two men viewing the glorious past—one of them legless, and the other with half a hair cut.

As he resumed cutting, the barber asked, 'What did you do when you were young?'

For a long time the white man didn't answer because suddenly he was forced to think back to his job, which had been the most contemptible on the face of the earth. During the war his job had been to gather the hair, bones, skulls or corpses of those that had just been cremated or gassed. His sunburnt skin in the mirror hanging from the tree, reminded him of the red skin he'd had when he worked as a burner of corpses in the crematorium.

'My past was very horrible'.

'What do you mean?'

'I don't want to talk about it now. Later when we get to know each other better I'll tell you'.

The dry season breeze kept making the faces in the mirror sway from side to side, but it also brought coolness so that the two men felt they were in air-conditioned premises.

'How'd you like to go out and have a good time?' asked the barber.

'Where to?'

'To my place'.

'Sure, I will some day when I can make it'.

'We could go when we get through here'.

'Can you spare the time?'

'No problem'.

The hair cut finished, the tools were tidied up and a pedicab hailed. Nimbly the barber got down from his stand and scrambled up into it. The white man followed, and sat down beside his new friend. They turned here and there, stopping from time to time because the streets were jammed or because a train was passing and at last arrived at a house that looked like a mosquito net because of the woven bamboo walls.

They had got out of the pedicab and were about to knock on the door, when a man's harsh voice was heard:

'Two weeks ago a Chinese came here, and eight days ago a Japanese and an American were here together all day. You can't hide what belongs to me'.

'Who told you?' said a woman's voice.

'I got reports!'

'Who from?'

'From my spies!'

'They lied!'

'You're the liar'.

Then it was quiet. In the lull the white man, who was standing stock still in front of the door, stooped down and asked 'Is this an international meeting place?'

'You could say that', whispered the barber.

Slowly the crab barber crept to the bottom of the door made of woven bamboo, jabbed his finger through a gap and peered inside. Then he signalled to his friend to do the same. By pulling aside a little of the woven bamboo at the top, the panorama inside was clearly visible. Good Lord! A man was bullying a young woman who had flawless marble-like skin.

'You don't know the meaning of gratitude!' snarled the man. 'I got you out of the village, bought you dresses and make up, provided your food in the early days, gave you a strategic place to stay, and I'm the one who protects you. Come on, hand over the money. You don't expect me to believe that not one out of ten customers has paid!'

From this it could be understood that the woman inside was a prostitute who was being interrogated by her pimp. He stopped speaking, but his bloodshot eyes could be seen fixed on the woman while she sat with her head bowed, scratching at her red painted fingernails. Then he suddenly took a draw on the long aromatic clove cigarette he was smoking, pulled her close and burnt her on the breast with it. She shrieked like a bitch that had been doused with boiling water. Before her first shriek had subsided, the end of the burning cigarette was pressed against her thigh several times. Her heart-rending screams grew louder but the man was unperturbed. He was absorbed in his game, as if he were pressing piano keys with one hand, playing a sadistic melody. His hand played faster and faster and finally, the woman fainted.

The white man was beside himself. His mouth moved like a man praying and only stopped when the barber pushed the door open.

'Leave her alone! I'll give you the money!' the crab shouted to the lout. Turning to his white friend he said, 'Meet a childhood friend of mine from the same village, who likewise became a tool of the Revolution and a two stripe railway track private, though now he's got three stripes now!'

'And this woman that he burnt, who's she?'

'She's our capital, which means she's yours to enjoy'.

Suddenly the woman regained consciousness and sat huddled with her arms hugging her body. The guest blushed red like a tomato. He throbbed all over and broke out in a sweat and, for a moment, he couldn't say anything. In the meantime the two men told the woman to tidy herself up.

'Where does she come from?' asked the guest.

'From a village. It was fate that she fell into our hands. Her village is well known for its rice production, but the farmers who are desperate for cash in hand sell the rice for a cheap price before it is ripe. Straight after the harvest the mature rice is taken away by the people who bought it to sell for a big profit and the farmers are left with nothing. Her parents lived under the pressures of this system, so after they'd sold all their possessions to buy rice for themselves, they finally had to sell their own daughter. We took her in as an investment, because there are a lot of people who are frightened or apprehensive of coming to me for a haircut because of my disability. As for sergeant three stripes here, how do you think he'd be able to feed seven kids if we didn't have a sideline like this? You can take her now'.

'No', the man blushed, even more, like a red tomato.

'I get it, you're impotent or you're a homosexual', said three stripes.

'I'm a doctor and you must put some cod liver oil ointment on those burns'.

Silence fell on the place and in the meantime the pretty girl sat on the bed holding a mirror and powdering her face. Very quietly the guest stood up and looked at his watch.

'I'm sorry, its getting late, and I've got work to do'.

'Why don't you stay and have a good time. She's just finished doing herself up for you'.

'Thanks, but the fact is as well as being a doctor I'm also a priest. You bring her to the hospital for treatment or buy some ointment at the chemist. Don't forget. Now, excuse me'.

He went out, leaving the three people looking at each other.

'Well, he wasn't wearing a cassock was he!' said the one who'd brought the guest.

'Shut up, you crab! Fancy bringing a useless customer in on a scene like that!'

The barber was silent. The whole room was silent. But suddenly the barber, who had been sitting on the floor, shifted away from the bed because the ends of the bedspread that hung to the floor, moved to reveal an old, white haired woman and a silent, sickly little girl about one year old.

The bully stared wide-eyed in astonishment as the old woman got to her feet and looked at the three of them. She was wearing an old *batik* sarong and on top she only had on an under-bodice. From the bodice she took out a square paper package like a packet of toilet soap and said, 'Here's the money, take it!' and she threw it into the pimp's lap.

'Tjutjun', called the old woman.

'Yes Mother', replied the woman who'd been burnt.

'Your child and I will go back to begging on the trains, and you listen to my advice. Look for a decent job, become a servant in a big house, sell things, do anything at all, but whatever you do, get away from this place!'

Then, putting on her blouse that had been hanging on the wall, she picked up her grand-daughter and left.

Tjutjun buried her face, streaming with tears, in the pillow.

(originally published as 'Oleng-kemoleng', *Horison*, 1968, 7(3), pp.200–01;223.)

Applause on a Journey

Gerson Poyk

translated by Jan Lingard

This thin, slight body of mine had been carried by Garuda jet far, far away from Jakarta to Surabaya. Then it was swallowed up again by a limousine that rolled along swiftly heading for the hinterland of East Java. I ended up in the town of Jember, in a state building jam packed with people, not one of whom I knew. I was very tired. When I had arrived in this town last night, my job had been just the same as it always was, to sit in the middle of a crowd of people and listen to The Honourable Minister's speech. There was no way I could avoid it! If it wasn't for the Honourable Gentleman I wouldn't be here. I am one of the forty members of his entourage. I'm not sure that I know what the significance of my job is, in being part of such a large party. I've heard that this is a 'getting down to grass roots' trip, but sometimes I feel that I'm not quite with it.

Look at the grand scale of it! Whenever our party enters a town, everyone comes out to welcome us. The town is decorated with streamers and coconut fronds and banners and posters saying 'Welcome to the Honourable Minister's Party'. Jaunts like this are just useless, colossal picnics! When we arrived at Jember last night the party went straight off and showered, had dinner and then listened to the Minister's speech being dispersed to the people of the town for hours on end. I'd already heard speeches like it many times in Jakarta and everywhere else. At first, I used to give them their due by listening attentively, but in the long run I got so bored that finally to me, it was like the noise of an old motor bike exhaust pipe. When that sort of thing gets under my skin I just leave or I doze off while I'm listening.

So we come to last night. The Honourable Minister was casting forth his speech. Quickly I worked my way out of the crowd and wandered round town all night. When I got home in the early hours of the morning I went straight to have a wash and eat breakfast. Then, in the motorcade of the Honourable Gentleman's party, preceded by a number of outriders with their motor-bike sirens screaming hysterically, this small thin body arrived at a state building in town.

Damn! How could I get over my tiredness? When I went into the building, the crowd was already packed in. On the stage a dais had been set up, and to the right and left of it were chairs for the members of the party. No matter what, I had to have a sleep while the Honourable Gentleman dispersed his speech. At the very least, I had to have a nap, or otherwise let my mind wander off on a private journey of its own. That's just what happened. Since I'd come into the building, I'd been wearing a pair of dark glasses which I purposely bought, not to keep out the sun, but to keep out the speeches. As the State Carriage of the Honourable Minister rumbled on to the hot Equator with his speech, the carriage of my memory travelled in my cool tiredness, heading for the South Pole with its vast cold snow-fields and its alien, silent creatures.

Last night, I had run into Margareta, walking along the footpath at the town shopping complex. I wasn't surprised, because I knew she'd married an army officer from the Brawijaya Division, who came from this inland town in East Java.

'This is my daughter', she said.

'My word, she's a big girl. Is she your first?' I asked, picking the child up.

We'd only got out these two sentences of greeting when a relative of hers, who was probably escorting her while she did the shopping, called her into a shop.

'You stay here with Uncle for a little while, all right?' Margareta said to the child, leaving us.

I carried the little girl all around the place where we'd met, and after that I bought her a bun and some sweets. Then I chatted with her—she was only four years old—till her mother came out of the shop.

'So how are things with you, Greet?' I asked.

'I'm fine', she said.

'And how is the father of this little one?'

'He's not in the army any more. He just stays at home now'.

'Oh, he's young to be retired', I commented. Greet smiled, then took the child from me, and put her down.

We walked slowly along the footpath, each holding a hand of the little girl, who was in between us.

'I'm only here for one night, Greet', I said.

'Where are you staying?' she asked.

'Over there', I said pointing in a direction that was probably wrong.

'And where are you going tomorrow?'

'I live in Jakarta, and I'll be going back there', I answered.

'And what are you doing here?'

'Having a picnic', I replied.

'Oh, go on with you! You've probably said to hell with teaching, and become a tobacco merchant'.

'No, I've given up teaching and become a first class tobacco smoker', I said.

Hearing the word 'tobacco', I remembered that I hadn't had a smoke for a while. I took out a packet of clove cigarettes, lit one and inhaled deeply.

'My guess is your husband is running a tobacco plantation, Greet', I continued the conversation.

'No, I've already said he just stays at home now', she said.

'In an inland town like this,' I said, 'a man could live securely in his old age if he had some land, or one or two hectares of rice fields'.

'Yes, that's what I'm hoping for. Just now I'm working very hard to get some money together to buy a rice field or some land for our old age', Greet said.

'So, you've gone back to teaching?' I asked.

'No, how could I be a teacher in an area where there are so many fully qualified teachers who are unemployed? As you know, I didn't finish my teacher training, so the most I can do is teach in a private school. Have you forgotten?'

Only then I remembered that Greet didn't have her teacher's certificate. She used to teach with me in a private school, only because there weren't as many teachers then as there are now.

'So, what are you doing now, Greet?'

'I'm working in a cottage industry', she said.

'Thank goodness that you've been able to get a job. But, if you can—I mean you and your husband—you ought to open up a business of your own, even if it's only on a very small scale. You could make clove cigarettes, for example, or noodles or bean curd, soybean and other cakes. You could get into any cottage industry at all. Besides agriculture, this country also subsists on small, unsophisticated industries doesn't it? When daily life has become stable from the results of enterprises like that, stable in the sense of people being able to eat three meals a day, then we'll be able to expand those industries, for example, by increasing capital, which means increasing the work force, looking for markets and so on'. I was amused as my rather long statement came out sounding like a speech.

'That's all theory, what's needed is practice', Greet said after a few moments.

'Cottage industry is practice; making speeches about it is not', I said.

'In that case, you should be the first one to set an example. Come here, and live among the tobacco plantations and open up a cigarette making business or whatever you like' said Greet, laughing.

'I think a cottage industry making cigarettes would have difficulties here, because tobacco is exported to Bremen, and the cloves would have to be bought from outside Java. Hey! Here we are chattering on about things that have nothing to do with our meeting. At this stage, I'm a man without a home, let alone a home industry'.

Greet threw me a sidelong feminine glance and I had probably stolen a glance at her too. Because of that our past began to flare up from a far away place of mountains and clouds in her native inland village outside Java, where I had once been a teacher. But, I had to put a stop to all that!

'I'd better take you home, Greet. I'd like to meet your husband'.

'O.K. but aren't you busy tonight?' she asked.

'No', I said.

We were only about a hundred metres or so from the spot where we'd met, and at this point Greet's child became a bit difficult.

'I want something to eat! I want a drink...' she whined, pointing to a nearby restaurant.

So, dinner was on the agenda, during which our conversation returned to the past.

Suddenly, a car pulled up in front of the restaurant and in came the young man who had been with Greet earlier. Immediately she left me and went over and spoke with him for a few seconds, then came back to our table.

'That young fellow is a pest, but the trouble is he's related to this one's father', Greet said, indicating the child.

'You're having me on, Greet', I smiled sourly at her. 'Your husband is probably a coffee or tea merchant; and you own a car, but you pretend that you work in a cottage industry'.

Keeping her eyes on her food and drink, Greet didn't say anything. When we came out of the restaurant, the car had gone.

'Where's the car?' I asked.

'I told him to let them know at home that a guest was coming'.

'There's no need to go to any trouble. After all, we've had dinner together haven't we?'

'All right. Let's go by pedicab', Greet suggested.

I got quite a shock when I went into Greet's house. After we'd got out of the pedicab, I kept asking where I was being taken to by the wife of this ex-army officer who now owned a car because he was probably a tobacco merchant. We passed through clumps of bamboo along a dark, narrow track leading down to the river, crossed a bamboo bridge, climbed back up through more bamboo and came out at a settlement of village houses, most of which were made of woven bamboo, with low roofs. Was this the residence of a tobacco merchant who owned a car? And, after Greet's husband came out: was this the director of a tobacco business, or a small industry? I didn't know what to think! Seeing what I saw, I felt weary in mind and spirit. This was all a journey. A mental exercise, and if my mind was tired, then there was nothing for it but to take a break.

That wasn't too hard to do. I just raised my dark glasses, opened my ears, and a kind of entertaining diversion was served up in front of me! The Honourable Gentleman's speech was still droning on like an old motor-bike exhaust pipe, and the masses in the state building were like swarms of worker bees buzzing. Sometimes, these humans became grinning monkeys, and sometimes they turned into dried fish, laid out in rows on mats in the sun, with bulging eyes that no longer functioned as eyes, gazing at the Honourable Minister. Sometimes they all turned into upturned turtles or crabs, with arms and legs reaching for the sky like the outstretched arms of the *kecak* dancers in Bali!

My break was over! I put my dark glasses on again and settled back comfortably in the chair.

Greet's husband was still alive. He was a human being and it's the human race in general that has created civilisations of soldiers with weapons that they turn on each other. Why do we have these industries of war? You see, Greet's husband was totally blind as the result of an explosion. Because of that, this blind man was serving Greet as best he could, by becoming the director of a cottage industry!

As we were talking about the past, and asking and answering questions about our respective presents, the young fellow whom I'd seen earlier arrived, and with a voice that sounded like a snarling cat. He said, 'This man who's sent for you isn't a nobody. He's a V.I.P. from Jakarta, do you realise that? Now get a move on!'

Then, in an instant, Greet had gone, leaving her husband sitting facing one ex-schoolteacher.

'Lieutenant!' I started to speak.

The man squared his jaw when I still honoured his officer status. Such a pose reminded me of the poses on the statues of heroes.

'If you will excuse me, I must go now', I said.

'Don't go. Please stay the night here...' then it grew quiet.

'Teacher', he called me by my former title. 'If a plane crashes, then at least the aluminium can still be broken off by the villagers and made into spoons, food containers, rice steamers and so on'.

'That's what you call cottage industry', I said.

'If a convoy of trucks is blown up by a mortar, the springs can still be collected to be made into machetes for working in the rice paddies and the fields', he continued.

'That's cottage industry too, Lieutenant', I added.

'But, in every war people too are destroyed. Those who die are gathered into heroes' graves. The maimed, who survive, are the ones like me', he said softly.

'Lieutenant, what you were talking about in the first case are fictitious industries, in other words, fairy-tale industries. What you were talking about secondly is the sex industry. Indonesia already has industries of that sort, and if they're on a small scale, they are still cottage industries', I said, taking a breath. 'It is appropriate for Greet to say that she's working in a cottage industry'.

'Yes, but how sad it is that I sacrificed my eyes for industries like that. I want our country to become a nation of large industries so that you, as a teacher working in the education industry, can be happy in your old age', he said, his voice savouring his hope as though he were dreaming.

'I left our up-and-down education industry a long while ago', I said, 'and now I'm working in a large industry with a big salary and plenty of perks'.

'Of course, you would expect Jakarta to be a city of large industries. Which one of them do you work in?'

'In the speech making industry. I'm a member of the V.I.P. party visiting here'.

'What? You're no different from Greet!'

'Yes, you're right. We're both examples of the people of this country under so much pressure, because, on the one hand we are drawn by the ideals of independence, moral goodness, pureness of heart, and so on, and on the other hand we are drawn by our needs'.

Frankly, I was mentally exhausted confronting this blind officer. I fell asleep on the chair in front of him, and only woke up when I was startled by the loud applause in the state building. I opened my eyes and joined in the ovation, turning to the front, to the right and to the left, to the people who were on their feet. The masses in the building stood up and clapped loudly as the party was leaving. I grew more silent in the noise of the ovation.

(originally published as 'Tepuk Tangan Perjalanan', *Horison*, 1970, 6(5), pp.170–72, 175.)

A Letter

Putu Wijaya

Translated by Marian May

A woman of indeterminate age woke before dawn to write a letter to her husband. In her crumpled nightclothes she sat at her husband's desk. He had been abroad for a year already. Her face was oval and pale. She was beautiful, strikingly so. But the sorrow which lined her face stole her good looks, making her dreary and plain. She seemed wretched and dejected. Suppressed passion, disappointment and loneliness had already turned to hatred.

Above the desk hung a photograph of her husband, taken when they were still boyfriend and girlfriend. He was dressed in his work clothes, which he wore rather carelessly. His hair was ruffled by the wind. He was smiling; there lay all his attraction. His beguiling smile made even the pillars of the factory behind him into an interesting background. He gazed straight ahead, right into the eyes of anyone looking at the photo. His eyes were full of understanding and protectiveness.

Meanwhile, on the bed which she had just left, their third child was sleeping soundly. On another bed the twins snored in unison. Everything seemed peaceful. Under the bed on a pile of books a cat, too, was sound asleep, completing the homely scene.

The woman yawned. Her eyes filled with tears. She forced herself to take a sheet of paper. After a good deal of thought she began to write.

My Husband,

For months I have waited for a letter from you, but till now not one has come. It's more than a year now since you left me and the children here at home. The children are really missing you and I am amazed that we haven't had any news so far. I keep waiting, but wait in vain, everytime the postman goes by.

You have to understand that you have a duty to consider our peace of mind. It is especially hard for me looking after our three small children who so very much need a guiding hand just now. Can't you take even a little responsibility for them? You at least have an obligation to consider them, if not me. I don't care what you're doing. Although you have never sent any word, I've heard from some of your friends that everything has changed. Yes, men will be men, I realise that. I'm not demanding anything; I realise that I can't make any emotional demands on you. So I won't.

The woman stopped for a moment to read it through again. She put in the date which she had forgotten. Then she became hesitant about whether she should add anything to the words 'My husband'. For the time being she decided not. Then she crossed out the part about the children missing him.

After that she tried to continue, but it seemed to become more difficult, because she had to get a feel for the mood again by reading what went before. But the more she read those sentences the more she felt they were not right. She crossed out a great deal, and finally decided to take a new sheet of paper.

On the fresh sheet, she began to write a new sentence. She felt she did not need to open it by addressing her husband. She went straight to the point. This is what she wrote:

Almost twenty times I have written to you. Now I have no more patience to wait for your generosity. I have to know where I stand. But remember that as well as me there are still three others who...

She could not finish this sentence. She took another sheet of paper and began this way:

From the outset I have been suspicious and apprehensive. But at the time...

But she seemed unsatisfied with this sentence too. She screwed up the paper and threw it in the rubbish bin.

She sighed and wiped her face with her hand. Her long hair hung down over her shoulders. She really was a stunningly beautiful woman, if only she could have freed herself from this depression.

She got up from the desk, trying to shake off her confusion. She was slender and alluring. In her dishevelled state, her full breasts were firm and prominent and her bottom round and smooth. She filled the peaceful room with the silent scream of a lonely soul. She moved towards her bed, and stood watching her child. She stroked his cheek, then was reminded again of her husband. The memory tortured her. She imagined all the things he might be doing. She remembered the sorrow and loneliness of every night. Her pointless loyalty. Her loving letters, not one of which was ever answered.

The woman became angry. Her eyes became wild and her breathing rapid. Quickly she went back to the desk. She wrote hurriedly:

> *I have been patient long enough. Now at last I understand what you're trying to do. Taking off, leaving your wife and family, not sending any news! It just doesn't make sense to me. I know what you're doing now. You're probably living it up at some night club with a student or a striptease artist. I don't give a shit! But you must take the responsibility for these three precious sons; they need a father's guiding hand. And...*

And that letter was torn up too when she felt she had gone too far in writing 'precious sons'. She wrote the same opening sentences, then continued:

> *I am not old-fashioned, but I really don't understand why you are doing this. What hurts me most is that I can't imagine why someone like you, whom I trusted so completely, could behave like this. How could you possibly build your happiness on the ruins of my heart?*

She read over these sentence several times, then seemed deeply moved by them. They captured how she really felt. She blinked. And her full lips trembled. Then she began to cry. Her hands were shaking but she continued to write:

> *I just cannot understand you. You're so smug, you must think you're really smart for getting away with doing this to me. To me! Always regarded by our friends as so sensitive. How could you leave me just like that; I didn't do anything. I'll never be able to do anything now. And you, I'll bet you're feeling great about it all. You must be feeling really proud of yourself. I can't imagine*

how you could bear to be so happy, when you've hurt me so much.

The woman could not continue her letter. Her tears flooded down onto the paper, smudging the writing. She hunched over with her head on the desk. She could restrain herself no longer. Both hands trembled as she toyed with the edges of the paper. Then without thinking she screwed it up.

Meanwhile the clock on the wall struck four. Outside a couple of roosters were crowing to greet the day which would soon be dawning. Inside the room the peace had been disturbed by her weeping. The smallest child woke with a start, stretched and began to whimper. When his mother paid no attention to him he too began to cry.

The woman quickly raised herself from the desk. She wiped her eyes, swollen from crying through the night. She put her arms around the child and soothed him lovingly. The child buried his head in his mother's breast. His face closely resembled his father's face hidden there. Then the woman kissed his cheek, as she had kissed her husband's when they were still together.

The child was soon calmed. In a moment he had gone back to sleep, stretching his little arms in the air as he dreamed. He had no awareness that his mother lay sobbing beside him, staring at the ceiling, as she pondered again the happy memories of better times. When they first met, when they married, the happy years, until her husband had to go overseas to continue his studies.

Half an hour later the woman awoke from her reverie. She let go the beautiful memories. She remembered that this was no time for daydreaming. She must finish the letter, because there would be no time later. Her friend, who was going overseas, to where her husband was, was coming at seven to collect the letter.

She got up slowly. Weary and desperate, she took another sheet of paper. Sitting at the desk as she had done dozens of times before, she started to rewrite the letter:

My husband,

This is my final letter. I can't be bothered convincing myself any longer. Tell me honestly. I will accept it willingly. All I ask is that you don't leave me in this uncertainty. Especially, with responsibility for our children.

She stroked the paper. Suddenly she felt fed up. What was the point in explaining it all. How could her husband possibly not know? It would only make him more arrogant. That was usually the way it worked with people like that.

Slowly she folded the letter. She folded it carefully then deliberately tore it up. She ripped it slowly into shreds. Then she heaped all the unfinished letters into a single pile. Next she went to the kitchen to fetch matches. And burned the letters.

The flames leapt like a dancer, while the woman sat on her chair watching the letters turn to ashes. Resting her chin on her hand, she gazed thoughtfully at the tongues of flame. Meanwhile, the cat which had been asleep under the bed woke up. Slowly it approached the fire and observed it closely.

The clock struck five. The woman came to from her daydream. She was sad and lonely, but had no more tears to express her suffering. Now she stood next to the cat in the room. She looked at her children. The three boys she loved so dearly. She looked at the books, the pictures and the clothing left by her husband when he went abroad. Then she glanced again at the photo her husband had left behind. Suddenly she felt very different. She saw herself. She saw herself as the one responsible for everything in the room.

She walked over to the mirror and tried to look at herself. She wasn't as beautiful as she used to be. She wasn't as young. But it was more than that. There was also something else. She felt she was no longer as naive as before. For a long time she remained gazing at herself.

Then with greater determination she went back to the desk again. She picked up the fountain pen which had earlier fallen to the floor. Now she wrote without hesitation. She wrote with precision, with no uncertainty. She did not even hesitate in choosing words. And while she wrote her eyes seemed to grow brighter. She bit her lip and narrowed her eyes. She really was an attractive woman.

The sun was rising just as she finished writing. The woman left the paper on the desk because she intended to add one or two more sentences later when she was to hand it over.

Calmly then, she went back to bed. She put her arms around her child and shut her eyes, trying to forget it all.

The cat climbed on to the desk to chase a gecko. There, right on top of the letter, it succeeded in catching its prey. Its tiny paw was right on the first sentence, which was followed by:

> *I am anxious and all the children miss you, but I am sure you are missing us far more. You have never written, but we know it's only because you are busy, or perhaps there are things which prevent you from writing. All of us at home will always try to be a comfort to you. Stay healthy and try to look after yourself properly for us. I'll keep on writing to you, to keep you company while you're busy. We're all well, and proud of you. You're the pride of your sons and my most prized possession...*

Six o'clock already. And the woman had not yet woken. She was dreaming peacefully. She smiled in her sleep. When her youngest son, lying on her breast, opened his eyes he looked at his mother in amazement.

Jakarta, 17 October 1969

(originally published as 'Ini Sebuah Surat', *Horison,* 1970, 5, May, pp.132–34, and reprinted in Ajip Rosidi (ed.), 1977, *Laut Biru Langit Biru*, Pustaka Jaya, Jakarta, pp.595–600.)

Jakarta

Totilawati Tjitrawasita

translated by David T. Hill

When the attendant handed him the guest book he felt a little hurt. It was strange, like having to make an appointment to see your own brother. After all, it wasn't as though his brother was a doctor. Holding the book he looked carefully at the attendant, then slowly he asked: 'Does everyone have to fill in this book? Even his brother or his father, for instance?'

The person questioned only nodded and handed him a ball-point pen.

'Please write: your name, address and the reason for your visit'.

Suddenly he felt an urge to make fun of it all. Restraining his laughter he wrote down: 'Name: Soeharto (not the president). Reason for visit: Family matters'.

'Is that enough?' he said while showing what he had written to the attendant.

'It's just a joke. A joke', he said several times, patting the back of the attendant who stared in amazement.

'He knows who I am', he said explaining.

'You haven't signed it yet, Sir. And your address?'

That was true. There was some wisdom in explaining his identity so the host would know and give him a warm welcome. Thus he wrote under his signature, in full, Waluyo ANOTOBOTO. He deliberately wrote the family name entirely in block letters and underlined it heavily. Once more he smiled, a look of pride etched upon his face.

'Like this?' he asked as if wanting the attendant's opinion.

He imagined his young brother hastily opening the door and embracing him, overcome with emotion, throwing all kinds of questions at him: 'How are Mum and Dad? How many kids has Tinah?' Then he saw himself patting this cousin (whom he called 'brother') on the back, and with the voice and manner of a parent, replying, 'Fine. They are all well. They send their love'.

When the door creaked he was startled out of his daydream. He stood up to greet his younger brother but saw straightaway that the person coming out was not him...but the attendant.

'Well?', he said impatiently.

'Have a seat, Sir, do sit down. The General has a guest at the moment. But I noticed that he was amazed to see your name there'.

Hearing this, he smiled and sat down again on the chair. He brushed off the dust that clung to his trousers, then took his cigarettes from his pocket.

'May I smoke?', he asked.

'Please do', said the attendant in a friendly tone. The guest's attitude really did induce a feeling of warmth. He held out the cigarettes under the nose of the attendant.

'Would you like one? Please!' The attendant answered with a shake of the head and a wave of the hand.

'Alright, but don't call me 'sir'. I'm no 'sir'. I'm just an ordinary man, just like you. My name is Waluyo. People call me 'Pak Pong'. Just you wait and see: your 'General' is sure to tease me with:

'Pak Pong, Pak Pong,
*you eat too much 'singkong',**
If you're so greedy,
you'll just have to eat dung'.

'Ever since we were young we have enjoyed joking around'. He laughed heartily, remembering his childhood, joking and playing around on the back of a water buffalo. As he laughed the attendant noticed that the guest had lost his teeth.

'Sir, er...Pak Pong, are you a farmer?' he asked hesitantly, afraid of hurting his feelings.

---

* Type of cassava.

'A farmer?

Am I built like a farmer? Oh, no! But when we were younger we did do a lot of martial art. That must have left its imprint upon my build. Or perhaps it's this Chinese-style shirt? I'm a primary school teacher in Nggesi village. That school has produced some important people. My first pupil became a captain. There's also been one who has become an engineer. But your General was a most outstanding student. He has a very sharp mind', he said while holding up his thumb in a gesture of praise for his younger brother's cleverness.

A bell, which suddenly rang three times, put an end to his tale. He saw the attendant stand up quickly saying, 'Wait a moment. You may be required'.

He was bewildered: 'Required…required?' he said to himself, sighing because he did not understand. He drew deeply on his cigarette and blew the smoke upwards. Again he imagined Paijo in front of him, thin as a rake, eating at the same table, sleeping in the same bed; his own little brother. Once when Paijo had an ulcer on his backside Waluyo had pounded *datura* leaves for a ointment. When his dry body was attacked by scabies Waluyo had cycled fifty kilometres to buy medicines in the city for his brother. Morning and evening he had ground sulphur, boiled water and soaked Paijo in a big tub. Thirty-five years ago, when they were both still children.

'Pak Pong, what would you like to drink?' As before the attendant came in suddenly, sat down and addressed him, scattering his thoughts of the past.

'The General said that I should keep you company because he is still busy. In a short while a special guest, the Minister, is coming. What would you like to drink? Juice, Coca Cola?'

'Anything at all will be fine. Coffee if you have it', he said humbly.

'Oh, but Jakarta is so hot. Why do you want coffee? But, tell me, are you really a relative of the General?', he asked pushing a cup in front of the guest.

'Yes. Actually I'm his cousin, but he was orphaned when he was small. His parents died in a cholera epidemic. There was just him and his younger sister, named Tinah. Then the two of them were taken in by my parents. We come from the same stock, raised in the same hovel in Nggesi. We were a real farming family but he was rather different, with an extraordinary mind. From the time he was small he showed talent, always doing astonishing things. For that reason we all agreed to send him to school in the city. At that time it meant we had to sell our cattle and rice to pay the expenses, then later when I became a teacher I sent all my wages to pay his way. In our village we got by somehow, finding things to eat. Oh, is that the Minister?' Suddenly he stopped his story and pointed to the street. As if stung by a bee the attendant who had been sitting near him leapt up and half ran to greet the guest who had just arrived. The attendant quaked as he opened the car door for him.

'Go straight in, Sir', said the attendant, ushering the Minister into the reception room.

Waluyo just sat there, flabbergasted. He noted the incident in his heart: when Paijo's guest was a Minister he met him straightaway without any delay. Then he counted up how many years it had been since they had seen each other. Was Paijo also as fat as that Minister? Suddenly a kind of longing seized him, rising up inside him. He wanted to see his young brother! He felt he wanted to kick down the wall in front of him. He stood up, restless, and walked towards the door. When he touched the door knob the door was pushed from the inside and someone appeared in front of him: the attendant. Laughing gleefully he slapped the elderly Pak Pong on the shoulder.

'Good news, Pak. Good news. They are both beaming. The Minister has lots of money; and that means I'll be getting my share. Oh, so you are the General's cousin. You do look like him, and the General has always been proud of his family. In his speeches he always mentions being a village boy, the people's suffering and the struggle against the Dutch', said the attendant to the guest, as he tried to remember again the things the General had once said.

'Yes, our house was once an army post during the guerilla war. Is the Minister going to be long?', he asked impatiently.

'Provided the General is prepared to sign, they usually settle things quickly. Would you like something more to drink?'

He shook his head wearily, silently cursing the Minister and other visitors who lined up there taking his brother's time.

Because he was mentally and physically worn out he dozed off. The attendant did not disturb him but just let him slump limply in the chair. After sitting like that for some time— even Waluyo himself did not realise how long—he suddenly heard the bell ring again three times. The attendant shook him by the shoulder.

'It's your turn Pak Pong. Let me take you in'. The attendant sounded genuinely friendly. He began to smile, sharing in Pak Pong's happiness.

When the door gaped open Waluyo was dumbfounded by what he saw in front of him. He cast his gaze around taking in all he could. The room was very beautiful. Cool air touched his skin. There was a freshness in the room. Amidst the luxurious furnishings sat a tall man wearing dark glasses. Was he really Paijo? Yes, Pak Pong was not mistaken; there was the mole on his cheek. Pak Pong rushed in, overcome by emotion. '...Jo...', he called out loudly. As he went to embrace the man sitting behind the desk he stopped suddenly because the man did not stand up, but kept sitting in his chair. The tall man took off his glasses slowly then held out his hand.

'Hallo, Pak Pong, how are you? I'm pleased to meet you here, brother. How are mother, father and Tinah?' he asked flatly without emotion.

The man called Pak Pong just stood agape. 'Brother, Mother and Tinah'?

He registered the new, formal-sounding Indonesian words. Not the Javanese terms he had used in the past. 'Fine, *Dik*, fine. They all send their love to you', he said nervously following his brother's lead. Saying '*Dik*', the Indonesian word for 'brother', sounded awkward. In the past, when they used to wash water buffaloes together in the river, he had addressed the man sitting in front of him with '*le*', the affectionate Javanese term an adult would use for a very young boy.

'You're just as you always were, still cheerful, looking as young as ever and wearing those Chinese-style shirts'. They laughed loudly together. But Pak Pong noticed something different in his brother's face: insincerity. His happiness vanished. The reminiscences that he wanted to pour out in lots of stories caught in his throat. He sank into a feeling of alienation. A barrier stretched out in front of him. While he did not know what created it he could feel it. Every breath his brother took suggested Paijo's nervousness at his presence.

'Where are you staying?' asked the man whom Pak Pong had coddled since he was young. The question hurt him deeply.

'Gambir. Are you busy, *Dik*? I've got something for you from Mother'. His voice trembled and he restrained a feeling of vexation. He heard himself how strange the formal Indonesian word for 'Mother' sounded, coming from his mouth. For more than half a century he had been living in this world and this was the first time in his life he had referred to his mother in this formal way.

'From Mother? Good. I'll get it later. In a little while I have to go to a meeting at Bina Graha, the Presidential Office. So you're staying at Gambir? If that's the case I'll get the attendant to take you back there. Later on tonight I'll expect you at home. Come around and have dinner at our place with the family'.

The man stood up and walked his brother to the door, calling and giving orders to the driver and the attendant.

Later the General's red car glided swiftly through the city, as quick as lightning.

'Which part of Gambir, Sir?' asked the driver on the trip.

'The railway station', he answered calmly.

'The station? On the left or right of it?' asked the attendant wanting clarification.

'No, at the station itself. What time does the next train leave Jakarta? I don't have any family here except for him. I feel sorry for my brother; he seems so busy. There must be lots of guests at his house, so that he has no room or time for me. I feel sorry for him. I'd better not disturb him', he said honestly, without prejudice, quietly as if talking to himself.

'Pak Pong...', the attendant said to him softly, 'if you'd like to, we could squeeze you in at my humble place. The train leaves

Jakarta at five o'clock tomorrow morning. There is one going this evening but tickets cost Rp.10,000'.

Pak Pong stretched out both arms. They shook hands warmly, each touching his chest in the common Islamic greeting of friendship.

'God bless you. You don't have any objections to taking me in? I'll only be staying one night'. The attendant shook his head gently without speaking, merely looking sadly at the man who sat near him.

That night Pak Pong walked around Jakarta with his friend, the attendant. The events of that day did not show in the slightest in his expression; his face still shone. He had accepted the reality as something natural: his brother was an important man, busy with many affairs of state. Every time he saw a red car pass nearby he asked 'Isn't that my brother's car? I hope he hasn't come to pick me up. We did promise to have dinner together at seven o'clock'.

The attendant patted him on the shoulder: 'There are hundreds of red cars here. And tonight the General is at the Palace welcoming guests from overseas'.

'At the Palace? At the President's house, you mean?' His eyes widened, expressing his great amazement.

'Yes. The President's residence. See that, the lights glittering: that's a Night Club. Do you know what a Night Club is?' Suddenly the attendant felt important, smarter than his guest, his General's cousin.

'A Night Club is the centre of night life in this city. A place where the wealthy throw their money around. Five watt lights, dim atmosphere, beautiful women, strong drink, nude dancing and wild music. In short, it's fantastic!' said the attendant holding out his raised thumb in approval.

'So, what do they do in there?' His voice caught in his throat suggesting a great fear.

'Dance, embrace. That's the way it is in Jakarta', he answered casually.

'Oh! May God have mercy! Does my brother go there often?' he asked softly and sadly.

'Not there. To the Paprika, but it's just the same. The tickets are more expensive there. In fact, six thousand'.

'Six thousand. Equal to two months of my wages', he sighed softly. He felt the glittering lights were piercing his eyes, while the noise of the city cut into his heart. Dimly he began to realise that he had lost his brother, his beloved Paijo.

The hapless Pak Pong gazed at the city with resentment in his heart. Jakarta, its hustle and bustle, Bina Graha, the buildings, the president's Freedom Palace, the Night Clubs, the red cars, had all separated him from his brother. He gazed at the small parcel sent by his mother. Then he gave it to the attendant.

'For you. A *batik* sarung made by my mother's own hand. Etched in it is a mother's love for her child. Lines from the land of his birth sent to bind the ties of family'. Two tears moistened the old cheeks, marking the event in time.

(Translated from the Indonesian version published in *Sebuah Cinta Sekolah Rakyat*, 1976, Pustaka Jaya, Jakarta, pp.38–45; originally appearing in *Mimbar*, 1972, 21(2), pp.39–41.)

Matias Akankari

Gerson Poyk

---

translated by David T. Hill

Matias Akankari was taken from the dense jungles of West Irian by a parachutist. In a night-time jump over the jungle, the parachutist had become entangled in a tall tree. With great difficulty he saved himself and when he had recovered, he set off on foot in search of his companions. But before he managed to find them he came across Matias—a sick and suffering Irianese man. He gave Matias what medical treatment he could and luckily Matias recuperated. Although unfortunately Matias could not speak Indonesian, he was a most trustworthy guide, and saved the parachutist from all sorts of calamities, enabling the man to return safely to Jakarta.

That briefly is the story of how he met Matias. But it did not end there, for Matias Akankari was then taken by the parachutist to Jakarta. Unlike other people from Jakarta serving in West Irian who went home bearing TVs, refrigerators, and all kinds of luxury goods left behind by the Dutch, the parachutist took his mate Matias, a friend in time of need whom he would never forget.

But Matias was more than a luxury good. He ate about three helpings a meal so in just one day nine plates of food would disappear into his belly. Of course the parachutist, who was only a private, was taken aback. How could he feed this 'luxury good' on his paltry wage?

After giving this a great deal of thought, the parachutist finally came up with an idea. He dressed Matias up in some smart, expensive clothes which he had bought in West Irian. Matias put on a wool suit, a shirt, a tie, and imported shoes. In a borrowed jeep the two of them headed for the bustling city centre. Matias had only been in the capital for three days, and was agog at all the neon glitter of the city's lights. He was bedazzled, amazed at the buildings, amazed at the human jungle. No-one looked like him. He blinked and blinked, turning his head right and left. Occasionally, when some fascinating sight was scattering from view behind the speeding car, it was as if his head was screwed on back the front.

Arriving at Senin, they went to the movies. It was the first time that Matias Akankari had seen a movie. Since all his attention was riveted on the screen, when the parachutist left him alone just for the hell of it, Matias did not sense a thing and was totally oblivious.

'I'm bored!', said the parachutist to a friend of his—another parachutist—who happened to be watching the film too. 'I slipped out leaving Matias Akankari on his own when he was watching the film. I'm curious to know how someone primitive survives in a big city. Who knows, maybe one day I'll make a fortune writing a book about it!' laughed the private to his friend, before hurrying towards the jeep and bolting.

As soon as the film ended, Matias started, and looked around him. It was only now that his heart began pounding, but because he did not speak a word of Indonesian he could not say a thing. His reddish eyes sunk in his black skin scoured amongst the forest of bodies, looking for his friend. In vain. He was swept outside with the stream of humanity. Once outside his heart drummed anxiously.

The man upon whom he depended totally—the parachutist he had met in the middle of his friendly jungle—had actually vanished. Matias was in the midst of a jungle—a jungle of lights, human bodies, pedicab and car wheels, and strange sounds; in short, a jungle of commotion not nearly as peaceful nor as friendly as his jungle expanse. He drifted along, totally alone.

Suddenly he heard the sound of a loud speaker. Ah! That was something he had seen once in West Irian when some important officials came from Jakarta. The loudspeaker crackled loudly but unfortunately he could not make out anything it said. He approached the loud noise, only because he felt drawn by memories of his home village. But while last time lots of people just like him had swarmed around the device with the loud noise, hearing their own regional language, now the people around it were unlike him, and the language was different.

Slowly he broke through into the centre of the circle, to see the person speaking. 'He must be a friend of the man who came to West Irian before', he said to himself in his own language. When Matias needed help, such sounds were useless. He needed someone who would take him home; to a home with a roof, a place to sleep and regular food. He needed someone to protect him.

Then, as he stood, anxiously hoping, there came a helping hand. A gentle, friendly creature, speaking to him with a distracting gaze, made his heart jump for joy. There followed a beckoning hand gesture. Then a pedicab arrived and the two of them left together for a district Matias Akankari had never visited before.

On entering the woman's bedroom, Matias was immediately sent into a spin by this small, delicate creature. And even the firm-bodied Matias submitted! He could do nothing else. He needed a friend, a home, a small island at which to harbour. He found it. Happily he spent that night sleeping beside this woman who had been so friendly to him. Waking early he was given food and drink, all of which had already been laid out on the bedside table.

After breakfast he was sent for another spin. And he submitted again. At the conclusion of all these goings on (which were very new to him) another ritual began.

Sitting facing the woman, it was as though Matias was watching a pantomime. He was bewildered. For a long time, for a very long time, he was puzzled. He only understood when the woman pointed to the pieces of paper. Her finger pointed accusingly at Matias' chest, then turned to her own breast again.

Matias shook his head and threw up his hands to tell the woman that he didn't have any paper like that. He didn't have anything except what hung on his back.

Then the woman grabbed hold of Matias' coat, and pointed accusingly at his chest. Matias understood that gesture. He took the coat off and gave it to the woman.

After this scene, the small, delicate creature turned quite rough. She dragged Matias to the door, and shoved him outside. Then slammed the door and had a rest.

Matias turned left and right. But there was no-one he knew. He felt like he had been cast back into a jungle not nearly as friendly as his in Irian.

Now he walked slowly away. In a city like Jakarta, to walk for hours just for the sake of walking was something of a record for people who usually lived on wheels, but Matias regarded it as quite normal. It was common for him to walk for days in his friendly jungle.

As evening was falling he came across a church on his journey. There was no other way for him to expiate the sins he committed unintentionally during that one night with the woman except by going into the church and asking Christ's forgiveness. And he went into the church to pray. When he came out, the day had turned to night. He sat down in front of the church reminiscing about his home village.

There, on his distant island, he went to church wearing a *koteka* (penis gourd) and stood amidst a crowd of people in the choir in front of the pastor and sang. He had been in the choir since he was a child. Almost all the choir members were illiterate but the hymns were like songs everywhere across the face of the earth—easily memorised.

Once Matias made such a nuisance of himself that he was expelled from the *koteka* choir. This was the stir he caused. When all the choir members were standing in front of the congregation and the minister to sing, Matias, who was right at the very front, took off his *koteka* which had evidently been made into a flute. When he played the hymn on it all the congregation listened in delight, but then broke out laughing, which shattered the solemnity of the worship. Because of this Matias was berated by the pastor and the other choir members and was kicked out of the choir... Well, that's the way it goes! Even now he took his *koteka* everywhere he went. He put his hand inside his shirt, and took his *koteka* out. Slowly he began to play.

It was getting late. A young man carrying a folder drifted shakily towards him from the distance. Matias observed him carefully. As he came closer, it was obvious that the sole of the man's shoe had come partially unstuck. He had first to lift his toe up high before putting it back down on the ground. And it was this that made him walk so unsteadily. Nevertheless he eventually arrived at the church, went inside and not long afterwards emerged once again.

'This church is always open. It's different from the other churches in the city', said the young man, sitting down close to Matias who was more smartly dressed than the young man holding the folder. Matias was still wearing the expensive imported long sleeve shirt, a tie, and woollen trousers. The young man was in second-hand clothes.

Matias did not understand what he said, but since the young man did not know that Matias could not speak Indonesian he went on talking.

'I have absolutely had it with trudging around this city! Now the sole on my shoe keeps flapping like an iguana's tongue! I am actually a university graduate but I haven't been able to get work yet', he said, toying with the iguana tongue of his shoe.

Seeing that, Matias took off his shoes and gave them to the unemployed graduate.

'Wearing shoes is torture for me! In dense forests and vast jungles full of thorns and prickles I never wore shoes and my feet never hurt. But after wearing these shoes my feet are killing me! Here, take them', said Matias in his Irianese language. The man only heard strange sounds and saw the new shoes heading towards his feet.

From the church porch the two of them headed to Banteng Square. There, without speaking, they fell asleep under the West Irian Liberation Monument. That night both slept very soundly. Waking early the graduate sneaked away, leaving Matias. He was afraid of waking him because if Matias woke, they would certainly both end up travelling on together. That would be too much of a spectacle. So he just left a letter in Matias' shirt pocket.

When Matias awoke his friend was no longer there. He saw the piece of paper in his pocket but because he could not read he turned the paper over and over then screwed it up and threw it away. He went back to sleep again on the cold, expensive tiles, blown by the wind of Banteng Square.

When he woke up it was evening. Although his stomach was empty, he was still energetic enough to walk. He wandered through a district with many homeless poor. Here he came across a woman giving birth, lying on sheets of paper. He remembered that Christ had once been born on hay and wrapped in swaddling clothes. This time he met another christ being born on sheets of paper! Then in the midst of the birth it started to rain. Fortunately the homeless woman had some sheets of plastic. But under this plastic 'roof' was spread only paper. Matias took off all that clothed his body and handed it over to the woman who was giving birth to the baby.

'Thanks, thank you', said the woman.

Matias put on his own traditional garb. He fitted his *koteka*. By that time the rain was getting heavier and heavier, and after everything had finished—he had given the woman all the help he could—he walked off in the rain.

He arrived at Thamrin Road, a highway fenced in by multi-storey buildings. Near the Hotel Indonesia he stood agog. All the cars dashing through the rain had to stop or slow down to check him out. At one stage a car passed which contained a creature like him, a black man wearing a suit, accompanied by a graceful, beautiful, sweet girl. The car pulled over near him, with the entire contents of the car staring. Seeing someone who looked like him, Matias leapt forward eagerly and clung to the rear of the car. It accelerated immediately but Matias managed to keep a hold. Finally the car headed for the Hotel Indonesia and dropped off the black guest. He was an American Negro. Matias had guessed wrongly.

When Matias noticed a large number of uniformed people beginning to crowd around him, gesturing as if they were trying to capture an animal, he bolted back into the heavy downpour.

The people were not brave enough to follow, because they were concerned about getting wet. Only, not long afterwards, he was tailed by a person in a raincoat. The man chased him. Of course, Matias took off like an arrow. As he was passing a multi-storey building, he ducked in. He ran blindly into a narrow room, the door of which opened then shut suddenly.

It turned out the narrow room was a lift which rose upwards and suddenly opened again into a dim room in which only a stage was illuminated by spot lights. On it were naked women wearing only skimpy coverings on their genitals, just like him: he wore a *koteka* while the women wore G-strings. And...would you believe it? The dance the women were doing was more or less the same as dances at Matias' home village. He leapt towards the stage with his *koteka* on, and danced with the women. Applause arose from the audience in their dimly lit seats.

But all this brought Matias' wanderings to an end. The newspapers published his story and Matias was re-united with his parachutist 'master'. But this time Matias had become wealthy. He had been given funds so he could be returned to his beloved village and lots of people there wanted to hear his stories.

He told the tale that the 'high class' in Jakarta are just the same as in West Irian: they all only cover their genitals!

('Matias Akankari' was originally published in Gerson Poyk, 1972, *Matias Akankari: Kumpulan Cerita Pendek*, Balai Pustaka, Jakarta (2nd ed., 1975).)

Coming Home

Wildan Yatim

---

translated by Jan Lingard

He stood opposite the banana plantation and inspected his house; it was still solid. It had bark walls, a roof thatched with palm leaves, a high, open space under the house and a jutting out kitchen. There wasn't a glimmer of light to be seen, and there was no sound of voices. With his heart pounding he turned off the road and went into the plantation. Leafy shadows played on his shirt.

'Limah! Limah! Limah! Limah!' he shouted.

There was no answer. The place was deserted. He went up the steps, pushed the door and pounded on it. It was locked from the outside.

'Limah! Limah!' he called again, pounding on the door as though he were pounding on and questioning his heart. There was no movement at all inside. But there was a faint voice from the house across the road. He went down the steps, and looked at the open and empty chicken coop under the house.

'Who's that?' a man shouted.

'There's no one there!' a woman called.

A cat came up to him, meeowing and rubbing itself up against his legs. He walked round to the back of the house, knocking into the cat. He stopped at the beginning of a path with earthen steps. At the bottom of a steep bank there was a water spout, gurgling and gleaming dully. The reflections of the banana leaves that bobbed up and down above him played on the water. A couple of fireflies flew by and perched on the bushes.

'It looks like Piko!' came another voice from across the road.

'Yes, maybe he's come home! Oh dear, and Halimah's not there!'

Taking a deep breath, he turned round and went across the road.

'Good heavens, Piko! It is you! Have you just arrived?'

A man wearing a white cap came down from the verandah and welcomed him and shook hands. He was followed by a woman who folded her prayer cape back over her shoulder but did not offer him her hand.

'Come on up to the house. Limah isn't there now. You'll spend the night here won't you', said the woman.

'There's no need for that Makcik Haji. I think I'd better go straight to my mother. Where have Halimah and our child gone to?'

'Oh, she's living in the plantation'.

'What for?'

People arrived from the neighbouring houses, crowding onto the verandah to shake hands.

'Come in and sit down', said the woman.

'I'd better go straight to my mother's house. Has Limah been living in the plantation for long?'

'Er, er, um...yes...maybe two months or so. That's right isn't it Bang Haji?'

Her husband nodded hesitantly, and lowered his gaze. Piko was surprised at their confusion. The others also lowered their gaze and turned away when he looked at them one by one. No one added anything to what Pak Haji and his wife had said.

Piko left. The young people, women and children crowded round in the yard, whispering secretively. Some followed him down the road. The shadows of the whispering coconut and *jambu* branches criss-crossed his body. The moon peeped out through breaks in the clouds, and the stars scattered in clusters as if they too were whispering secretly about him.

He stopped in front of a big house built on low poles. It had a pointed roof made of palm fibre and wooden walls. The verandah was small, with only enough room for three or four people to sit. He went up the steps to the verandah and knocked on the door.

'Who is it?' came a voice from inside.

'It's me, Mother, Piko!'

'Piko's come home, Aunty!' called a man at the bottom of the steps.

The bar of the door was heard being lifted and a woman wearing a prayer cape with its ends folded back appeared.

'God be praised!' she said, clasping Piko and hugging him tightly. 'I thought we would never see each other again my son', she said, weeping.

Piko disengaged himself and went and sat on a rattan mat in the long front parlour. The mother wiped her eyes with the edge of her blouse, and invited the people crowding around on the verandah to come inside.

'Get some mats, Ros!' she said hoarsely.

Ros, a girl about ten years old, started up from gazing at Piko. She hurried inside and came back bringing two white pandanus mats and unrolled them. Piko went and sat on one of them and the guests sat around him. Tobacco pouches and young *nipa* palm leaves were laid out in front of the men. They rolled cigarettes, and smoke wafted up and drifted out through the open windows. They'd been sitting for a few minutes when a married couple appeared. The husband was tall with a beard like a newly reaped rice field.

'Torkis, my brother!' Piko leapt up to greet him.

Torkis sat beside Piko, and his wife took a place among the women who were sitting close together opposite the doorway to the parlour. Some of them were peeling *areca* nuts, cutting them into pieces and handing them around. They were chattering or listening with the nuts held in their mouths.

Piko answered questions, at times faltering and lapsing into thought and coming back with a start if there was a sudden query. Coffee was passed around and in the kitchen women were busy boiling sweet potatoes and frying bananas.

Some asked questions about such things as whether Jakarta was crowded. Piko described how congested it was by pointing out that at least one or two people died every day in traffic accidents. He told them if you want to cross a street you have to do it in two stages. First you cross and stop half way waiting for the stream of traffic to ease, then go the rest of the way. You have to cross quickly too, and sometimes even run. It's better if you cross in a crowd—there's no fear of being hit. Now there are areas so congested that they've built bridges for getting across. Normally, bridges are used to cross rivers but in Jakarta they're also used for crossing roads. There are so many people packed together that there are never enough houses. Hundreds of thousands of people live in shacks or small huts alongside the railway lines or canals and sometimes these places are no better than the shelters we have here in the fields. Here, if you walk a distance of twenty-five kilometres you reach a new district. In Jakarta, you can walk fifty kilometres and still be in the city.

The people present clicked their tongues and nodded their heads in amazement.

When Piko was asked about his trading he said that as a man with no capital and little education he couldn't keep going. Men like him had to compete with tightly organised groups of Chinese traders who had plenty of capital. In addition, there were already too many petty traders on the footpaths, so earnings were only enough for a hand to mouth existence. He said he'd once been offered a place in a multi-level market that was being built so that the roadside and shop awning pedlars would move there. But he and a lot of his friends were in the same boat; they didn't have the money to pay the price for the place—between Rp.200,000 and Rp.400,000.

'The fact is that the multi-level market is only filled by the Chinese now and our people go on trading at the roadside and under shop awnings. What's more they are constantly being chased away and forced to move on'.

Piko said he was sorry because he hadn't brought any presents—he could only afford to pay the boat and bus fares home. The people reacted noisily, telling him that it didn't matter and they were thankful that he was back in the village safely, and that he wasn't hurt and hadn't come to any harm living in Jakarta all that time.

'That's the main thing', they said.

They took it in turns to tell Piko what had been happening in the village while he was away. They told him who'd died, who'd gone away to seek his fortune and who'd got married. They also mentioned the rice irrigation channels which hadn't been repaired again since the time of the 'upheaval'. They were still like they were before, and in fact, there was even less water. Bedah, the widow of Tapor who had been set on and killed by a gang of youths, had remarried and moved to another village, taking her children with her. Kabidin, someone who'd been lucky enough to be classified as 'C' (a suspected communist sympathiser' but against whom no proof could be found), no longer had to report or work as a street cleaner without pay. Smiling, the young people embellished their conversation about Kabidin, saying how he zealously went to the mosque and devoted himself to religion nowadays.

What made Piko relieved hearing their stories was that there were no longer any soldiers or police in the district, except in the subdistrict centre. He got the impression that the villagers were no longer under the continuous pressures that they had been before. Nevertheless the sources of livelihood were still inadequate. There wasn't enough water for the paddy fields, the rubber plantation didn't produce much, and the fish in the river were getting scarce. All these things made the people disheartened and want to escape by going away to try their luck elsewhere. He heard that almost half the young people had gone to Sidempuan or Medan. There were also some who'd gone on to Java, though Piko said he hadn't come across them. None of those who'd finished Junior High School, let along Senior High, had remained in the village.

As he thought about this Piko felt exasperated as to why people were so foolish going away in large numbers to look for opportunities. He'd only just realised that that was the wrong thing to do. He'd experienced the difficulty of making a living in Jakarta, whereas a person who stayed here only had to dig the soil and a livelihood was there. In Jakarta, although they worked desperately hard and sometimes staked their lives, the prospects for any livelihood were still dim.

When the cool evening breeze blew in through the windows, the visitors took their leave and one by one went home. The glasses and sweet potato skins were cleared up and taken away.

Finally Torkis, his wife and their mother were left. They sat close to each other and continued the conversation.

'Why isn't Halimah living at our house any more?' Piko asked them.

'You tell him, Torkis', said their mother.

It seemed that Halimah and Piko's son, Anwar, had been living for two months or more at her own parents' plantation. She'd had an argument with Torkis and his mother. Torkis said he saw Halimah associating with a married man who had a lot of children. His name was Abdullah and he came from across the Batang Kundur River. People said that Abdullah had given Halimah presents such as a pendant and a piece of batik cloth. That's why Torkis had driven her out of their house in the banana plantation, and she'd moved to the hut in her own parents' plantation. Later, Abdullah felt ashamed that a lot of people knew about his behaviour, and he took his family away to Medan. Torkis had wanted to write and let Piko know what had happened and tell him just to divorce Halimah, but unexpectedly Piko was home. If he wanted to go back to Jakarta, Torkis suggested that he just find another wife.

Their mother said that Halimah had behaved like a mad woman since she'd been ordered out of the house in the banana plantation. She had chased after Torkis in front of everyone in the market, pelting him with stones. So a lot of people knew about her behaviour—probably the news of it had spread far and wide. This was what made the family ashamed.

'How is she now?' Piko asked.

'She's isolated herself in the plantation. She never goes to the market or to see the neighbours. Her mother takes rice and so on to her'.

'Is Anwar all right?'

'Who knows!'

The mother went and shut the windows. Piko and Torkis sat lost in thought for some time, smoking one cigarette after another. The wind rustled in the rubber plantation, blowing on the fronds of the coconut trees beside the house.

'Do you all want to sleep here Torkis?' said the mother.

'No, Mother, we'll go home'. Torkis and his wife stood up and he said, 'Think it over carefully Piko. I think my suggestion is the only course you can take. If you're going back to Jakarta, and you want to find someone here, it's easy—there are plenty of girls. The other important thing is, don't let Anwar stay there with Halimah, or he'll end up crazy too. Bring him here as company for Rosni and his grandmother'.

Torkis and his wife went inside, then left, each carrying a dribbling, sleeping child. The mother barred the door and Piko continued staring into space. His mother sat beside him and stroked his shoulders.

'My poor Piko, coming home with no wife or child to greet you. So, what's to be done next?'

When he had left for Jakarta, Piko hadn't told his mother, only Halimah, and he'd told her not to say anything at first, until he wrote when he was half way there. He had told his mother he was going deep into the marshes at Batang Lingkung for a week with a lot of his friends, to go trapping fresh water fish. But in fact, he had gone straight to Simpang Empat and waited for a truck to Talu which could take a letter to the village saying he was going to Jakarta to try his luck.

For a year Mukdan, a friend from the same village who had lived in Jakarta for ten years, had helped him get started trading. From then on he'd lived in the heat, rain, dust and wind, frequently chased by the police or the cunning market inspectors. Later, he separated from Mukdan but he still traded at the roadside. At night he slept at his friends' houses or at Mukdan's. These places consisted of shacks with dirt floors, musty with the smell of bed bugs. Because he only made enough for two meals a day, he was always thinking about ways of making more. But it seemed that there was no way open in Jakarta for a man who was a sincere and honest worker. Then he got caught up in the world of lotteries and gambling, which seemed to be the only lucrative activities—that is if corruption isn't counted as a problem anymore because it's so common. Piko no longer realised that he was betting between Rp.50 and Rp.100 every week, and he was no longer aware that he had never hit the jackpot. Like madmen, he and his fellow roadside traders were absorbed in unravelling the code of the numbers game, while they were waiting for customers. They made guesses about every form of poem or picture in the newspapers, as to whether they were put there intentionally as clues to help figure out the betting numbers.

Towards the end, he was very worried and always dreaming about Anwar and Halimah. Heaven knows what was going on in the village. Finally, he decided to go back. Probably the political climate in the village had calmed down too. Surely four years were enough to dispel the hatreds which had arisen one after the other. First there was the resentment of the Muhammadiyah or the banned Masyumi Party towards the people of the left wing Islamic Party, Perti and the Communist Party. This resentment erupted when the Banteng Council and the Republican Revolutionary Government were in power, before Padang was bombed and the forces of the Central Government landed there. The vengeance of the Communists and Perti was unleashed against the Muhammadiyah when the Republican Revolutionary Government was pushed out of the district. They were branded as rebels, and members of their families were very severely abused. At that time, Piko was in 3rd year of Junior High School and with his classmates he avoided the trouble by going away to a remote village. The situation reversed when the 30th September Movement grab for power, dubbed 'Gestapu', erupted in 1965. Piko had taken a leading role in the ensuing events. He had been directly involved in inciting the emotions of those who had taken part in beating up the prominent figures in the Peoples' Youth and the Trade Union in that area. While the people they had attacked still had breath in their bodies, he'd helped to drag them to the channels and hold them underwater until there was a gurgling sound and they were drowned. There were even some of his friends whose vengeance was so extreme that they wanted to crush the testicles of the men they were torturing or to suck their spurting blood. When all the violence was over, Piko laid low.

'Do you want some *areca* nut Piko?' He was startled.

'Is there a piece?' he answered slowly, still deep in thought.

'You won't go away again, will you?'

'I don't know, Mother'.

'There's no need to go again son. Stay here and keep me company. I'm old. Who knows, if you go, we mightn't see each other again. Divorce Halimah, and then we'll look for a young girl here in the village. Everyone understands, son, and it would be natural for you to take that attitude'.

Piko went inside. He came back carrying a bag. His mother sat very close to him, to see what was in it.

'This is all I could bring, Mother', he said, taking out a piece of batik cloth in a plastic bag.

'Oooh, it's very beautiful Piko! Very beautiful!' she said, spreading it out on her lap. 'Don't you have anything for Torkis and his wife?' His mother refolded the cloth and put it in the bag.

'I didn't have enough money, Mother'.

'It doesn't matter. Later on you buy a piece of batik and a sarong on the quiet to give them. I'll give you the money'.

'It's a bit late isn't it Mother? They'll find out later anyway'.

'Ah, no they won't'.

'All right Mother', he said with a sigh. Actually, the length of cloth he'd just handed over to his mother had been for Halimah.

***

The sun was already directly above the roof tops of the houses when Piko went down to the river bank. Opposite his house he stopped and looked at it closely. The roof was old and thin but the rest of it was still solid. Would he go back there to live and work his paddy fields again? Was he going to be separated from Halimah and Anwar and take a new wife in this very house? For a moment a girl who had come to visit the previous evening came to mind. She was fair-skinned and had looked at him shyly. He remembered long ago, before he'd left here, how every day she had passed by the house, bare footed, on her way to school and back. Now she'd grown into a pretty young woman. Oh no, he argued with himself. Then Halimah's face rose up in his mind, blotting out the face of the young girl, and he imagined that now Halimah too, was still a young virgin.

He walked to the mosque, made the ritual cleansing at the water spout and performed his prayers quickly. After that he went down to the rice fields via the track that descended, terrace by terrace, with bananas and taro growing beside it. Here and there men could be seen hoeing, while the women turned over the rotting stubble, piled it up or put it on the embankments. In several places in the distance, some people were already planting rice. As far as the eye could see the mountains soared and a few tree trunks stood out starkly. From within the mountains echoed the song of a band of gibbons. Piko breathed deeply, feeling a great joy at being back in the midst of his calm, peaceful village. The hustle and bustle, swirling dust, whining of mosquitoes and scratching of bedbugs in Jakarta seemed like a terrible dream.

'Where are you off to?' a man said, stopping his hoeing. His pants, which reached to his knees, clung to him in folds and his face and hat were spattered with mud.

'I'm going to have a look at the fields for a while. Where's Aunty?'

'She went to the plantation earlier'.

'I'll keep going, Uncle'.

'All right. Just now I saw Ja Sangkutan already there'.

Piko crossed over the channel, walking along the embankment. Soon he reached the boundary of the neighbouring paddy field. Bananas and sago palms grew there. Fanned by the wind the leaves trembled, as if greeting him. He came to a hill which formed a small island in the middle of the rice fields. At the foot of the hill was a rice mill standing idle. He went up to a man who was stooped over, working.

'Ho, Piko!' The man looked up, taking off his hat. They both put their hats back on as they walked towards a small hut, and sat down on a bench outside. Piko examined the floor of the hut, remembering his life with Halimah. They'd worked there from the time they were first married, working as they joked, and joking as they worked.

'Is there enough water now, Pak?'

'That's the trouble at the moment, Piko. Only half your fields can be worked. The one beside the water mill there can't be irrigated any more'. The man pointed. Piko looked at the field overgrown with weeds and long grass. In several places bushes and sword grass grew wild.

'It's a shame. When I left home, all the fields could still be worked'.

He got up and looked inside the hut. There was no door. He used to put the rice grain there before carrying it to the house. He and Halimah even slept there often when they were first married. The grass roof was rotten and full of holes.

'Are you going to work your fields again Piko?'

'I don't know yet, Pak. Just carry on as you've been doing. Maybe later I'll work the one there near the hill again. We'll fix up the channels first. We'll all work together on the mouth of the channel'.

'The people are fed up with working together, Piko. It's every man for himself, not like it was before when my brother Ja Dolok was still alive. Nowadays no one wants to be organised or told what to do any more'.

'We'll talk about it later, after the Friday prayers. How can we just go on ignoring things?'

'If you can do something it would be great Piko. Who knows, maybe all the fields in this village could be worked again. Torkis can't get the people moving. Maybe you can open their eyes because you've just come home.

'All right, I'm off now'.

'Where to? Won't you have a drink of young coconut milk first? Let me climb up and get one'.

'Another time, Pak'.

He looked up at the coconut trees growing at the side of the yard. There were some trees whose fruit had turned black. Apparently his mother had forgotten about the picking. He continued on his way, up into the hills. At a certain spot he stopped and looked to the east, shading his forehead with his hand. He saw a hut, surrounded by trees. Round the edge of the yard were mango and *areca* nut trees. Apparently neither Halimah nor his mother-in-law was there, only his father-in-law, Pak Haji, was tending to the water at the edge of the channel.

Piko went down, heading west. Several times people called out greetings. He called and waved back. He reached the banana plantation. The rustling of the flowers drowned out the noise of the wind in the bushes and branches. He walked through a field of *gelegah* and *pimping* grass, his hands brushing the leaves. At the end of the field he climbed up a steep bank at the top of which was a rubber plantation. He walked towards the plantation, and the lapping sound of the river faded away, lost in the whistling of the wind and the singing of the cicadas. The white rubber sap was running through the tapping grooves, dripping slowly into the coconut shell containers. Just then he saw the back of a man bending over behind a tree.

'Ho!' shouted Piko.

'Ho!' came the reply, and a young man appeared from behind the tree. 'Piko, where did you spring from?'

'The paddy fields. Do you tap Pakcik Haji's rubber now?'

'Yes, I do. Where are you going? Across the river?'

'No'.

He crossed the main road. He could see the house of Bedah, the widow of Tapor. Tapor used to be the chairman of People's Youth in this village. His house had walls of woven bamboo and a palm thatch roof. It stood off by itself at the edge of the village. Now it was closed up. Piko remembered when they'd beaten him up. He remembered the great commotion in the overcast moonlight in front of the house across the river that Tapor was imprisoned in. Before the mob attacked him, Tapor spoke to them. He said that in time to come his children would demand vengeance for what was done, and revenge would follow revenge. 'Our children are six and seven years old now, so in ten or twenty years' time of course they'll find out who attacked their father and they won't let it rest', he said. Piko was nervous when he heard Tapor's threat, but his friends couldn't control their fury any longer, and they dragged Tapor from the steps. Each one of them tried to get at part of his body, until he no longer moved. Echoing now in Piko's ears was the noise of the four or five hundred swarming attackers who came from the villages of the Tanjung Aur district, the groans and cries of their victims and the moaning of the prisoners getting louder and louder calling their mothers and fathers, frightened their turn would come too.

He reached the cemetery. On the other side of the fence proper, there was a long grave scattered with pebbles and sheltered by a frangipani tree, but it had no name on it. Piko stopped, bowed, and took off his hat. He pulled out the grass in the cracks and under the shrubs. Some lizards scuttled out of the way. For a moment he conjured up the image of his father, whom he only knew when he was a little child. He had the impression that his father was very big and powerful with a waxed handlebar moustache and brightly shining eyes. Beyond that he knew more from what people said. They said that his father had magical powers. He had a guardian—a tiger. They said his father could move from one coconut tree to another just by swinging from branch to branch. They also said with his bare hands his father could stir the seething curry in the big pot, when there was a ritual meal.

Piko didn't feel that he or Torkis had inherited his father's magic powers. Torkis certainly used to be known as a dare-devil and good fighter when he was a child and in his youth, but Piko didn't think he was a man with magical powers. When they had gone 'outside' together previously to join the guerillas for a year, Torkis hadn't been one of the daring members of the force who'd killed a lot of the enemy. On the contrary, Piko heard that he hadn't even killed one. Piko had never been able to verify that he himself had ever killed an enemy in battle either. He had been as frightened as everyone else. As far as the tiger that was said to be his father's guardian was concerned, he and Torkis never got a turn of being guarded by it, and they were as scared of the King of the Jungle as other people were.

He stood up and walked among the graves. Now and again he stopped and looked at the names and dates of death inscribed on the headstones. He stopped as he read the headstone of a long grave, almost the same length as his father's. This one too was scattered with pebbles and shaded by an ornamental tree and a big shrub. On the stone was written: 'Ja Dolok, died Friday, 23 April, 1962'. Taking off his hat he squatted down and pulled out the weeds growing on the grave.

The man buried here used to be the village chief. How good hearted he was, and how great was his prestige! At the time of the Dutch he was treated like a king, and in the Emergency period he was once chosen to be the District Head for two years. When the upheavals were on he gave a lot of help to Piko and his friends who were 'outside'. As soon as the Central forces found out, he was arrested and sent to Military Headquarters. There he was interrogated and tortured with electric shocks. When he was released after peace was restored he was always in pain until the day he died.

Piko stood up, blinking away tears, and walked towards the clove plantation. He walked through it for a while and then it led into a rubber plantation. He walked through this, going downstream, parallel with the village road. At the edge of the rubber plantation, where its borders where planted with cloves, he stopped. On the other side of a patch of *lalang* grass there was a grove of banana trees and in the middle of it, higher up, was a hut with a grass thatched roof. Whisps of smoke from a rush fire rose from the yard. A child could be heard crying, followed by the sound of a woman talking. The crying grew softer but it went on and on, fading to a whimper. Piko went and sat on a rotting tree trunk under a big clove tree. Honey birds and *jantung* birds squawked about him and pollen from the clove flowers sprinkled his head and body. He put his hand in his shirt pocket and took out a little toy car, red in colour, strongly built, made of steel. He examined it as though he was just seeing it for the first time. For a long time he fondled it, while now and then he looked at the hut. The child's whimpering had stopped. Now a woman came out of the hut, and Piko's heart beat faster. She was wearing a headcloth wound around her hair, its ends hanging loosely at the nape of her neck. 'Is she really mad?' he whispered. It didn't seem possible, she looked so normal. Piko put the toy car back in his pocket and in its place he took out a packet of tobacco and some young *nipa* palm leaves and rolled a cigarette. He watched the hut as he smoked. The wind rustled in the branches of the rubber trees and ripe fruit fell with a thud, scattering its seeds in all directions. A blackbird chattered in the clove branches.

The woman pounded the rice and chickens roamed around cackling busily, squawking and clucking. The woman called and the child appeared and chased the chickens away. The woman was winnowing beneath the banana clump at the edge of the yard. Piko saw her earrings sparkling as they swayed, played with by sunlight. He remembered they were still the same ones she'd had before.

He was startled when a rubber tapper appeared in the plantation, emptying the sap from the coconut shell containers. Piko felt embarrassed and slipped away stealthily to avoid him, circling around to get back to the village.

***

When the Friday prayers were over, Piko made a long speech, trying to get through to the people who were set in their indifference and stubbornness. Because he'd just returned from a trip away, and perhaps also because he was the younger brother of the village chief, the community listened intently and respectfully to the speech. The old men sat with heads bowed in the front row, nodding politely every so often.

'In Jakarta, gentlemen', said Piko, 'the people make use of a span of land by the railway track. It really is one span brothers!' said Piko, showing the distance with his hands. 'They plant it with spinach, onions and *kangkung* and water it with water carried from hundreds of metres away. What happens here? Land is plentiful, and water is abundant too and flows freely. But we don't make use of it. The rice fields by themselves are inadequate to feed us all the year round. We can only produce half of our normal crop. Why does this happen? Not because we don't have water but because the irrigation system is no good. The river is big and it's only two to three hundred metres from our fields. You can clearly hear it flowing. Aren't we stupid and foolish if this is the case, brothers? What's the use of praying five times a day, going to Friday prayers and hearing the mosque official or the preacher giving religious instruction. Every day our ears are stuffed with religious teaching telling us to always be aware that in our labours we must think—to distinguish us from animals! Right now, we are like animals, and that's why we just labour mindlessly. We're already too stupid to work out how to get the water of the Batang Kundur River into our fields to grow our rice'.

'What are the consequences of this? There are many, brothers! First, we can't live entirely off the paddy fields, but we have to supplement by cultivating dry fields, and this means our forests keep getting thinned out each year. The forests are stripped, there's no longer any storage of water in the wet season, and the water overflows downstream, and flattens everything. Up comes the flood, washing away our properties, and the main road and then the bridge collapses. What happens next? The main road has caved in so cars can't come to our village any more. It's difficult to bring the things we need in, so prices go up. Our contact with the outside world is cut off too and our village becomes isolated. It gets lonely. Our children get restless living here, not seeing any bright future. Especially the ones who have a little bit of education feel disappointed and the situation kills their desire to go on living in the village. Then they go away in droves looking for something better. Even when they're away their prospects for a livelihood aren't as good as they expected. They need capital and perseverance and they very seldom succeed in the struggle. Maybe they could hang on living in the cities, but only providing they can eat. They can't branch out, and what's more they create a problem in the cities too'.

'That's why we have to wake up, brothers. We have to repair our fields' irrigation system immediately, so it's back to the condition it was in when the Dutch were here'.

When Piko finished, Torkis stepped forward to give the members of the community time to give their responses and reactions to the speech. Not one man contradicted what Piko had said. The old men even said how grateful they were that Piko wanted to warn them in a kindly way. Who else would do it if not one of their own family? Although what he said made them feel uncomfortable, they deserved it!

When a complaint came up about how hard it would be to get the funds together, Piko quickly leapt up and said there was no need for any money now; what was needed was enthusiasm and the will to work. He urged everyone to go to the mountains the next day, Saturday, to look for rattan. After that they would use it to make a dam framework. On Saturday too, or otherwise if they ran out of time it could be continued the next couple of days, they'd fill the framework in the middle of the river with lots and lots of stones. They all said they agreed, and promised to come along the next day to the mountain. Then the group dispersed.

The next day only five men turned up to go with Piko to the mountain. They included Torkis, Ja Sangkutan, who worked Piko's fields and also Piko's father-in-law. Piko led the way, not saying even one word about Halimah. Silently they cleared a track to the middle of the forest, pulling out the rattan and dragging it in bundles as big as a man's thigh to the head of the irrigation channel. When the band of workers crossed the main road leading into the village, they met a few of the old men. They spoke evasively to Piko, saying that they needed to go across to tend to the rubber sap, or that a child was sick and had to be taken to the medical assistant, and all kinds of excuses. Piko nodded and just smiled bitterly in reply to their pretexts.

'Yesterday they spoke sweet words at the mosque! Now where are they?' grumbled Piko, at the river's edge. Torkis stood beside him, silently wiping his sweat with a piece of cloth.

The head of the channel was downstream from a long curving water hole, protected from the surge of flood waters by a steep rocky bank. In the water there was in fact a dam, all askew, blocking the river all the way across. But, there were a lot of breaks and leaks. Piko and his five companions plaited a framework from rattan, fifteen metres long and two and a half metres round. When it was time for the afternoon prayer they stopped, and went home. The job of restraining the frame so that it wouldn't float up and wash away would be very difficult. It would have to be packed closely with big stones from end to end. After the framework had been sited properly and firmly, they would also have to fill it to the brim with small stones. Piko calculated that if thirty men turned up to work they could finish the job in just two days. But it turned out that there were only six of them for those two days. On the third day Piko was amazed when he saw five more new workers who had arrived, dragging bundles of rattan. Silently they plaited a new framework, and after it was finished, with Piko and the others, they planted the second framework beside the one that was already filled. On the fourth day, ten more men came. They were able to speed up the work of filling the baskets, with the result that after five days' work, the water in the channel was three times as high as it had been before. The next job was to fix up the connecting channels leading into the rice fields.

A week later everything was finished—water flowed abundantly and streamed everywhere.

After the Friday prayers, Torkis stepped forward beside the mosque official. On behalf of the people, he expressed gratitude and thanks to Piko, who had succeeded in raising the level of water in the channels to its normal height. Thus all the rice fields could be worked and the water wheel, rice mortar and rice pounder were able to work again. After Torkis, several of the elders also stepped forward to express their feelings to Piko. Piko saw among them, quite unashamed, those who only came to help when the easy work of repairing the connecting channels was being done, and even then only when it was opposite their own fields.

The people dispersed, their faces glowing smugly, all the time smiling broadly at Piko and slapping him on the shoulders.

Piko was the only one not happy. He responded to their grins with a sad, bitter smile, and every now and then he lapsed into thought and sighed.

When Torkis and the others accompanied him to the main road he said, 'I'm going across the river'.

'What do you want there?' asked Torkis, raising his *peci* cap from his forehead. 'Come on. Let's go to my house. We'll have lunch there'.

'Another time, brother. I want to go for a walk over there'.

'Come home with me'.

'No, I'm just going for a walk'.

'Maybe you want to buy some cigarettes? Can't you get them at Mian's place? He's got 'Kansas' and 'Escort' too'.

'No!'

Piko left the crowd of men, and strode away upstream. They watched him in astonishment. When he'd passed the cemetery he turned and went into the *lalang* grasses. He didn't continue on towards the cable bridge which crossed the Batang Kundur River (some 400 metres on from there is the village of Tanjung Aur, where there is a market day once a week).

Leaving the *lalang* behind, he walked through the rubber plantation, turning downstream, parallel with the village road. He reached the spot under the clove trees where he had sat about ten days ago. He felt in the pocket of his shirt and took out the toy car. For a while he fondled and contemplated the toy and spelt out the writing on it. 'Match Box, Made in England, Pontiac'. Some of the paint was worn off because he often took it out and fondled it. He put is back in his pocket and rolled a cigarette.

A boy about five years old was playing under the hut. A young woman came out of the hut and fetched something from the yard. The woman and the child went inside. Thick smoke billowed out through the roof. Half an hour later, an elderly woman came from the rubber plantation, and went into the hut. She was inside for a quarter of an hour, then he saw her go, and the younger woman went with her to the edge of the garden and then went back inside.

The boy appeared again, holding a stick. He poked it at dragonflies, or grasshoppers in the yard. The insects flew out of his way and he kept on following them, poking the stick at them. Apparently he wanted to catch them. The child wandered away from the hut, engrossed in following the insects. At one point he came to a big fallen tree trunk blocking the way. The dragonfly he was chasing flew to the other side of it and the child clambered over. As he got to the other side his foot slipped and he tumbled over.

Piko sprang up and ran to get him. He picked up the child, who looked at him in surprise. The child did not cry, or call his mother. Piko brushed his elbows and pants and carried him.

'I didn't bring much, 'War! Only this! I brought it from Jakarta. It's beautiful isn't it?' he said holding out the toy car.

The child didn't take it, but his eyes gleamed and he swallowed hard.

'Here, take it! It's for you. After all, I'm your father aren't I? I'm just back from Jakarta! Your mother said something about me didn't she?'

Hesitantly the child took the toy he was holding out. Piko hugged him and kissed him several times. Apparently the woman in the hut heard the man's voice. She came down the steps. When she saw Piko she gazed at him wide eyed, blushed deeply, and turned away, knotting her loose hair up into a bun. She climbed up the steps, hitching up her sarong. Piko carried the child to the hut. At the foot of the steps he put him down and went up by himself. The child hesitantly began to pluck up courage to push the car, very carefully, with amazement, along a bench.

Piko pushed the door wide open with a bang. The woman who had just now run away sat near the stove, with her back to him. He sat down and leant back against the wall near the door.

'I didn't bring any present for you 'Limah, only for Anwar', he said. He stuck his head out the door and called, 'Come here, Anwar!'

The child shook his head and went on pushing the car, growing more daring.

Apparently the woman was crying. He heard her sobbing and she was wiping her eyes with the edge of her sarong.

'Is there some rice left Halimah? I haven't had any lunch yet'.

Now she shook her head, wiping her nose and her tears.

'All right. I'm taking Anwar to my mother's house now. I'll bring him back here later this afternoon'. Piko went down the steps. 'Come on Anwar, we're going to Grandma's'. Anwar squatted down, reluctant to go. Piko pulled him to his feet and piggy-backed him away. They took the plantation road heading straight for the village. The wind rustled and fruit from the rubber trees fell with a thud.

The village was quiet. A few children were playing in the yards or on the road. Some played pole-leaping or marbles and others played with rubber balls. When he reached the house, his mother had just returned from getting firewood.

'Where have you been all this time? I've been waiting since everyone got home from the Friday prayers. Torkis said you'd gone over the river. Oh, you've brought Anwar? So, you've been to the plantation!'

The mother wiped the perspiration from her bright red face. Piko put Anwar down in the kitchen.

'Ugh, look at this child!' said the mother, an expression of disgust on her face. 'Probably his mother even forgets to wash him. Typical!' Anwar wiped away the green snot running from his nose and his cheeks were dirty with crusted mucous.

The mother took the lids off the dishes of food under the plate shelf and Piko and Anwar ate—red rice and fern-shoot curry mixed with fish.

She lit the fire in the stove and filled the cauldron with water from a bamboo container.

'Is that a toy you brought, Piko?' she said, noticing Anwar pushing the car on the floor while she was putting food in his mouth. As he sucked in air to cool his tongue because the food was too spicy, he sniffed up the mucous that kept running from his nose.

Piko finished eating, and went and leant back against the wall, and belching softly from time to time, he rolled a cigarette and lit it. Anwar finished eating too.

'Come here now, 'War!' called his grandmother. 'I want to wash that face of yours'. She pinched the end of his nose, threw a glob of mucous out the window and washed his face with water in the wash basin.

'Mother', said Piko. 'I've been doing a lot of thinking and it would be better for me to go back to my own house. I'll work my field again. Uncle Ja Sangkutan can work a section and I'll work the rest. There's plenty of water now too, and we can irrigate our fields. If I get on with it straight away the crops won't be too late. What do you think, Mother?'

'It's up to you. But are you going to live there by yourself with Anwar?'

'Anwar can stay here with you. That's if Halimah lets him. Where's Rosni? Has she gone home to her mother for a while?'

'Whether Halimah lets him or not, Piko, you must see that Anwar stays here. The child's upbringing will be terrible if he's allowed to stay there with his mother!'

Piko's mother took some coconut from the shelf and grated it.

'Did Halimah really act like a mad woman that time at the market, Mother?'

'Why do you want to know?'

'I saw her earlier and she looked and acted normally. There were no signs of any madness at all'.

'So, what do you want?'

'Well, I've thought it over, Mother...'

'Oh, you want to make it up with her don't you? You want to bring her back to your house, don't you?'

'Yes, Mother. That's what I'm trying to say. What if we live in our house again like we always did?'

'Halimah has disgraced the name of our family, Piko. Try to listen around; you'll realise how people are talking about her'.

'I have thought about it a lot, Mother. I was wrong too. I left Anwar and Halimah for four years without sending even one cent. We have to look at it from both sides, Mother. We have to be fair'.

'What do you think is unfair? She's been working your fields all this time hasn't she? She's had coconuts and she's had the plantation'.

Piko didn't say anything, and his mother didn't either, going on with the grating. Finally it was finished and she threw the shell out the window, and went on staring out. A few minutes later she turned to Piko, heaving a sigh. Piko crushed his cigarette on the bamboo floor.

'I don't know why, Mother, something deep down inside tells me I have to take Halimah back. I have no intention of divorcing her, nor of finding someone to take her place'.

'Perhaps you've been bewitched, Piko. You'd better discuss this with your brother'.

'What for, Mother? Isn't Halimah still my wife I haven't divorced her have I? I think it's really typical of Torkis to want us to split up, so that he can control all of our hereditary land, while I'm far away in some other place'.

'Don't talk like that Piko. It's terrible! Your own brother!' Piko went to the door and called Anwar to climb up on his back.

'Where are you taking that child?'

'To the plantation'.

'Why are you taking him there again? Let him stay here!'

Without replying, Piko disappeared. His mother looked at the vacant spot at the door, shook her head and went and stared into the fire that was licking the sides of the cauldron. Suddenly she was startled because the lid was dislodged by the boiling water hissing at the edges. She lifted the lid and poured the water on the coffee leaves.

***

Now, on the western horizon the sky was turning a reddish orange colour. The twilight crickets chirped in the rubber trees. The wind whispering in the rubber plantation welcomed the evening. The old leaves that had made the sap turned orange too in the golden glow, then reluctantly settled on the grass. A mimic bird called far over yonder in the middle of the clove plantation.

'Uncle! Uncle! Aunty's coming! Aunty's coming!'

A girl came running up. Her face was pale as though it had been washed in ice water. She was panting and she spoke out of breath. Piko patted her head to calm her down.

'Which Aunty, Ros?' said Piko. 'Where is she coming from?' In fact his own heart was beating fast, thinking of Halimah.

'Anwar's mother, Uncle, from her plantation'.

'If she's coming, what is she doing?'

'She's carrying a big stone, Uncle. Everyone's afraid'.

'What did she say, Piko?' said his mother. 'Limah is coming with a big stone? She's probably having another attack! You see Piko! We told you!'

'Take Anwar inside, Mother. Hide him in his room'.

Piko went out and looked up the road. It was deserted. Usually in the late afternoon there were a lot of children and their parents at the roadside playing or chatting and smoking. Some people were hurriedly shutting their windows and doors, peeping up the road through the cracks or the chinks. Piko heard his mother behind him, closing the windows too.

At the bend in the road, Halimah appeared. With one hand she hitched up her sarong and with the other she held on to a stone as big as a man's calf. She was shrieking and yelling in the Indonesian language. (To this day, Piko wonders why the speech of anyone who loses his memory or is mad, whether he is from Minangkabau or Mandailing, will suddenly change to Indonesian or High Malay, if he is having an attack.) Some of the people in the houses opened their windows a little and peeped out as she passed by.

'Come inside, Piko!' his mother shouted from behind him.

Piko trembled when he saw Halimah already five metres away from him. The stone she was holding had sharp edges. Her expression seemed to show that she neither noticed nor recognised Piko. Now she waved the stone about, threateningly.

'Limah! It's me, Piko! Your husband! Say something to me, Limah!' he said, trying to coax her into handing over the stone she was holding.

Halimah went straight past him, walked up to the kitchen door and threw the stone she'd been waving around at the shuttered window. The house shook.

'Give back my child, you criminal! Pig! Bitch! Give back my child you old nagger! You green bellied old woman! Give him back! Give him back!' She picked up another stone and threw it too. The kitchen door shook and rattled.

Piko heard his mother shouting from inside the hut but couldn't hear what she was saying. Halimah walked right around the house. When she got back in front of the kitchen door she pushed it hard. Apparently there hadn't been time to bar it before. It suddenly flew open and Halimah almost fell head first.

'Bring my child here, bitch! Pig! Bring him here! You have no right to keep him! Give him back, bitch! Pig!'

Halimah picked up another stone. 'She'll smash the crockery', thought Piko. He chased after her and tried to wrest the stone from her. She resisted him, twisting and turning and shrieking, 'Bastard! Bitch! Pig!'

Her lips were white and trembled crookedly.

'Limah! Remember! Say something to me! It's me! Piko! Your husband!'

'Bring my child here, bitch! Nagger!'

Halimah was incredibly strong. Piko heard a lot of voices behind him. Suddenly he felt the stone he was trying to snatch from her hit his forehead. He fell and everything went round and round and he saw stars. People came crowding around. Piko's father-in-law, wearing his white haji's cap, held Halimah tightly, helped by two or three other men. Piko's mother came down the steps, without Anwar. Inside, he could be heard crying and banging on the door. Halimah struggled, but she couldn't get away. Suddenly she looked shocked, seeing Piko fallen on the ground, his forehead bloody. It was as though she had only just seen that he was there. Her face, which had been strained and flushed, now looked as though water had been splashed on it, and it was downcast, limp and deathly pale. It was the face that Piko had known. Feelings of compassion for her arose, making his heart beat painfully.

Halimah struggled again, and they let her go. She ran away up the road weeping. Piko was helped up to the house. Torkis fetched a bottle of iodine, and their mother cleansed the wound and dabbed it with the cork of the bottle.

'Where's Anwar, Mother?' said Piko a little while later.

'He's inside. What do you want him for?' His mother went away and then Anwar came out and sat on Piko's lap.

'We'll go to your mother, won't we, Anwar? Poor Mummy, all by herself at the plantation. Do you want to?'

Anwar was confused. He stiffened and shook his head.

'What do you want to take him back again for, Piko? He's used to it here, now'.

'No, Mother, let me take him. Poor Halimah has no friends there'.

'I don't know, Piko. Why are you like this? Do you see what I mean Torkis?'

Torkis turned to his mother, but didn't say anything.

'Your father-in-law will take Anwar, Piko. No good will come to you there!'

'Yes, I'll take him Piko. Forgive us, Piko!' said his father-in-law, moving to take Anwar.

Piko shook his head and told Anwar to come outside. At the steps he sat, and Anwar climbed on his back. Torkis, Piko's father-in-law and others gazed at the backs of the father and son getting further away until they disappeared around the bend. Torkis looked as though he was reading an important announcement on Anwar's back. In the bushes in the rubber plantation, the magpies were calling, signalling that it was evening. From the mosque too, the beating of the drum could be heard followed by the faint roll of the call to prayer. When Piko and Anwar vanished into the plantation, the father-in-law and his wife slowly followed. The wind blew over them, making a rustling sound which travelled afar, and branches and leaves fell with a cracking sound beside them. Crickets sang everywhere.

The hut was in darkness. Piko shouted from the bottom of the steps. There was no reply. He pushed the door and put Anwar down on the floor.

'Limah! Here, I've brought Anwar!'

Halimah was sitting on the small stool used for grating coconut, near the stove. She was sobbing and kept sniffling and wiping her eyes. Piko sat down and leant against the door and Anwar sat on his lap, staring at his mother in the twilight gloom. When Piko saw his parents-in-law coming, he edged forward to sit in the middle of the room. Silently his mother- in-law lit the lamps from the flame of the stove. His father-in-law went and sat in the corner, keeping quiet.

'Here's Anwar, Limah', said Piko again. 'Give him some food! He hasn't had anything to eat yet!' He pushed Anwar towards his mother. Anwar touched her shoulder, hesitantly, and now she embraced the child, weeping loudly and kissing him again and again. Anwar didn't say anything, his eyes wide with astonishment.

'Haven't you eaten yet?' Halimah's mother stroked her shoulder. Halimah stopped crying and wiped her eyes and rose, shaking her head. Her mother took the lids off the cooking pot and the wok and brought the lamp closer. Piko remembered that Anwar hadn't been home for three days since he'd taken him off to his grandmother.

'You say you're sorry to Piko, Halimah. His forehead is hurt because you struck him earlier. Do you remember? Your behaviour was shameful Limah!'

Halimah bowed her head, sobbing again and wiping her nose and eyes. Now Anwar went back to his father and sat on his lap. Piko stroked his hair.

For a while the only sounds were Limah's sobs and the chirping of crickets. From the direction of the spring in the valley frogs were croaking and under the hut there was a dog scratching and making a scuffling noise. Halimah's father cleared his throat, rolled a cigarette and lit it.

'Tomorrow I'm going to fix up our house again, Limah. After that we'll work our fields again. Ja Sangkutan is only working half. We will work the whole lot ourselves. We'll plant two crops each year like they do in Java'.

'What do you mean, Piko?' said Halimah's mother.

'Yes, I'm taking Halimah back to live in our house in the banana plantation. Then we'll grow our rice together like we did before'.

'Torkis and your mother will be angry Piko! Have they agreed to this?'

'Don't bother about them. Halimah is still my wife. I haven't divorced her and I'm not going to'.

'Halimah has behaved badly Piko! Haven't you heard about that?'

'Let bygones be bygones. I'm to blame too for leaving Halimah and Anwar for so long'.

Suddenly Halimah wept loudly and buried her head in her mother's lap. Her mother stroked her hair.

'Do you want to come back to our house, Limah?' said Piko softly, touching Halimah's hair gently.

'Don't you hear Limah?' repeated her mother. 'Do you want to do what Piko says?' Halimah nodded her head over and over again in her mother's lap. Then she moved and buried her head in Piko's lap, sobbing again. Anwar started crying too.

Few a few minutes Piko and his parent-in-law just kept quiet, letting Halimah cry herself out.

Then her father moved and got to his feet. 'We are going now, Piko, Limah', he said. 'We haven't said the evening prayers yet. We'll come back again in the morning. Come on Masriah!'

Piko and Halimah watched them go. After a while they were lost from sight, swallowed up in the darkness of the rubber plantation. The wind blew and the *lalang* grasses rustled. Piko closed the door.

They looked at each other for a long time in the dimness of the reddish glow of the lamp. Piko smiled and Halimah smiled back at him.

'We'll cook some more rice will we?' she said, going to the stove. 'We only need to cook a bit extra. It won't be long'.

'What sort of curry have you made?'

'Ah, there isn't any, Bang, I'm ashamed! There's only some taro mixed with *belanak* fish'.

'That's just my favourite, Limah. I've been longing for it!'

They laughed. Piko gave Anwar an affectionate squeeze and the child laughed too. The wind whistled in the grass roof and the cracks in the walls. Forest frogs croaked noisily in the valley.

After being back in the village for two weeks, it was only now that Piko felt he had really come home.

(originally published as 'Pulang', in *Budaya Jaya*, 1973, 63(6), pp.491–512.)

Drought

Mohamad Fudoli

translated by Jan Lingard

Ustaz Somad, the Islamic religious teacher, had just come out of the village mosque when he met a man waiting for him outside. As he stopped a moment and wiped his eyes, Somad answered the man's greeting. The man came nearer and Somad was able to recognise his face in the glimmer of light from the oil lamp in the mosque.

'Bakri, is anything the matter?'

The man he had spoken to smiled.

'There's something I want to tell you'.

Somad was very well acquainted with the man, who always attended prayers and the Thursday evening Koran recitations at the mosque.

'What about?'

'It's to do with what I told you yesterday'.

Still dabbing his eyes, Somad smiled.

'Actually I waited inside for you for quite a while just now, but you seemed to want to pray for some time after the service'.

Still wiping his eyes, Somad smiled again.

'How is your youngest child, Bakri?'

'Fine', answered the man, rather taken aback.

He didn't understand why Somad had suddenly asked about his child, specially since Somad had visited him at his home only two days ago.

Somad smiled again, feeling in his shirt pocket with his right hand. In the pocket was an envelope containing a letter and some photographs.

'He's well, is he?' Somad continued.

'Yes'.

Again Somad felt in his pocket. The letter was from his only son who lived a long way away and it announced some very exciting news.

'I...have a grandchild'.

'Oh...Somad!'

'I got a letter from my son this morning telling me of the birth of his first child. Yes, it's my first grandchild and it's a boy'.

'God be praised! I share your gratitude and joy'.

Somad lapsed into silence for a moment. When he had prostrated himself earlier during the prayers, he had been unable to hold back the tears that wet his cheeks. The blessings that God showered upon him were too great. A fine grandchild, who would, in his turn, take his grandfather's place, carrying out the tasks entrusted to him in this life. He had not realised that the prayers he offered up after the service were so long, nor had he the strength to hold back his tears.

'But I still have to see him with my own eyes'.

'Won't they be coming here?'

'Probably not till Lebaran, but they've sent some photos'.

Somad felt in his pocket again and took out the envelope. From his other pocket he took a small flashlight. He showed the photos to Bakri, who took them and looked at them with delight.

'My goodness! He's very good looking. He looks just like you, and he's got such thick black hair'.

Somad just smiled and dabbed at his eyes, feeling that his tears were going to start again.

'Let's walk along while we're talking'.

Leaving the grounds of the mosque, they came to the village road and turned south. It was a dark night with stars studding the sky. Now and again Somad put the flashlight on to show the way after he put the envelope back in his pocket.

'Perhaps I can guess what you're going to say, Bakri'.

'As I said earlier, it's about what I told you yesterday'.

'About how angry they are'.

'Yes'.

'I heard all the things they were saying outside the mosque'.

'And what do you think about it?'

'I think we have to do much more than just talk a lot'.

'But it's as though the people don't want to understand. On the contrary they're showing their anger more and more'.

Somad smiled and looked up at the sky. Except for the tiny flickering stars scattered across it, the sky was clear with not a cloud in sight.

'So what are they angry about? Is it because the settlements and this village have been hit by such a severe drought and there's no sign of any rain?'

'That's it'.

'We've already tried hard to do something about it. We've deepened all of our wells. I even helped dig the one alongside the mosque myself, as well as the one at my own home. What more can we do?'

'These wells are almost dry and they can't provide use with enough water'.

'That's true. I've talked to the village head and told him to press again for help from the city, and if he still doesn't succeed to go on pressing them'.

'But the people are much angrier with you than they are with him'.

Somad smiled again and looked up at the sky.

'I can't do things beyond my power. I've done everything I can and I've also held a special prayer service to pray for rain. It's up to God whether the prayers are granted or not'.

'That's why the people are very angry now'.

'Yes, I've heard it all. It's because it's almost two weeks since those prayers were held and there's still no rain. And they were saying outside that I'm nothing more than a liar and a fake'.

Somad gave a short laugh and then turned to the man walking beside him.

'What else can I do besides what I've already done? I'm not the village head, and I've got no authority at all'.

'They're putting too much faith in the success of your prayers'.

'Hmmm, prayers are certainly a good thing, but more concrete efforts have to be made too, don't they?'

'That's why they're very disappointed that so far there hasn't been a drop of rain. It's as if they are blaming you, because you are an incompetent religious teacher. I'm sorry, that's what they are saying'.

They walked on. Somad felt his pocket for a moment. In the distance a cart loomed into sight before them. They could see its two oil lamps swaying and the sound of its cow bells could be heard clearly too.

'I'm worried that our hearts have been afflicted by this terrible drought, far sooner than our village has'. Suddenly it was as though Somad was talking to himself.

'Yes, Somad?'

'It's as though we've lost the warmth of the simplest contacts altogether: helping each other, sharing all kinds of joys and sorrows with our neighbours, calling on sick friends, paying respects to the dead, speaking kindly when we pass by in the street. We are too preoccupied with chasing after wealth in every way we can, wanting to get rich quickly by any means, no matter whether the way we do it is decent or not—such as gambling and setting up brothels on the outskirts of the village with the excuse that they are being kept right away from the city's crowds'.

They walked on very slowly. Now and again Somad switched on his flashlight to show the way. And the cart and the sound of its cowbells came closer and closer.

'Have you heard what else they're angry about?'

Somad was looking straight ahead, in the direction of the cart.

'The ceremony to placate the spirits that was put off that day. They're angry because you forbade them to hold a sacrifice at the sacred graveyard on the hilltop', said Bakri.

'Yes, just imagine it. A few cows would have been slaughtered and placed in the so-called sacred graveyard as an offering to ask for rain, not to mention all the food and money, even though the people need these things themselves. I ordered them to divide up the food among the village people and as a substitute for their sacrifice I held the special prayer service', said Somad.

'And so far', said Bakri, 'there still hasn't been any rain. That's what the villagers were talking about just now. And Pak Miun, the guardian of the graveyard, has been stirring them up and saying that if the sacrificial ceremony had been held in the graveyard, rain would have certainly fallen, whereas the prayers have been useless. He's got them quite worked up'.

'So now they're very angry with me', said Somad.

'That's right. As well as branding you as a liar and a fake, they also threatened to burn down the mosque or wreck your house if it still hasn't rained by the end of this week. This is what I've been wanting to tell you'.

Somad was quiet for a moment, and then he smiled.

'And what does the village head think?'

'He can't do anything either'.

They walked on. The cart was very close now. It drew level and passed them and the sound of the cowbells faded slowly in the distance. Somad stopped a moment and turned to the man beside him. They had now reached the front of his house.

'Would you like to come in for a while, Bakri?'

'Not just now, but thank you'.

They shook hands and said goodbye. Then Somad smiled as he felt his shirt pocket.

'Oh yes, don't forget to give my love to your children!'

They parted. Somad went in to the yard of his house and the man walked on towards the south.

After dinner, Somad and his wife looked again at the photos he had received. Then he put them back in his shirt pocket. As he was going to bed he remembered his conversation on the road with Bakri after the late afternoon prayers at the mosque...about the long drought that was torturing them, about the long-awaited rain and also about the wells that were starting to run dry; about the village head, about the guardian of the graveyard that was considered to be sacred, and the villagers who had begun to get very angry and their threats to do stupid things.

Somad was up very early next morning. After he had finished his ritual cleansing, he left straight away and walked north, heading for the mosque. It was still quite dark, and the dawn call to prayer could just be heard.

Suddenly, on the road, not far from the mosque, a figure stood in front of him. Before Somad had a chance to say anything, the man plunged a big knife into his stomach and chest several times. Somad groaned and collapsed immediately, but he just managed to catch a glimpse of the man's face in the dim light. It was the guardian of the graveyard. Yes, it was him!

Somad's body lay sprawled on the roadside. Meanwhile, in the mosque, a few people were waiting for him to lead the dawn prayers. For a long time they waited. Finally, one of them, whose name was Bakri, came forward to lead the prayers that morning.

And without the village people knowing, all at once great clouds gathered and covered the sky; and before the people in the mosque had finished their prayers, suddenly, completely unexpectedly, heavy rain started to fall. The village people, amazed and astonished, leapt outdoors and ran around in the street, shouting with joy. And so did the people in the mosque. When the prayers were over and they had recited the Koran briefly they too rushed outside. Bakri ran off home, intending to stop by for a moment at Somad's house to ask him what had happened. Usually Somad was never absent from prayers unless something such as illness prevented him.

But not far from the mosque, Bakri saw a crowd of people gathered at the roadside. He also heard some of them cry out. He moved quickly and pushed his way through the crowd to the front. Suddenly he uttered a cry and stopped abruptly. In the early morning light he saw Somad, sprawled there, lifeless. For a moment he lost control of himself and started to tremble violently.

He looked at the corpse bathed in blood. Sticking out of an envelope lying nearby it was a photo of a dear little baby. Bakri could not restrain his tears, and sank to his knees. The rain kept falling on him, on the dead body and on the earth and on the villagers crowding around him. But he had the feeling that the drought was still not over in that village, no matter how heavily the rain was pouring down, on him and on the dry earth.

(originally published in *Dari Jodoh Sampai Supiyah*, 1976, Radio Nederland Wereldomroep & Djambatan, Jakarta, pp.70–76.)

Telephone

Chairul Harun

---

translated by Marian May

The news had already travelled far and wide by word of mouth that the Bupati, the district head, in the district of S was to be replaced. Several names of Bupati Ramli's possible successor had been bandied around. Those most mentioned were Lieutenant Colonel D, Mr M, Lieutenant Colonel Rs and the lawyer N.

A few coffee stalls in the main town of S were the centres of information, spreading the latest news on the Bupati situation.

'This month the Governor will make the change-over. The Governor has already agreed that Lieutenant Colonel D should be Bupati. Ramli's going to be frozen out by the Governor's office. Lieutenant Colonel D's father-in-law gave me the whisper yesterday'.

Sutan Gareseh swallowed the last of his coffee, then studied the reactions of the people around him. His statement had succeeded in catching their attention.

'Impossible! M's nephew has already been told by his uncle that the Governor's given M the job of Bupati'.

Lenggang Dunia's sole intent was to undermine Sutan Gareseh's statement. And Sutan Gareseh did not like his assessment of the situation contradicted.

The transistor radio in the coffee stall played loudly. Some new hot song by 'Limestone' distracted them.

'Malin...can't you turn off that radio?' called Sutan Gareseh. Malin Permato switched the transistor off. Sutan Gareseh was a well-respected character at the stall and an ex-member of the regional parliament. He was disappointed in Ramli because the

Bupati didn't take any notice of him, even though he'd tried to flatter the man.

'The Commander has already agreed. The word is that the Lieutenant Colonel is the Commander's only candidate. Defence and Security have already given their blessing, and the OK from the Regional Commander in Medan has already been received in Padang'.

'There won't be any change in Bupati. Ramli was a close friend of the Governor's; they lived in each other's pockets'. Rajo Mangkuto's words made Sutan Gareseh's eyes widen.

'The Governor didn't get an accurate report. I know for sure even if he was a friend, the Governor would crack down right away on anyone who stepped out of line. Do you blokes know what Ramli's mistake was?'

'Having an affair with someone in the Bupati's office?' said Rajo Mangkuto.

'That wasn't important. The most important thing was that Ramli gave himself contracts for the Five-Year Development Plan projects. And as well as that he's not sympathetic to the Armed Forces'.

All eyes were on Sutan Gareseh. He felt that his explanation had convinced the coffee addicts at Malin's stall.

'If the Lieutenant Colonel becomes Bupati, the road in front of this stall will be sealed', said Sutan Gareseh.

'Because it goes to his parents-in-law's house?'

'Yes'.

'And you'll get the contract', Lenggang Dunia pointed accusingly at Sutan Gareseh.

'Hope so', Sutan Gareseh answered, with a smile.

***

Ramli, the Bupati, was standing in the ricefields. He was looking carefully at the rice around him. The fields were all parched. The yellow-leafed dwarf rice was getting on towards maturity. He looked at Yus Rahman, the sub-district official in charge of the area.

'Are these ricefields part of the rice improvement project?'

'Yes, Bupati'.

'Have they been fertilised?'

'We didn't have a chance. The fertiliser was late. I've already reported that, haven't I?'

'Did the farmers get the complete rice growing package?'

'Yes. But because it was late, a lot of the fertiliser was put on the market. Some people used it to fertilise their vegetables instead'.

Ramli frowned. The mid-day wind was biting into his cheeks. The unrelenting noise of the cicadas did not enchant him any more, but made his hair grey faster.

'Can't the water get to these fields?'

'No. The reservoir system was blocked by a landslide. I've already reported that, haven't I?'

Ramli nodded. He didn't know whether the report existed or not. He didn't have a chance of keeping up with all the reports from subdistrict heads which made their way to his desk.

On his tour of inspection during the week he had found things which made his hair stand on end.

'What's the production estimate for this subdistrict?'

'There's been a big drop. In several areas rice pests, mice and birds have done a lot of damage'.

'Yes...yes. Make an official report'.

'Right. Will you be spending the evening here, sir?'

'Unfortunately...I can't. I'm going to report on this situation to the Governor. He's going to Jakarta to an executive meeting of governors from all around Indonesia'.

'I've prepared an itinerary for you, Bupati. The people asked if you would give us some guidance with regard to the general elections coming up. And tonight there's an entertainment programme as well'.

Ramli thought for a moment.

'We'll discuss it again later'.

He moved towards his white Toyota jeep. He climbed in, and Yus Rahman and his party followed.

After lunch at the subdistrict head's residence, Bupati Ramli whispered to Yus Rahman, 'There won't be any briefing tonight. I'm not very well'.

'How about we just have the concert then?'

'Don't bother about it. If there's someone who wants to play the flute, send them along later tonight. But otherwise, I'm too tired. Tomorrow morning I have to leave and in the evening I've got to see the Governor'.

Yus Rahman couldn't do much to entertain his Bupati.

That night from his bedroom, Ramli heard someone playing the flute. He fell asleep after being massaged by an old woman.

***

Travelling in his Toyota towards Padang, Ramli was feeling really confused. What sort of report would he give the Governor? He was capable of writing a report from behind his desk which would please whoever happened to be reading it. He possessed a talent for writing and great powers of imagination. When he was still a student, his writing skills had been a great help, bringing in money and enabling him to graduate in political and social sciences.

Would he report on the farmers who sold the fertiliser because it came too late? Would he report that the irrigation channels had not yet reached the ricefields, even though the reservoir and many of the main channels had been officially opened with ceremonies reported in the newspapers?

If he passed on all these facts to his superiors, they'd really be upset. And he'd be going against the practice of other Level 2 District Heads. Did he have the nerve to make his boss upset? Could he expose him to ridicule from the Minister and make him the butt of jokes from other Governors?

Ramli's Toyota entered the courtyard of the Governor's residence towards sunset. From the Governor's aide he learned that the Governor had a cold and needed to rest.

'Tell the Governor I've arrived and am ready to report to him'.

'He's sleeping, Sir', said the Governor's aide.

'Fine, well maybe later then, when he wakes up. I'm staying at the Hotel Jakarta. Later, if the Governor would like to receive me, please ring me at the hotel?'

The Governor's aide nodded. Ramli felt relieved. He still had a chance to rest and consider the tone of his report.

Arriving at the hotel, he immediately took a sleeping pill. He told his personal assistant, who doubled as his aide, to prepare a report on the progress of the rice improvement scheme in his region.

'Don't make the production estimates too far from the target which was set. Don't forget to recommend that the fertiliser arrive on time and that the Public Agricultural Service become even more active'.

Ramli lay down on his bed. He massaged the bridge of his nose and stared at the ceiling.

'What else, Sir?' asked his assistant who was all prepared with paper and typewriter.

'Don't give the impression in our report that the failure of the rice improvement scheme is the fault of the sub-district head. Or he'll be the scape-goat. Everything is the result of a technical problem or beyond our control. Type it up straight away. Five copies. Is the ribbon still OK?'

'It's just been changed'.

'I want to sleep for a while. If there's a call from the Governor later, say I'm having a bath or eating. Don't leave the hotel until I wake up'.

'There's something else I wanted to ask you'.

'What?'

'About the format of the report'.

'Just do what we usually do. The Governor thinks our reports are most systematic. Did you bring a copy of the last one?'

'Yes'.

'Base this report on the statistics in the last one. It must demonstrate the consistency of our regional development. The statistical ups and downs must have a logical clarity. The main thing is that it be logical. It doesn't need to be entirely true'.

'And the report on the political situation...?'

'Not necessary. I'll give an oral report'.

Ramli yawned several times. Suddenly he needed to relieve himself. He got up, and went straight to the en suite. He trudged unsteadily. He couldn't make it in time and wet his pants. He stripped off his underpants and pyjamas and went back to bed, naked, his eyes almost closed.

His personal assistant looked on, open-mouthed, then gave a chuckle.

***

The bell rang. Ramli's assistant stopped typing. He glanced at his boss sound asleep, snoring. He covered him up with the sheet.

He opened the door.

'There's a telephone call for the Bupati', said the messenger boy.

He went to the phone.

'Hallo. This is Mr Ramli's aide. Who's speaking?'

'The Governor's aide. Where's the Bupati?'

'Having a bath'.

'The Governor wants the Bupati right away'.

'Fine'.

Ramli's personal assistant put down the telephone. He returned to the room and woke his boss, without difficulty.

Ramli's face, weary earlier, was now refreshed. Several minutes' sleep was enough to restore his energy. He threw off the sheet and was astonished to find himself naked.

'Where're my trousers?'

'You left them in the bathroom'.

'What happened?'

His personal assistant grinned, and changed the subject. 'The Governor wants you to come immediately. There was a phone call just now'.

'Could you get my towel'.

Ramli covered himself with the towel and went straight to the bathroom. He smiled seeing his clothing lying on the bathroom floor.

'I'm becoming a bit absent-minded for someone so young', he sighed.

He was used to moving fast. He bathed and ate quickly.

'There's no need for you to come along. Just finish the report. We'll deliver it tomorrow morning', he told his aide.

Ramli whistled as he walked to his car. He was in a good mood.

'Where to, Sir? Something to eat?' asked the driver, starting up the engine.

'I'll have something later. We're going to the Governor's residence. If you're hungry, you go and eat when you've dropped me off'.

The weather in Padang in the dry season was usually pleasant. There was a gentle breeze. The sky was clear. There wasn't too much traffic.

Ramli was still whistling. His driver was surprised to see how happy he was. He had been down in the dumps all day but now seemed bright and cheerful, on top of the world.

***

The Governor received Ramli in the spacious reception room. He was seated on a dark red sofa, wearing a short sleeved sea-blue tetron shirt. As usual, when receiving guests in the late afternoon or evening he wore only a pair of Bata sandals on his feet.

'I hear you haven't been well, Governor', said Ramli, sitting down opposite.

'When I went to Tanah Datar yesterday I got caught in the rain. It wasn't very heavy. Just drizzle. But it gave me a chill. I'm very sensitive to the weather'.

'You should take some leave', said Ramli. The comment was actually directed towards himself.

'I'd like to. But obviously it can't be done. Sometimes I just feel I'd like to empty my mind of all the burdens that pile up every day'.

Ramli took advantage of the congenial atmosphere to bring up the problems confronting him. If the Governor had begun on an informal note then there was a chance that their conversation would progress as he had hoped.

'When are you leaving for Jakarta, Governor?'

'Tomorrow afternoon. Have you completed your report yet?'

'Yes. I'll deliver it to your office tomorrow morning'.

'I hear relations in the Regional Council aren't too cordial. Why is that?'

Ramli lit his cigarette. He looked at the Governor. 'Well, here we go!', he thought to himself.

'They tell me Colonel Hs is very angry. What's wrong?' the Governor continued.

Ramli saw that his problems with Colonel Hs would have to be discussed sooner than he had hoped.

'Well, it's like this, Governor...some time ago he telephoned me, supposedly on official business. But in fact, there was absolutely nothing official raised in the call'.

'So, what did he talk about?' asked the Governor, curiously.

'He asked me to send him some eggs and rice. I told him that shouldn't be discussed over the telephone. If anyone else heard it, it could be embarrassing. He was very angry. I hung up. I didn't want to encourage that kind of thing. If it were only a hundred eggs and a sack of rice I wouldn't have any objection to handing them over, but I didn't like him using his position. Especially since he's not my superior. I don't like that kind of thing'.

'He said that you were rude'.

'If he thinks that was rude, that's his problem...I don't know whether any other district heads would want to send such bribes, but I don't. I don't want to give the contract to the contractor he is recommending either, because there were problems with the work they did elsewhere'.

'I don't want this matter to become an open conflict. Last week Colonel Hs asked whether I'm going to retain you as Bupati...'

The Governor paused. He gulped down some cold orange juice. Ramli too took a drink.

'I replied that this depended on conversations with the Commander and other Level I Council members. He said that he was in possession of facts which would incriminate you. I asked him to provide authenticated evidence. He said he would'.

'The climate isn't favourable for the implementation of development. It's not that there's discontent from below. The discontent is coming from above. I've been accused of being unsympathetic towards the Armed Forces. They forget that we were in the army together during the struggle for Independence. We gave up our rank so we could go back to school'.

'Don't pay too much attention to Colonel H's behaviour. That's just his personal style. It has nothing to do with Defence and Security's general policy. Be careful not to get caught up in discussions about particular branches of the Armed Services. Let their superiors make the appropriate assessments'.

'I'll take your advice'.

'And the Chairman of the Regional Parliament, why did he join in the speculation about a new Bupati?'

'It was like this, Governor. He came to ask me for help in finishing his house. I told him I didn't have the kind of money he wanted'.

'How much?'

'One million'.

'Phew…'

'I felt I'd helped his household enough. I'd also provided for his kid's marriage. Every month I gave him fifty thousand. But when it came to building a house, Governor, frankly I just couldn't do it. I haven't even got a house of my own yet. You know that'.

'Well, carry on with your work as usual. Pretend that none of this ever happened. Later when I return from Jakarta I'll visit S district. I'll crack down on anyone who's shooting off at the mouth'.

Ramli was relieved. The political matter was settled.

'And how about development problems, especially the rice improvement scheme?'

'The implementation of the scheme isn't particularly encouraging, Governor'.

'I know. Just make sure that no-one dies of starvation before the harvest's in. I've already received inside information on the global food and fertiliser situation, also some estimates for Indonesia. The long dry season and the high price of fertiliser can be relied on to explain any future deterioration in the food situation'.

'My report discusses the facts fully. It's up to you how you use it in the executive meeting in Jakarta'.

'Reports at the Jakarta meeting are hard to predict. One minute all the Governors are groaning. Next minute the reports are full of optimism, even if it's unfounded'.

Ramli felt relieved. His intuition was obviously right. He heard the noise of the geckos playing on the ceiling. He looked up. The Governor smiled.

'I hope you will be able to visit S before the end of the month, Governor'.

'I hope so. I don't like the feudal way of doing things'.

'I understand, Governor'.

Ramli took his leave. Back in the car he began to whistle again.

'Where to, Sir? To eat?'

'No. To the movies'.

***

Ramli invited Sutan Gareseh to dine at his home. After a tasty meal, Ramli invited him to speak privately. He didn't discuss his position or the question of development.

'Sutan, you know it's not long until the general elections. You've a lot of experience in these matters. The government's likely to ask for your advice and suggestions'.

Sutan Gareseh nodded enthusiastically. He jumped at the opportunity to talk at length with Bupati Ramli.

'I've thought a great deal about the general elections, Bupati. I've been waiting for the right time to contribute my ideas. I'm very pleased that you've begun to give them some thought. I'm acquainted with the local leaders and people all through this District. I've been involved in politics since my youth'.

'I'll need your suggestions and advice later in determining the candidates for membership of the Regional Parliament'.

'Is there a definite date for the elections?'

'It'll be in twenty months' time. It's not long, Sutan'.

'No, not long. We'd better be ready this year'.

'You're ready, Sutan, aren't you?'

'Certainly…certainly, Bupati. As long as I'm still fit and healthy I'll help you'.

'When he returns from Jakarta, the Governor'll be coming. I'll arrange a meeting with the Governor for you. Tell him what you feel, what you think needs to be done for the advancement of our District. He likes frankness. I've already told him that you've helped me a great deal in bringing political stability to the region, and in encouraging the people to participate in development'.

Sutan Gareseh chuckled. Ramli laughed loudly too.

'I haven't done much, Bupati. I'll feel embarrassed if you praise me in front of the Governor'.

'I'm objective, Sutan'.

Before he went home, after initially refusing, Gareseh finally accepted a carton of Dunhill cigarettes from Ramli.

'Perhaps your friends in the market will want to switch brands too', said Ramli. Sutan Gareseh pocketed the cigarettes.

Ramli accompanied Sutan Gareseh as far as the street. For Sutan Gareseh, the meeting with Ramli had its own significance. He began to imagine himself as a member of the Regional Parliament again. Better than being a contractor.

'In two more years I'll be elected to the Regional Parliament. Maybe I'll be Chairman or Deputy Chairman. There are lots of fringe benefits. There's a car, travelling allowance, maybe even a house'.

For Ramli, the success of his approach to Sutan Gareseh was a sign that his birds were coming home to roost. If it worked, good. But if it didn't work, it didn't matter. But for now it looked as though he'd hit his mark. He could prepare for his next move.

'Fat chance he's got of getting elected to Parliament! Ah, the pipe-dreams of a politician!' muttered Ramli.

***

Malin's coffee stall grew more crowded every night. The facts about Lieutenant Colonel D's failure to become Bupati were being discussed.

'It's very unfortunate that his energies are required for a more important position', said Sutan Gareseh.

'If that's the case, then there's a good possibility that M will be next in line', said Lenggang Dunia.

'No, no. Apparently the Governor is keeping Ramli on. You can understand his reasons. If someone new became Bupati there'd be a good possibility that the implementation of development plans in our area wouldn't go smoothly'.

'What about the present Bupati's blunders?' Lenggang Dunia was not satisfied.

'We can fix that. I've heard the Governor's coming. We can pass on our complaints. We can criticise regional development here. Of course, we'll do it in a subtle way which'll only hint at criticism of Ramli. The Governor's an intelligent man'.

'Some people are saying that you'll be standing as a candidate for parliament in the next general elections. That's pretty good, Sutan', said the bloke with the hare-lip.

'Ah, that's not true. I'm too stupid to be a member of parliament'.

Sutan Gareseh finished his coffee. He went home straight away, and directly to bed.

And he dreamed that after he had been elected as a member of the Regional Parliament for his District, he was proposed as the sole candidate for Bupati. And the Regional Parliament elected him by acclamation.

He began to learn to drive. Several times he had to step hard on the brake. And he woke with a start when he kicked his wife out on to the floor.

(originally published as 'Telepon', *Horison*, 1976, 10–11(XI), October-November, pp.332–35)

The Lebaran* Prayers of a Group of Political Prisoners in a Concentration Camp

Sides Sudyarto DS

---

translated by David T. Hill

In fact, as he understood it as just an ordinary run-of-the-mill bloke, today is also yesterday. This afternoon is yesterday afternoon too. This day and night will become yesterday, and tomorrow will become the present, and so on, all with absolute certainty. The present will become yesterday, the day before, the dim distant past, seconds, days, through pre-determined hours becoming months, years, centuries, continuously, thus becoming history.

He didn't understand what history meant. Because he hadn't had an opportunity to study, let alone attend university. Of course, he accepted his lot, in the sense that he lived out his life as a destitute child who was born, grew up and lived in a poverty-stricken country.

Because he didn't understand history, he could make no projection about his future (which was now still his present). His present could not yet pass. In fact, he had already seen a lot of time go by. He was 25 years old. But the present, whether it was the seal for his situation, the condition of his life, or whether it was what holy people call 'Fate', was just 'so so'.

---

* The 'Lebaran' festival (or 'Idul Fitri') ends the Islamic fasting month of Ramadhan.

As a logical consequence of not having an understanding of history, he could not know or understand the meaning of the word 'Revolution'. Nevertheless there were people in his current environment who had indoctrinated him to parrot over and over again that one word: Revolution.

His understanding now about Revolution was simple: an event which has to happen or is brought about by people to change their fate. The event has to take place quickly, said the indoctrination. The problem of just how quickly and for how long, the indoctrination did not make clear. The indoctrination went on to say that it all depends upon the efforts of the people themselves, plus several other factors of environment, situation, place and time.

Because, as he pictured it, Revolution was so attractive, beautiful, romantic, inevitable and overdue, he accepted such a definitive interpretation. Because he accepted that understanding, as a logical consequence, he was now in a Camp. From the outset he had not understood that this...this place, was called a 'Camp'. He did not even know whether this name should be completed with the word 'Concentration' or not.

What was clear was that as a political detainee, he began to write a diary out of his loneliness and prolonged introspection. However in his note book he rarely wrote the date. Because obviously, in his present home, or more precisely the building called the 'Concentration Camp', it was very difficult to remember what date and day it was now or tomorrow, let alone the days of the past so much more distant. On his first page he wrote: 'In this Concentration Camp, for the first time I understand that, when I am not free, I really appreciate what my freedom means'.

While on the second page he continued, 'Evidently, from what I have experienced, I have to conclude that freedom means a space in which one is able to do anything—eat, defecate, breathe or sleep, or do anything at all with his or her life—without being disturbed'.

He became very preoccupied with his diary, like a young child preoccupied with a new toy. He sat alone now, while the other inmates of the Camp were busy lining up to receive packages from their families. He did not line up like them because, from the time he had accepted the prescription of Revolution to overcome poverty and sustain his life thereafter, his family no longer acknowledged him as a member. Consequently he did not get any packages, nor any visitors. Because of that, he had the chance to write some more in his diary: 'The first thing that I got from the Revolution was this Concentration Camp. Then secondly, I was no longer acknowledged as a member of my family. What happens now? Surely this question mark will be answered by another question mark. But usually, as is customary with a question mark, it will answer itself, later, in the future or whenever. Or it may also get no answer at all'.

Into his daydream came a number of relatives. He did not investigate the exact number any further. Actually he wanted to count them exactly, but because they came only in a daydream he realised it was all in his imagination. And because he realised that this was only his imagination he did not need to count them. He was sure that they all came. A mother, which means someone who had been forced to give birth to him, then his father, which means someone who was the exponent and component of his being born. The rest, younger siblings, older siblings, who did not determine, but did have an influence upon, his being born, and his life afterwards. He immediately bowed, taking the hands held out to him, shaking hands to ask forgiveness, to be forgiven, and to forgive the hands and their owners all at once.

In the wide yard stretching in front of the Camp a large crowd had gathered. Because they did not have mats or things which could normally be used as prayer mats, they spread out their towels to pray on. If he was not mistaken these mats were called *sajadah*. Maybe this meant 'a place to pray'. They did indeed bow in prayer on their towels. And those who did not have towels used the leaves that the cooked rice had been wrapped in, washing them with water. Those who were not able to get leaves or something like that just bowed in prayer on the earth. Because the earth had a lot of sand and gravel when the prayers had finished many of their foreheads bore the imprint of pieces of gravel with several grains of sand still clinging there.

Seeing them gather there in increasing numbers the camp guards became more and more worried. Automatic and other weapons were loaded immediately. All the rifles were cocked for firing. The guards were all ready to fight, taking position, ready to shoot should the prisoners make the slightest suspicious move.

The political prisoners still continued their ceremony—the *Idul Fitri* prayers—according to their wishes. It was a spontaneous ceremony. They did not ask permission from the Camp Commander beforehand. Neither had they made any collective decision previously about it. As a result, even the appointing of an *imam* to lead the prayers was extremely incidental. It was a case of whoever wanted to, whoever was willing, whoever was devoted, and also of course, whoever was able to lead the prayers.

In the initial stages, the Camp guards ridiculed them. They mimed the movements of the people's prayer. They mimicked them standing, folding their arms. Then they aped their bowing down and so on. They did not imitate them when they bowed their foreheads to touch the ground. Perhaps they were afraid of getting dirty from the dusty floor.

At the next stage, the guards began to grow tired. The people being mimicked did not take the slightest notice of the movements of their spiteful imitators. The political prisoners became more deeply immersed in their devotions.

By the third stage, the camp guards began to stop their imitating. It was not that they were tired of it, but because they were confused about what to do next. The confusion arose because they were becoming moved by the massed prayers of the political prisoners. Then one by one the guards began to shed a tear.

This was a good opportunity for the Writer of the Diary to take a picture, not with a camera, but with his diary. Immediately he wrote briefly: 'It appears that even men wearing uniforms to enhance their macho appearance, with weapons loaded with bullets and sharp bayonets, are capable of tears when watching people drawing before their God. Maybe not because they themselves are not praying, but because they are amazed that people who have become the victims of Revolutionary theory, appear still able to believe in God'.

By the fourth stage, the Camp guards had put down their loaded guns, bolted tight, upon the table. They came down, leaving their guard post, joining the political prisoners to pray together with them. They too intoned a series of long verses, melodious, pleasant, and yearning for the mercy of the Most Exalted. Their voices worshipped Him.

The skilful Writer of the Diary again wrote about this event in his own words: 'The Guards and those guarded are like cat and mouse. Today, mouse and cat pray together'.

After writing this, he immediately went away, leaving them calling, worshipping the Exalted. He went into his room. A room like a house, a house with only one room. A room with no real walls, but with something that resembled walls: dry banana leaves hanging by their stems from a piece of rope made from a banana palm too, which was stretched across the corner of the wall with the toilet.

Suddenly a man dressed in clean clothes came up to him. His clothes were all white and spotless and he was wearing spectacles which were also crystal clear. The person came into the room of the Writer of the Diary, this occupant of the Camp. The Man in White approached the Writer of the Diary with a smile on his lips.

'May I ask your name?'

'I shed my name a long time ago, Sir. That name was given to me by my parents who now no longer acknowledge me as their son. So I gave that name back'.

'Your age?'

'I honestly don't know how old I am, when or where I was born. I really don't know, Sir'.

On getting such an answer the Man Dressed in White was not the least bit angry. He still kept smiling.

'Any aspirations?'

'Yes, of course'.

'What?'

'To die'.

'Die? Why exactly is to die an aspiration?'

'Beyond that, what else is there? In a place like this, that is the most appropriate thing, isn't it? Because that is the one thing that is most likely. Most likely'.

'How long have you wanted to die?'

'Since this morning, immediately after the prisoners' *Idul Fitri* prayers'.

'What was it about the prayers that have just finished?'

'That incident made me realise. That a man—or at least I—must be allowed to carry out prayer. And a man can only pray when he is able and whenever he has a kind of 'permit' to pray, can't he?'

'Where did you study?'

'Primary school, Junior High School, Senior High School'.

'And then?'

'I read papers, books'.

'What books were most interesting?'

'I enjoyed reading on Religion, and Literature. And the thing that I most enjoyed, unfortunately, was that which I understood least. I didn't really understand it at all'.

'What was that...this thing you didn't understand?'

'Philosophy. A word which terrifies me, like a ghost'.

'But did you really like to read about religion?'

'I did. It was good just for fun'.

'Do you know why you are here now?'

'I have no idea at all. But what is clear is that I am here, aren't I?'

'But you also want to go home sometimes?'

'Go home to where? I don't have a home. Don't have an address. Don't have a place to live. Nothing. Nowhere'.

'What if you were released, what would you do?'

'I would go out. Those are the rules, aren't they'.

'Do you think there is any advantage in you being outside this camp?'

'Maybe it would be an advantage, but maybe not'.

'Does the concentration camp also afford you any advantages?'

'A lot'.

'What are they?'

'Here I can feel and think, that I am Me'.

'Will that be lost when you are outside the camp?'

'I am not prepared to make an *a priori* judgement about that. What is clear is what I have experienced since I was put into this camp. The problem about what happens after I leave here I haven't yet had to deal with, have I?'

'So you don't want to leave this camp then?'

'It is not a question of whether or not I want to, but rather, of where am I now?'

'Do you know who I am? I am crucial to determining whether you can go free, or not. Because I am religious'.

'I had guessed as much from the beginning'.

'You guessed that that was my job?'

'Yes. You also presumed that I knew that while you carried out religious practices, you do not yet truly *live out* your religion'.

'I've got some news for you which, with a heavy heart I am forced...with a heavy heart I have...to pass on to you: You are to be executed by firing squad tonight. What is your last request?'

'I have only one. Give permission for them to pray'.

'Who are "them"?'

'Just them'.

'Any other requests? A second one?'

'The second is the same. Permit them to pray'.

'A third one?'

'Give them a chance to carry out their prayers'.

'Do you think that up till now people here haven't been permitted to pray?'

'They are in a camp here. A camp is not a good place for prayers. They are in a camp because of their acceptance of an ideology at variance with the prayers. That acceptance was not because they understood. But because they were attracted to it to end a state of poverty which had become just too desperate for words'.

'So is that your conclusion?'

'Give them the opportunity to pray when they want to'.

Night came. Heavy drizzle fell on the camp. The electricity blacked out, extinguished, black, dark and gloomy. As usual, when there was a black out it meant that someone was going to be 'paid up'. In the jargon of the political prisoners to be 'paid up' meant to be taken out and shot dead by a firing squad. That's the way it was. On that drizzling night the Writer of the Diary was taken away by truck, escorted under tight security by fully armed men with bayonets fixed. The next day he had already been buried in a shallow grave. His feet protruded, tugged out by stray dogs. A Catholic Priest who was standing near the grave squatted down now in his swathe of white clothes, and clear spectacles. In his prayer he was able to utter:

'Forgive me. For, although I knew that you did really live your religion, I could not set you free. Because I am not the Commandant: I am just responsible for religious affairs. I have never come across the problem of actually living a religion. I admit it. But be patient. The considerations of Our Lord Jesus are different from ours'.

Beside the shallow grave lay a diary. The dead man's. When the Priest glanced at it, blown by the wind, it opened precisely at a page which said: 'I assume one proof of a backward nation is where people have difficulty getting the right to say their prayers'.

The Priest moved on. A gentle breeze blew. The book lay tossed aside, like a hand waving itself at the leg which stuck from the shallow grave.

(first appeared as 'Sholat Lebaran Kawanan Tahanan Politik dalam Sebuah Kamp Konsentrasi', *Horison*, 1977, XII(8), August, pp.249–51.)

The Critic

Pamusuk Eneste

---

translated by David T. Hill

Morning.

When the prison warder came to his cell, snow was still falling outside. Snow was rather unusual at this time, although the fall was not as heavy as last year.

'Hello', said the warder. '*Get up*'.

There was no reply.

'Hello', he said again. '*I have brought a letter for you*'.

There was no sound.

So the warder threw the letter onto the floor, locked the cell window and went.

The body remained still, without movement. Sprawled across the cot, with no mattress and no sheet.

I can still remember—as a journalist I covered the trial proceedings—when he was tried several years ago, without any clear charges. At that time he had only just returned home after several years studying abroad.

The public prosecutor claimed that the Critic hadn't written anything critical for a long time, despite the fact that criticism was absolutely necessary in the era of 'development'. By some stroke of fate he was the one and only critic in the Republic of What's-a-Name Land.

'Formerly, when you were still a student you wrote criticisms with great enthusiasm. But, after graduating, you have become lax. What is the cause?' asked the first member of the judicial tribunal.

The Critic remained silent.

'That's right', continued the second judge, 'you used to criticise officials, generals, corruption, authoritarianism and such like frequently. But after studying overseas you only write travelogues, about wandering in and out of museums and that sort of thing. Why is that?'

There was still no comment.

'I was surprised', countered the third member of the judiciary, 'that on returning home from overseas you no longer wrote the fiery criticisms you used to, when, after all, our country needs criticisms to support the development of the nation and the state. Why have you changed so drastically?'

I watched as the Critic remained silent. His expression unchanged. Calm but cold.

The trial progressed without protest. The Critic answered none of the questions from the prosecutor or the judges. Neither was the Critic supported by defence counsel, although that was his right, as prescribed by law.

Finally, the Judicial Council decided on a life sentence for the Critic. What weighed heavily against the accused was the apparent attitude that he had done absolutely nothing wrong, and the fact that he had not assisted the proceedings at all. None of the questions had been answered or contested.

'This constitutes serious contempt for the court of the Republic of What's-a-Name Land', said the Chief Justice reading the verdict, 'which also means a great insult to the country itself'.

Noon.

The snow was still falling when the prison warder came again to the Critic's cell, accompanied by several other colleagues. The body was still in the same position it had been that morning. It had not stirred at all. Silent and rigid.

When the cell door was opened the warders could read the writing on the back of the door: 'But I am no hero…' Congealed blood was spilled over the floor. The Critic's wrists were torn and gaping open.

The snow was still falling as the warders lugged the corpse of the Critic from the cell.

Hamburg, February 1980

(Originally published as 'Sang Kritikus', *Horison*, 1980, April, p.125.)

Generals

Pamusuk Eneste

translated by David T. Hill

Once upon a time there was general inflation in the Republic of What's-a-Name Land. You came across generals everywhere. The taxi drivers, bus drivers, semi-trailer drivers and the ushers at the cinema were all generals, not to mention the lecturers in the universities too. No-one knew why there were so many generals in the republic. There had not actually been a war for ages.

Initially people were not too concerned about the situation, but gradually they began to get annoyed. The civilians started to grumble that the generals had seized all their job vacancies. The passengers who travelled by city bus each day began to complain about the manners of the bus drivers, who were generals.

'They are really arrogant', said one person, 'and they drive the buses so recklessly'.

'Even crazier', said another, 'sometimes they don't pull up at the bus stop, even if there are lots of people waiting to get on'.

As time went by the frustration of the people turned to hatred. But the President of the Republic of What's-a-Name Land (himself a general) did not take any action over the behaviour of the generals. So, in turn, the people hated the President, accusing him of approving of the generals' behaviour.

But one day a miracle occurred in the Republic of What's-a-Name Land. The Military Government was successfully overthrown in a bloodless *coup d'etat*. A Civilian Government was formed immediately. The generals, including the President, were arrested. Despite this the Civilian President did not want to punish the generals from the military regime arbitrarily. This

Civilian President wanted to be democratic. He turned the decision as to what should be done with all these generals entirely over to his people.

To ascertain the people's verdict the Civilian Government launched an essay-writing competition. Anyone could enter, except the families of the generals. There was only one condition: the composition could be no longer than one sentence. The topic was: How can the generals be eliminated in an humanitarian manner?

The number of compositions that came in exceeded all expectations. After selection by the Civilian Arts Council ten compositions were declared finalists. Because the Civilian Government wanted to encourage openness in the Republic of What's-a-Name Land the contents of the ten compositions were made known to the public.

The first finalist wrote that the generals should be sent to Siberia to 'open up land there'.

'In Indonesia there is still a lot of jungle which has yet to be opened up', wrote the second finalist, 'so banish the generals there!'

The third finalist ventured the opinion: 'Send them to fight the war in Vietnam!'

'If it was up to me, I would prefer it if the generals were ordered to open up land in the Sahara Desert', said the fourth finalist.

The fifth finalist suggested: 'I would rather the generals were exiled to the North Pole where they would eventually freeze'.

'It's easy', said the sixth finalist, 'just order the generals to walk around the world and eventually, one by one, they will all croak it in the end'.

Said the seventh finalist: 'Who cares what you do with them!'

'So as not to hurt the families who would be bereaved', wrote the eighth finalist, 'it would be better to exile the generals from our beloved Republic of What's-a-Name Land'.

The ninth finalist said 'Why go to any special trouble; just lock the generals in a dungeon and feed them on soya-bean patties each day'.

'In accordance with the spirit of national development', said the tenth finalist, 'I suggest the generals be directed to build a bridge linking London with Citeureup'.

The ten finalists still have to be brought up for interview before the Civilian Supreme Council, which consists of Civilian professors.

Actually as I write this story it is not clear who among the ten finalists will turn out to be the ultimate winner. However, if you go to the Republic of What's-a-Name Land now you won't find a single general any more!

Hamburg, 2 January, 1980

(Originally published as 'Jenderal-jenderal' in *Horison*, 1980, April, p.130.)

The Debt

Jasso Winarto

translated by Jan Lingard

If a friend, a relative or a neighbour owes you money and he doesn't want to pay it back, then be careful! Coax him one more time to pay part of it, or to pay it off in instalments. If you have time, keep calling on him until he feels embarrassed. Or snap at him and abuse him till he shakes in his boots. But, don't report the debt to the police or take it to the courts. Don't! Of course its unjust that you don't get your money back, but seeking justice by involving the police in a matter of that kind only makes trouble.

Slamet was really good natured, although he was inclined to get upset when his wife was angry. He was the son of a village school teacher, and now lived in Jakarta, in the same local district as me. Because he was the son of a teacher, he became a teacher in a Junior High School in Cipinang Cempedak. His salary was Rp.25,000 per month. Life had plenty of shortcomings with a fierce wife and two sons who behaved like their mother. Because his income was inadequate, Slamet used his spare time for a second job. He was a tout, for anything at all, housing contracts, land or used cars. There were two reasons that made Slamet get involved in working at a second job until all hours of the night. The first, of course, was so that he would sometimes get a reasonable income, and the second was, he could not put up with his wife if he stayed at home for long. He said his wife always criticized his job as a teacher.

'Of course, teachers used to be respected. They were looked up to by pupils, neighbours or the district head. But now? With a month's wages that are only enough to keep us for ten days?

You were determined to be a teacher only because your father was a teacher. You had a nerve marrying me! Bah!' she said in her Batak dialect.

Frankly, I was surprised myself at how Slamet here, had had the courage to marry this woman of the Hutagalung Clan.

'I must have been out of my mind when I proposed to her', Slamet sighed one day.

Because he was always short of money, Slamet often came to my shop to ask for help. Actually, I was very tight fisted with money. But, Slamet's father had been my village teacher and had taught me to read and write. So, yes, I helped him a little by putting aside part of the day's takings. The first loan was for Rp.1,000, then it was Rp.2,000, and once in a while I lent him Rp.5,000. When I added it all up, it came to Rp.95,000. His wife came with him for the last loan, and they borrowed Rp.50,000 to go home to their village for the Lebaran feast, as she said in a threatening tone.

Actually, I strongly objected to lending as much money as that for going home for Lebaran. Especially as nothing at all had been paid off the old debts.

'The backpay that's due to me hasn't arrived yet', Slamet said in a piteous voice.

But, I was a trader. I had financially squeezed a lot of people as they sat about in my shop, so there was no harm in it if I made up for my sins by giving a loan to Slamet's wife. It was better than having her go berserk in the shop.

So the total loan to Slamet was one hundred and forty-five thousand rupiah. I stressed this to him when he got back from the village. He promised to pay his debt when the backpay eventuated.

Three months ago, he came to the shop again, bringing a letter from the State Treasury Office stating that his accrued backpay was due to him. He showed me the letter. Altogether, he was entitled to one hundred and seventy thousand rupiah.

'Please help me out with twenty thousand rupiah now, Besil. My wife needs money today, but the money from the Treasury only comes due the day after tomorrow. I'll hand the whole lot over to you then. I swear it!' he said.

But, business had been really bad that day. There had been no customers, so of course, there wasn't any money. I explained this to Slamet. I even opened the till to convince him. Naturally, he was disappointed. I really did want to help, so as not to disappoint him and so that the backpay would be sure to fall into my hands the day after next. But, he finally left the shop without even a cent.

The day after next, I waited for him. But he didn't turn up with the money. Tomorrow maybe, I thought. The next day he didn't turn up either and I lost my patience. What's more, I was suspicious. Slamet had received a lump sum of money. One hundred and seventy thousand rupiah! What would you do if you had as much money as that at a time when you were blanketed by poverty? Would you pay off your debts? Not even a 20th century Prophet would do that!

Slamet really was a good man. He was a devoted teacher and I knew that his honesty was highly praised, like that of the long line of teachers he was descended from. But, as soon as he received the backpay, he kept out of my sight. He did not want to pay his debts. I was sure he was using his money for living it up, buying *sate*, expensive clothes for his children, or things like that, just so that he would be treated like an ordinary human being by that wife of his. On the other hand, I had helped him as much as I could with Rp.145,000, and interest free! The one time I hadn't lent him money he had complained, whined, and pleaded. He had been scared to go home, frightened he'd be eaten alive by that Batak woman.

That night, after I shut the shop, I went to Slamet's place in Lane V. In front of his small house, I heard the loud voices of Slamet's family who were obviously very excited and happy. And my nose was assailed by the smell of durians. They were having a durian feast for sure. I coughed a few times and knocked on the door. Immediately there was a deathly hush. For quite a long time, no one opened the door. I knocked again. Finally the youngest child, the rude Icang appeared.

'Is your father in?' I asked.

'He's out', he answered firmly.

'Your father? Slamet?'

'He's not here!'

'Where is he?' I continued. I was sure that this child had been told to lie! Icang thought hard. Finally he shook his head.

'Don't tell lies', I hissed. He was frightened and ran inside. Then Slamet's wife came out. I put on a gloomy expression. She put on a gloomier one.

'He's not here. He's gone home to his village', she said belligerently.

I left straight away and the door was shut with a loud bang. I felt hurt. They were playing games with me. They were lying. I knew it. Just now I had heard Slamet's voice, and also his children calling to him, 'Father, father, open that big one'. Slamet was definitely hiding from me.

The next day I waited for him at the entrance to the lane. But, he didn't turn up. I was surprised. Which way had he gone? Not long afterwards I chased after him on the way to school. I caught up with him. Clearly he was already different. He was wearing new gaberdine trousers and a new shirt. His hair was neatly combed and it shone with hair oil. Even his speech was affected. The only reason he had for putting on airs was that he'd just got all that backpay.

'I can't give you the money now', he replied.

'But you said, when you got the backpay...'

'My wife has it. Ask her for it'.

And so I left the school. I went straight to Slamet's house to ask his wife for the money. I was actually terrified. And rightly so. Certainly I was able to see her, but she chased me away immediately when I told her that the reason I had come was to ask for my money back.

I went back to the shop feeling angry, resentful and upset.

'They have to be taught a lesson' I thought. Obviously they were not going to pay back their debt. Imagining that Rp.145,000 being thrown away like that, my blood boiled. Intending to teach them a lesson, I went to the police station to report the incident. On duty at the time was Police Corporal Slamet. Yes, by a coincidence it was the same name. Of course, in Java there are millions of Slamets. God only knows why there are so many Slamets on this island.

This corporal wrote out everything I reported, and questioned me about the smallest details. I related the whole story, how much the debt was, the details about Slamet's promises and how he had replied after his backpay came, how his wife had chased me away, and so on.

Two days later, Slamet and his wife came to the shop. They both looked furious. I pretended to be unconcerned.

'You've reported us to the police have you?' snarled the wife.

I didn't answer. I only glared at them in disgust.

'Right! We'll take this matter to the courts. You'll know what it's like to be poor!' Slamet's wife threatened bitterly, waving round a police summons for Slamet. Then they hurried off to the police station by motorised pedicab. I was satisfied. I imagined how Slamet would soon be shaking in his boots because of the dressing down he would get from Corporal Slamet.

That afternoon, Corporal Slamet came to my house. He said that he had interrogated the teacher and that he still had to get more information. Then the corporal complained about a policeman's low wage. Of course I wanted to give him a little money, but because I was scared that later I might be accused of bribing a servant of the State, I complained too, about how bad business was.

When he left, I didn't even give him a cent. He seemed disappointed. At the gate, he said he had to take his sick child to the doctor.

'Oh, go to Dr Suner. He's a specialist', I said rather stupidly.

Wearily the corporal took his leave. He headed off in the direction of Lane V where Slamet lived. I had very much wanted to help but I was scared of being accused of bribery. Now the policeman was heading for Slamet's house. What for? I began to feel uneasy.

My anxiety proved to be justified. Three days later an official from the Police came to deliver a summons. I was told to report to Lieutenant Colonel Abas Suryadimeja the next day.

After a sleepless night, I went early the next morning to Metropolitan Regional Police Command in Semanggi to face the said Lieutenant Colonel. The police station was full of people who all looked like criminals. Of course, I look like one of them now, I thought.

It turned out that I was dealt with by a Corporal anyway, after waiting more than four hours. His name was Police Corporal Ali Sujana. His eyes were sharp, his skin was dark and his face was pock-marked. He sat facing an old typewriter.

'Do you know why you've been summoned here?' he asked in a serious voice.

'No, Sir'. I replied.

'Do you know a schoolteacher called Slamet Danudirjo?'

I nodded.

'You have reported to the police that this teacher owes you money and you accuse him of refusing to pay?'

I nodded.

'Well, you have been summoned here because you have made a false report and slandered the said teacher', the Corporal said, making me feel as though my head had been struck by lightning.

'But...'

'Look, it's the judge who will decide whether you are guilty or not. But, my superiors have given me the task of taking a verbal statement from you, about the charge', he cut in quickly.

'Your name?'

'Besil...Besil Eudarmin', I answered nervously.

And the policeman typed it loudly. He asked about my family, my job, my connection with Slamet and my 'false' report. When he asked me for proof of the debt I was owed, I shook my head, for indeed there was none. He snarled at me that I had made a false report. He tried to force me to admit it, and I refused.

It was now 4p.m. I was hungry, resentful and angry. To myself, I abused that madman Slamet. But I also regretted going this far and bringing these corporals into it.

Corporal Ali took a deep breath and said 'You'd better think it over again, whether or not you admit that you made a false report'.

I shook my head. I asked permission to go home but it was refused. My downcast face paled. My blood froze.

'What's going to happen?' I asked.

'You have to spend the night at the Station. It's nothing to worry about. Haven't you ever tried it?'

I shook my head in fear. Then he got up and led me down to a cell. I cried all night long. I didn't think things would turn out like this, that my legal position was so poor because I had no proof at all about the money I was owed. Therefore, as far as the Law was concerned, my report was false, the Corporal had said.

After two nights shut away in the cell I was interrogated again. I had become a dazed creature. I could no longer think. My eyes were red and swollen. And when I was ordered to sign the verbal statement I just signed it automatically.

'Can't I just be left in peace now, Sir?' I asked.

'You can only make peace with Mr Slamet. But not with the State! This is a criminal case—making a false report, slander, and disturbing the peace. You could go to jail for five years', he replied sternly.

'Please, can I go home first—there's the matter of my shop...'

'I haven't finished cross-examining you yet'.

'I mean...can I get out on bail?...I'll definitely come if I'm sent for'.

'How much would you pay?' he asked with a wink.

'However much you like. I'll leave it to your discretion', I answered, catching on.

That afternoon, I was allowed to go home. However it may be, it was good to be home. I'd only been there for half an hour, when the Corporal arrived. He wanted to get the bail money. Straight away I opened a cupboard and handed over half a million rupiah, the amount he'd said. He left, and I began to think how to get myself out of this mess.

A week later the Corporal came again. He said he would be able to shelve the case if I would pay another one and a half million rupiah. The file on the case would be put away and not re-opened.

'I haven't got that much money', I answered, but I continued, 'If it's one million I can organise it'.

After he thought it over, he finally answered, 'All right. One million. But you can pay the other half million later when you've made some cash'.

I agreed. It was better than having to go to court, pay a lawyer and then serve the sentence. Frankly, I was very frightened. The next day I drew out all my money and paid the Corporal.

Then I fell bankrupt and became really poor. My shop was closed up for a month and I struggled to get back on my feet again. I never want to set eyes on anyone called Slamet, whether it's Slamet the teacher, Slamet the policeman or any other Slamet.

I'll say it again, don't report it to the police if a friend or a relative refuses to pay back money he owes you!

(originally published as 'Utang', *Horison*, 1980, 5(15), pp.160–61;165.)

Long Life for Mr Joyokoyoroyo and his Cronies

Hamsad Rangkuti

translated by Jan Lingard

Joyokoyoroyo, a corrupt official, had smiled when the servant handed him the morning paper at the dining table five minutes earlier. Now he folded the paper and sat leaning back in the carved Japara chair, looking at his pretty young wife and smiling to himself. He sat like that for a long time, then he called the servant who came running and tripped against the table. As a result of the knock he was actually in a lot of pain, but because his master wanted him he smiled as if it had only tickled him.

'Get me my most expensive cigars from the cigar case'.

'Which ones sir? I can't tell the difference between all your cigars'.

'You fool! Don't you know the alphabet?'

'Yes, I know it sir, but I can't read it'.

'In that case, get me the ones with the letter 'V' on them. Hurry up!'

The servant went to the parlour and Mr Joyokoyoroyo, who hadn't had his fill of his wife's pretty face earlier, went on looking at her. When he'd finished reading the morning paper, her face looked ten times prettier to him than it was before. But because he soon had to be in a luxury hotel to sign a forest concession, he controlled his mounting desire to take her into the bedroom and make love to her.

You'll keep, he thought, there's still a night of pleasure ahead to take you in my arms.

He stood up to go to the telephone table, but heard his wife say, 'There's your honey, darling. Didn't you see it? I've broken two eggs into the glass. All you've to do is put the honey in and add the pepper. Weren't you just looking at my legs, under the chair?'

'Yes, I was... But you'll have to wait until tonight'.

Mr Joyo gulped down the eggs, honey and pepper, and went to the telephone table. Clouds of smoke billowed up to the ceiling of the parlour from the cigar in his mouth. He dialled a number and started speaking into the phone.

'Is that you Mangkualamnusantara?'

'Speaking', Joyo heard in his ear.

'How are you? As happy as I am!'

'What are you happy about?'

'Are you blind? Or didn't you read it on the front page of the morning paper?'

'What about?'

'Heavens man! The fact that we're safe! We're protected! We'll live to a ripe old age! Weren't you frightened all this time that if we were caught, we'd had it? The main thing is the opportunity to make ourselves rich is still wide open. If we get caught, we'll get life. As soon as they forget all about us, we'll bribe the warders and we'll be free! But if it was capital punishment, that'd be the end of us. And now they're fighting to have it abolished!'

Joyo put down the receiver and dialled another number.

'Hallo?'

'Yes, Hallo'.

'Is that you?'

'Yes, it's me, Mangkubuminagorokoyo. What's up?'

'Have you read the morning paper?'

'Yes, I have'.

'What do you think?'

'I think—a party! We'll throw a party to welcome the decision'.

'Do you know all their addresses?'

'What for?'

'We'll invite them. We'll ask them to the party. And if they want to...'

'Of course they won't want to. They're honest'.

'In that case, we'll just say thanks a million'.

'What do you mean?'

'They've saved our lives. You arrange the time and place'.

Mr Joyo put down the phone, walked to the sitting room and looked out the open window. It was from there that long ago he'd once seen the university students shouting and demonstrating. On that occasion he'd quickly drawn the curtains. In the streets, the students had chanted, 'Hang Subandrio, the running dog of Peking! Hang the corruptors, the enemies of the people!'

In those days, Mr Joyo already had a reputation as a big-time corruptor. But he was saved. He sheltered behind his wealth and he sheltered behind his friends who held power in legal circles. He was saved. He'd been sentenced to life imprisonment, had bribed the prison officers and was free. Then he started up again. Now he had enough wealth for seven generations. And when he read the morning paper he made up his mind to go on cheating the state of its wealth till he had enough for fourteen generations.

Suddenly, Mr Joyo could hardly believe his eyes. Only a few hours after the publication and circulation of the morning paper in the community, some university students were coming down the main road, right in front of his house, demonstrating and carrying slogans. And it seemed to him that he agreed with what the demonstrators were shouting. He listened intently. However the shouts didn't alter, but were just the same as he'd heard since the chanting started.

'Abolish capital punishment!' shouted the demonstrators.

'Save the corruptors!' they shouted next.

Mr Joyo ran to the dining table. His wife was straining her ears to hear.

'Did you hear them?'

'I heard. Are my ears deceiving me?'

'I doubted my own hearing too. I know my ears are very good at twisting the meanings of things, but are these demonstrators really saying what I think they are? Did you hear what I heard?'

'You're not wrong. I heard what you heard. What they're shouting is quite clear. I still trust my own ears. What you should be doing is thanking those people'.

'There's no doubt about that, I certainly should. You probably can't understand how frightened I was when I heard them shouting fifteen years ago. You don't know what it was like. The hair on the back of my neck stood on end when I heard them shouting. It felt as though all my joints and bones had turned to jelly. Oh, most loving and merciful God. You always save even the greatest sinners on the face of this earth'.

Briefly Joyo hugged his wife and kissed her. Then he got the letters promising forest concessions, bills of sale for islands, bills of sale for coastline a few miles from the mangrove swamps, and bills of sale for mountains, which he was shortly going to sign in the lobby of the Hotel Borobodur. The overseas guests had, no doubt, been waiting there for him for a long time.

When he reached his car door, he didn't get in, but went back into the house to his study.

'What did you leave behind?' said his wife.

'The mining contracts'.

Then, having arranged all the documents neatly in his briefcase, Mr Joyo got into his car, clutching the briefcase tightly. The driver took off quickly.

In the middle of the road, they encountered the demonstrators. 'Save the lives of the corruptors!' they chanted in Mr Joyo's ear.

'That's splendid. You all know my aspirations', replied Mr. Joyo unconsciously from behind the car window. Suddenly he opened his briefcase and told the driver to slow down. He wound down the car window then threw out thousands of ten thousand rupiah notes. He roared with laughter watching the demonstrators scrambling to pick up the notes scattered everywhere in the middle of the highway.

'Why did you do that?' asked the driver.

'Didn't you hear what they were shouting?'

'I heard'.

'Hasn't my life been saved?'

'You're mistaken. They weren't shouting on your behalf. They're fighting for the lives of the small-time criminals, who kill one or two people because of economic pressures. You're wrong. They weren't shouting for the likes of you. I think you've misinterpreted what you heard to suit yourself'.

'I heard it that way and I can interpret it that way'.

'That's not what they said. They're demonstrating on behalf of the petty crooks'.

'But it's to save someone's life. What's different about my life? We're all human beings. They're saving lives, all lives—the lives of all criminals'.

'But you're different. You've killed millions of people by impoverishing them. You've robbed them of their land and their possessions. You've killed them slowly. Now you must be killed'.

'Shut up! What sort of driver are you?'

'I may be only a driver, but I can take a stand. If the meaning of what they said has changed to mean save all lives, including yours and the lives of all corrupt people, then I'll have to be the one to punish you myself. I'll be the one to execute you!'

'What are you talking about? All this time I've known you, you've been a good driver. What's got into you?'

'Sure, I was a good driver while I could still hope that others would carry out the law properly. But if I can't count on anyone else to do it, I'll just have to change my ways'.

The car changed direction. They appeared to be heading out of the city.

'What's made you like this? Where are you taking me to?'

'Just calm down. People always have plans'.

Mr Joyo had a nasty premonition. He took a pistol out of his briefcase and pointed it at the driver's head.

'Just remember, you're still young and so is your wife. You have small children. I know everything. You told me about them once. You've got a young family. Let's go back to the hotel. Pull yourself together. Slow down'.

The car was doing 120kph. A moment later they had reached the hills area.

'Are you going to stop this car or not? Can't you feel the muzzle of this pistol at your head?'

'Go ahead and shoot, and we'll die together'.

'You're really mad!'

'Those demonstrators drove me mad! Abolishing capital punishment saves you'.

'Think of your children. Think of your wife. You're still young. They still need you. You have a long life ahead of you. What's more, you've got a degree and haven't been able to get a good job yet. Remember, Sutrisno, you're still young. Look at your life—why do you want to end it?'

'What's the use of all of that? What do my three children and my wife mean, if millions of people fall victim to you'.

'Will you stop this car? Do you want me to pull the trigger?'

'Go ahead! Pull it! We'll both go into the gorge and die together in the blazing car!'

'What do you really want? Do you want to be a hero? Or...ah, I get it, I forgot to make you an offer. Pardon my delay. How many million do you want? Five? Ten? Twenty five? Just name your price. Say it, Sutrisno. I'll sign a cheque. I'll look after you, you needn't worry. I can fix it all properly. I won't call it blackmail. Trust me. I'll keep my word provided you don't kill me. Try and think calmly'.

'Nothing you've offered will make me change my mind'.

'In that case, are you trying to be a hero?'

'This isn't the way to become a hero. Chanting in the streets and getting shot, that's how you become a hero. No one will remember me. And that's not what I want'.

'Then you are taking the law into your own hands'.

'It's no good hoping the real judges will do anything'.

'You're mad! Help! Help! He's mad!' screamed Mr Joyo to people they passed by. But they didn't hear what he was shouting. They thought he was being friendly and waving to them. So they responded with friendly waves.

'You're really insane! Oh, God, save me!'

'It won't be long now. It's nearly time. Where the road climbs up there, see the ravine down below? We're going to go over the cliff together to the bottom'.

'Help!...Help! I still want to live. Why take me with you! You're mad, mad! You're insane!'

The car raced at high speed to the crest of the hill. A steep valley dropped away to the left, with huge rocks scattered everywhere. When the car reached the highest point of the steep road it veered sharply, hit the embankment, leapt over a pile of dirt and crashed through the safety fence. It appeared to be flying, then plummeted down at high speed heading for the rocks below. A fraction of a second later it hit the bottom. The sound of an explosion shattered the silence. Flames leapt up through the trees. It looked like an ordinary accident. There was no telltale evidence to prove otherwise. They were both incinerated.

When they recovered the remains of the dead men from the wreckage, all they carried were pieces of charred bones. And a mix-up occurred. They put Mr Joyo's bones into the coffin that had been prepared for his driver, and they put the driver's remains in the coffin that had been prepared for Mr Joyo. They were both buried on the same day. They buried the driver, whom they thought was Mr Joyo, in a hero's cemetery with a state funeral accompanied by a rifle salute. And they buried Mr Joyo, whom they thought was the driver, in a public cemetery without ceremony.

In my opinion, they made a good mistake, for thereby they decided who was the real hero. And I think how it would have been good, so as not to waste the bullets, if all Mr. Joyo's friends had been lined up in front of the firing party, with their eyes blindfolded, when the salvo was fired.

(originally published as 'Umur panjang untuk Tuan Joyokoyoroyo CS', *Horison*, 1980, 8(15), pp.267–70.)

The General Smiles on 17th August

Hamsad Rangkuti

translated by David T. Hill

I raised both my hands high into the air. I could feel the tip of the bayonet jabbing into the jacket on my back. Stretching back from the end of the bayonet handle was the barrel of a rifle, cocked to fire. And at the end of the rifle butt a Dutch NICA (Netherlands Indies Civil Administration) soldier stood at the ready. The crunch of boots on the gravel indicated that there were more than three of them.

'Search him! See if he is carrying any grenades!'

One of the soldiers came forward, frisking me around my waist and the legs of my trousers. They found two grenades at my waist under my jacket, and a pistol.

'Show us where your friends' base is. Where's the base? Where's the hidden ammunition dump? Come on, tell us! I will count to ten. On the count of eleven I will pull the trigger of this gun. Tell us!'

I turned around. Five rifles were pointed at me. The NICA soldiers had their index fingers wrapped around the triggers of their rifles.

'Tell us where the stolen ammunition and the seventeen other soldiers are hidden'.

I stared at them. My hands had been too long in the air.

'Speak up, quickly! Or we'll shoot! I'm starting to count! One! Two!...'

'Wait! What's in it for me?' I was beginning to betray them. There were always traitors in time of war. Perhaps I was one of them. I was not cut out to be a hero.

'Your life'.

'Is that all?'

'What do you mean?'

'That's not enough for what I have to tell you! One life for seventeen plus an ammunition dump?'

'So you want to be fixed up with some sort of a job, do you?'

'I want safe protection'. A traitor always asks for more.

'We will take you into town as a prisoner. And you will be safe in the barracks. Your friends won't know that you betrayed them. You'll be safe!'

'Can you guarantee it?'

'What I say guarantees you your life!'

'Thank you'.

'Now, tell us, where is your friends' base and the ammunition dump?'

'Go along the bank of the Progo river. Follow the direction of the current. There you will find a large banyan tree. It's the only banyan tree along the length of the river bank. That's how we usually find it. Go along the foot track. Follow that track until you get to some houses. The largest house with the thatch roof is the ammunition dump. Seventeen soldiers guard the store. Get the raid over with quickly before General Sudirman moves it!'

'Hang on to him! Take him to the barracks. Don't send him to town until we can prove that everything he has told us is true'.

The following morning I heard the ammunition store on the bank of the Progo river blown up by the NICA army. Five soldiers died in the engagement. Twelve freedom fighters were captured. They were herded to a bridge across the Progo river. Their eyes were blindfolded tightly with black cloth. They could not see me, the traitor, sheltering behind the bushes. The NICA soldiers fired a barrage from the barrels of their rifles. Twelve freedom fighters fell from the bridge above the Progo river, their bodies full of bullet holes. The water in the river turned red.

***

Today, decades later, I go to the podium and shout into the microphone, in the centre of a vast square, in front of a crowd of thousands. I shout out the catch-cry, 'Freedom!' three times in succession to them. They respond with a tumultuous cry. I take the folder which contains the text of the proclamation and the text of the Independence Commemoration speech from the adjutant's hand. I finish reading the proclamation with the names of the nation's founders, 'Sukarno—Hatta'. Then at the end of my speech I say, 'In remembrance of the souls of the heroes who have fallen, let us observe a minute's silence. Let the silence begin'.

I come down from the podium and am ushered away. The masses want to shake my hand. The hand of their leader.

'Make way for our hero!', they say. I smile. They open the car door for me. I sit in the car and smile again. I raise my five fingers to my forehead in a salute, in response to the young soldiers standing at attention, showing respect for their leader.

'Don't forget, Sir, that this evening at 7 o'clock you have to give a speech at the evening reception commemorating the 36th anniversary of Independence at the '1945 Veterans' Building', says the adjutant.

'Aren't you mistaken? 36th?'

'No, I'm not mistaken. It is the 36th'.

'Oh yes, I am forgetting this is 1981'.

'How on earth could you forget that this is 1981, Sir?'

'I always forget the year. But I will never forget the struggle for Independence! Each year seems to speed by'.

'Yes. A year does seem to pass quickly. But sometimes one hour seems longer'.

'Depending on whether you are waiting for something or not. A year passes quickly for someone who is not waiting for anything. But, one hour seems much longer for those waiting for something'.

'There is something I want to say, General'.

'What is it?'

'There was an old man who was saying to me just now that he remembers seventeen soldiers and an ammunition dump which was blown up by the NICA army on the bank of the Progo river'.

'Why did he suddenly say that?'

'He remembered it all when he saw you. The old man used to be in the pro-Dutch KNIL army'.

'Why is it taking us so long to get back to the house?'

'It's only another five minutes, General, and we'll be there'.

'It's taking far too long'.

The adjutant orders the car to speed up. The escort behind follows suit.

At the house I call for the adjutant. We talk in the room.

'Here is a pistol and money. Kill that man. Do it now. Don't delay'.

'But why, General?'

'It is now 1981. It will soon be 1982. Don't let him live any longer. I am worried that he might be able to influence the number of votes that I will get in the 1982 election. I am the strongest candidate in our party! I think you understand. You are my best adjutant'.

'Thank you, General'.

'Go and do it'.

'I have never failed in my tasks. That is my duty'.

'Excellent! I know!' I say, and smile.

The next day the adjutant comes to report on how things have gone. We sit in the reception room.

'I have done it, General, and left nothing to implicate me'.

'Excellent'.

I stand up and go to get drinks for us both. I take two glasses. In one of them I place some poison. I pour the whisky. I give the adjutant the glass of whisky with the poison in it.

'Let's have a drink, to your success'.

'Thank you General'.

We touch glasses in the air and toss back the contents. I smile as I put the glass on the table. I know that the poison will work slowly and that any person who drinks it will die in three days.

Three days later I receive a telephone call. The doctor says on the phone that the adjutant has died in his sleep. Possibly a heart attack, he says, giving his diagnosis. I replace the phone. I smile.

At that moment I am brought back with a start by the comment:

'We have arrived General'.

'Oh, yes. Have we?'

'Yes, we're there'.

I get out of the car. I step onto the red paving.

'Don't forget this evening at the '1945 Veterans' Building', General. An evening reception for the 35th Anniversary of Independence. Have your speech ready, Sir'.

'Yes, thanks. The reception for the 35th anniversary of the Independence of the Republic of Indonesia. You are my best adjutant'.

I stride into the house, opening the door. At that moment I hear a shout.

'Put up your hands!'

I spin around. I can see my grandson pointing a pistol in my direction. I don't have a chance to raise my hands in the air before the child pulls the trigger of the pistol in his hand and 'Bang! Bang! Bang!' I clutch at my chest, startled, and fall down upon the sofa.

'Grandpa, you've been hit by three of my bullets. You're dead!'

'You fired at just the right time, my child. But unfortunately you only have a toy pistol'.

The small child does not understand what I am saying. He runs off, aiming his toy gun in all directions. 'Bang! Bang! Bang!'

Jakarta, 1980

(originally published as 'Senyum seorang jenderal pada 17 Agustus', *Horison*, 1980, 9(15), pp.303–05.)

The Factory

Nh. Dini

---

translated by David T. Hill

For the umpteenth time the man came, bringing his thin black briefcase clasped under his armpit or dangling nervously first from his left hand and then from his right. Then back again from the right to the left. This time he was not alone. He kept bowing over as he walked beside two yellow-skinned men with slanty eyes. They talked animatedly in strange accents. Off and on Ma could hear them saying the word 'hai'. Every few minutes one of the three would say it, as if they had reached some agreement. The two with light skins Ma would have called Chinese. They looked like the soldiers whom she had known decades before, during the time when most people in the village had had to wear clothes woven coarsely from palm leaves or cut out of old gunny sacks. It was only that in those days their heads were shaven and they wore uniforms. Now these men had thick black hair standing up stiffly like black sugar-palm fibre.

The three of them got out of the car which they left far back by the side of the road. Ma watched them as they walked. After making their way along the edge of the dry fields which lay side by side with Karmo's wet rice fields they headed for the house. There, of course, they would meet Sarpin. And, for the umpteenth time, they would discuss the price of land, and go looking for Ma, to flatter and try to coax her into relinquishing their fields.

But Ma will let them look for her for a while. She hid, as she usually did, in those parts of the land where the feet of city people do not care to go for fear of getting muddy. Maybe she will try something different this morning. For the past few days the clusters of corn had grown tall and thick, quite enough to shelter someone squatting there. Only when she grew tired of hiding, did she reveal herself.

So that is what she did this time, too.

When Ma's back began to feel stiff and her feet numb, she stood up. She walked slowly to and fro, massaging her calves and thighs. Then she strode off in the direction of the roof looming far off in the middle of the greening fields.

On entering the yard Ma already knew where the men would be sitting. There were two sets of tables and chairs on the front verandah, and newcomers were always invited to sit at those on the left. It had been that way ever since the old days when Ma was just a child. Only now the furniture had changed. It was no longer made from wood or shiny bamboo shaped by the skillful hands of local people, in harmony with the rural environment which protected such traditions. The chairs now had seats and backrests coloured red. 'Practical', said Sarpin, 'made of plastic'. If they got dirty they could easily be wiped clean. The armrests and legs glistened, made of a white metal like silver. Ma did not like them. When someone sat down on this kind of chair it made a suspicious noise, as if they were farting. And on days when it was sweltering this type of chair made people feel very hot. Sitting on them was like sitting on a charcoal stove which had only just been extinguished.

But Sarpin was proud to change the furnishings. He said you have to change with the times. But the home improvements, which he had carried out little by little, had turned Ma's way of life upside down. And added to this, even the chairs had been 'improved'. Ma did not feel at ease anymore; she did not feel she was living in her own home. That was why she took to wandering more in the fields, in the rice paddies, circling this expanse with which she identified more intimately, which she knew and which knew her. There she would ponder, remembering the past, with its difficulties but its peace. She recalled the tranquillity of a verandah full of potted plants, bamboo chairs and benches which gave a gentle creak whenever anyone sat down on them. But they were cool and did not stick to your skin nor leave embarrassing sweat marks behind. Then she would think about Father. Fortunately he had gone to eternal rest before her. He would not have been able to accept these changes to the house. Or would it perhaps have been better if he were still alive?

'Morning, Mother', the man said greeting her when Ma stuck her head in through the doorway.

And the two newcomers followed his glance, turning to the door and then bowing from the waist in Ma's direction.

'We have been searching for you and calling out for ages, Mother!'

Sarpin repeated the sentence he had uttered so often over these past few months. Ma noticed that this time her son did not fumble when calling her 'Mother'. On ordinary days, when there were no city guests visiting, he usually called her 'Ma'.

Ma did not answer but walked over to Sarpin who stood up and helped her over to a chair. A 'pssss' sounded as her body dropped down into the seat. She placed her feet, still wet with well water, as politely as was possible. Ma also pulled here and there at the borders of her blouse.

'These gentlemen have come to repeat their offer', Sarpin explained.

These words too she had heard many times before, only the word 'gentleman' had now become 'gentlemen'.

'These two visitors are from Japan. This is the director, the boss. This one here is the architect, the one who draws the sketches of the buildings'.

Ma looked them both over. How small their eyes were! Their eyelids which protruded as if they were heavy, formed a thick folded layer. How could they possibly see clearly? One of them said something. This strange language that Ma had heard in the past seemed even more unusual at close range.

'I was just saying to your son, Ma'am, that these gentlemen are prepared to increase their offer'.

Ma listened. She sat there because she wanted to. Because she liked to observe other people, things around her, listening to voices and conversation. But she felt absolutely no obligation to answer or comment. So she just kept her silence. Her two hands bunched modestly upon the *kain* in which she was clothed.

'The offer these men are making would be extremely profitable, Mother', continued Sarpin. 'With attractive provisions for us'.

'For 'us'!' Ma felt the need for clarification. 'Who is 'us'?' she asked.

'Well...for all of us: *Mas** Dir, *Yu* Kam, Mas Wongso, Ma and me'.

'For you! Not for me!'

'You have to look at the practical side of things, Mother', Sarpin resumed, correcting himself by addressing his mother formally.

Ma had already noticed just how much Sarpin liked the word 'practical'. When she heard it for the first time Ma did not know what it meant. He was talking away in the regional language and then suddenly he threw in this word from Indonesian. More and more frequently her children were using foreign words which she did not understand.

'This is the highest offer ever made to the people here by these foreign visitors, Ma'am', interrupted the man who had brought them along. 'So don't let it pass you by just like that!'

Ma did not reply. She looked carefully at the man. Why do there have to be people like him in this world? Patiently and tenaciously coaxing farmers to sell their dry-fields and their land so that foreigners and Chinese could build factories there. On the slope of the mountain, towards Pingit, Karmo had already sold his rice-fields. Now there was a factory producing a reddish-yellow drink called 'Fanta', when all this time in the neighbouring village there was already a Chinese-Javanese person who had a business making soft drinks which had the real taste of fruit: Ambon bananas, *mandalika*, raspberries, all picked on the mountains beside the village. With the competition from such an enormous factory full of machines the sales of the small trader had now slackened. Quite soon he would be killed off, strangled by his shrinking market.

Ma took a deep breath. It seemed that God permitted the fields to shrink so that people will not have enough to eat. Then the lean time before the harvest comes and the number of

---

* *Mas* is the Javanese term for elder brother, *Yu* for older sister.

people will decline and Judgement Day itself will arrive. Then perhaps a new world will arise, a new divine creation, with new people in it. Ma would have already departed this life by that stage. She did not care. But now, as long as she still breathed, the land left to her by her ancestors she would hold secure.

Dir, Kam and Wongso had left for the city.

Each had married and sought their fortunes far from the smell of the rice-fields, wet and dry. They had tasted the accursed easy life of the city. Each time they returned home to visit Ma their children would call out in amazement whenever they saw a *pijer* butterfly, which to Ma foretold of an impending visit from afar; they would squeal in fear at the millipedes crawling on the floor of the house, which to Ma indicated that it would rain that day. On one occasion her favourite grandchild came tearing out of the out-house in the garden. It said a frog was watching it having a shit.

Ma knew what her children really intended.

Sarpin, who up until this point had followed his parent's wishes and managed the land and its harvest, could not hold out much longer against the temptation of life in the city. The village was becoming deserted. One family after another had moved. Initially to the side of the road which linked the towns, then taking buses and transport trucks, bludging by the walls of markets or stations no longer in use. Sometimes they did not care if they had any shelter or not. They had become fed up with working the land. Meanwhile, for those who were left in the village it had become harder to find the labour needed to work the ancestral rice-fields.

The times had really changed. Especially during the last ten years. More and more foreigners had appeared. They would stop to buy fruit at the road sides. The cars and small buses were often full of people with various skin colours. Those with the same coloured skin as Ma would, of course, be the guides who also worked as interpreters. They always seemed respectful and apprehensive. As if these foreigners were their bosses.

Now these foreigners had put pressure on the rice-fields. Factory after factory appeared in the middle of the dry fields. Left and right houses were built for the senior employees responsible for these factories. But not that many. For the buildings were equipped with machines to replace human labour, even human brains. If any of the local people were lucky enough to be invited in to work, it was only one or two as sweepers or guards. Then strange sorts of trees would be planted; types of shrubs which produced absolutely no fruit of any kind. These were planted along the edges of the roads specially constructed to lead to the housing plots. It was even odder in their yards and gardens. Generally there were only stones and grass. Tamarinds, persimmons and manggoes, which Pudakpayung was famous for producing in abundance were of no interest to gentlemen newcomers from the city like these.

Ma could guess what was in her children's hearts.

They wanted to get their share of the family inheritance immediately. In the form of land and rice-fields, it was a complicated nuisance. What they needed was a sum of money. Several times Kam had repeated his hope that his eldest child would be able to go to university to become a doctor. Though this meant very high fees. He had also repeatedly expressed his desire to buy some land on the edge of town to build a house. Wongso, the most successful, who already owned a house, also often said that he dreamed of buying the house next door to them in order to convert it into a shop. If the family land were sold all of Ma's children would receive their share and would be free to spend that money. It would be more 'practical' as Sarpin would say.

Ma was old. Every day she woke a little earlier and went to bed a little later as if she could make time last longer this way. So that the remaining years could hold more living for her. But her body was frail and tired. Her feet which she used to be able to invite to go down to the town, treading rocky paths and crossing streams, were now often aching and stiff. She still had a full head of hair which she could still fix without a hairpiece in a bun like a large clenched fist. But it was flecked with white. Each market day she still washed it with a mixture of water and soot from the burnt rice husks and then conditioned it with coconut oil scented with herbs. Once her daughter-in-law from the city had given her some shampoo. It was in a nice yellow-coloured bottle. But when her hands touched it Ma did not like the bottle. It was just like the material used to cover the front verandah chairs which Sarpin had bought. And so Ma continued to use the water and soot mixture to wash her hair.

Ma would not live forever. She had felt and experienced much both with the father of her children as well as since he had passed on. She had been through harvests of plenty and those scourged by pests. She had gone through changing times. Not to mention the pain caused by her life-long male companion's fancy for women and gambling. Yes, Ma had tasted the totality of life, in all its joys and sorrows. She had known the pleasure of holding a wedding ceremony, of marrying off her only daughter after an harvest regarded as extraordinarily abundant in those times. Grandchildren were born, grew up and received their schooling. Ma could not cope with a sense of ignorance: What was it all for? It was enough education if you could read, write and add up. The village had emptied because as the children grew they moved in droves to the city. No local person who had completed school wanted to remain a farmer, working the land and associating with livestock. They disliked manual labour, getting their hands and feet dirty, with mud or water-buffalo shit. They dreamed of becoming officials, teachers or police, if not doctors or other professions that required higher education. They wanted office work, with authority and without any further contact with stench or filth. Not one of those who had left the village ever returned to live in the increasingly empty Pudakpayung. There remained only three familes, seven goats, four water-buffaloes, three cows and several chickens and ducks. Part of the wet rice-fields could still be worked but the dry-fields were left fallow here and there and the land became barren because no human hand stretched out to tend it. In Pucangayu it was the same. There the scenic beauty had been ruined by the smoke-stack from the pharmaceutical factory built by the foreigners.

Once more Ma drew a long breath, a breath full of inexpressible regret.

'All you have to do is bless the sale, Mother. *Mas* Dir will arrange everything since the four of us are already in agreement'.

Why wasn't Sarpin shamed to coax her like that in front of outsiders? Family problems should be kept in check, hidden from the gaze of other people. To say that the four of them were all in agreement! To display before the guests just how Ma's children had ganged up to deny her the authority of a mother? The times had certainly taken a giant leap towards Judgement Day. People no longer knew how to restrain themselves, speaking without concern for the way things should be done properly according to family rites. Even the seasons had gone mad, coming with no regularity. Over two hundred baskets of *manggis* fruit had been picked from the garden this year, where last year there were not even fifty. That was because the rains disappeared or came after the flowers had blossomed when they should really have come after the fruit had been picked.

'Before the document of sale is signed there is to be an agreement first, Mother, a contract that the land will be sold to these gentlemen here after the harvest'.

Ma turned to look at the broker. The polite manner of his speech irritated her. How much were people like him paid? Did their work simply involve taking people around and helping them make their deals? Suddenly Ma thought, perhaps every time some land is sold he gets a reward, some percentage of the agreed price. He might even make something out of it from both sides: from the seller and the buyer! Ma turned her glance in her son's direction. How much were Sarpin and Dir giving him? Perhaps there had been some bargaining too, because he had said before that the price proposed was the highest ever to be paid by these foreigners. It might be true, it might not. People lie easily enough, especially in doing business!

If they are willing to pay such a high price they must badly need the land. But why does it have to be this land? Ma suspected Dir or Wongso, who had lots of connections and acquaintances in the city. Perhaps one of them initiated this deal. What kind of factory would the plots of eggplant and corn become? Part of the rice-fields will also be taken. Flattened by iron wheels, planted with cement, stones and bricks. What would grow on top of it?

'Why do they want this land so much, son?'

'As we have explained to your children, Ma'am, these gentlemen want to set up a factory'.

'What kind of factory?'

The man did not answer Ma's question but turned to the foreign guests and said something. They conversed for a moment. Then the broker turned back to look at Ma.

'A factory to make food, Ma'am'.

'What kind of food?'

The broker shifted in his chair as if his backside was getting tired.

'Dry biscuits or canned food?'

One of the foreign guests said something directed to the broker. Shortly afterward they said to her, 'The factory will be a *mi* factory, Ma'am'.

'*Mi*?'

'Yes, *mi*, Japanese noodles. Perhaps you have already seen them in the shops at the market. They are called "*Super Mi*".'

What was that? Ma had never heard of '*Super Mi*' before. She knew that noodles could be cooked in all sorts of ways, in soup or fried. In the kampungs there were even special noodle vendors. There they called it *mi kopyok*. But '*Super Mi*'? That was just another strange word which was sure to have come from the city!

'This is the best kind of *mi*, Mother'. Sarpin felt it was necessary to interrupt in order to explain. 'It tastes very good and what's more it's very practical. It is packaged in individual servings. Just enough for each meal'.

Ma rose from her chair.

Everyone followed suit, standing up.

'What do you think, Mother?' Sarpin asked hurriedly. 'Do you agree?'

Did Sarpin catch her flash of tiredness and irritation? The voice in which she spoke was definite and resolute. 'No!'

And without turning to the others Ma made her way down from the front door. She did not put on the sandals ready at the bottom of the stairs. From beside them she grasped a broad bamboo peasant hat hung on one of the stair posts. She walked outside.

It was burning hot. It would soon be time for the call to the mid-day prayers from the Pucangayu prayerhouse. The loudspeakers, one more influence from this new style of life, would ruin the tranquillity of this expanse of green. Ma walked to the lip of the paddy-fields in the direction of the valley slope, then continued to the edge of the main road. By the side of a dyke she stopped. Let her gaze take in how tranquil and serene it all was. The wind whispered through the rice-stalks, heavy with their swollen grains. With the new moon it would be harvest time. For the last time on these fields. Despite her refusal the sale would go through. Ma knew that for sure. Her children had become greedy, for the land had become theirs with their father's death. Only the house and the yard around it remained Ma's by right. Here packets of *mi* would spring up. *Super Mi*, they said. As if the villages, *kampungs* and cities needed a factory to make *mi*! As if the small-scale producers with their little capital could not supply the needs of their country's people!

Ma bowed her head. She rubbed her naked feet in the mud by the edge of the wet reddish dykes of the paddy-field. Mountain soil promising fertility for decades to come. Hazily, through the veil of her tears, she could see the ants and water-insects scuttling off. Seeking refuge? Perhaps they had already heard today's latest news?

Sekayu, 1980

(Originally published as 'Pabrik', 1982, *Tuileries,* Sinar Harapan, Jakarta, pp.37–48.)

Cancer

M. Fudoli Zaini

translated by Sam Nunn

I first happened to meet this family several years ago through the retired colonel. As I was moving from my seat towards the waiting plane, the colonel suddenly pressed a rather large package upon me. Once he introduced himself I realised immediately he was the father of a friend of mine.

'Amin', he said, 'Could you please deliver this package to the address noted here'.

It appeared that he already knew my name. I had long been familiar with his own moniker, having heard it from my friend. So having been put on the spot so unexpectedly, I could not refuse. He was my friend's father and it had all occurred so quickly that I agreed to do it.

'Do you mind if I ask what's inside?' I asked.

'Oh just some food and a few small gifts'.

I took the package and put it in my hand luggage, which, as luck would have it, still had room.

The day after, in K, I just lay in bed for the whole day. The flight had taken a dozen hours or more and had made me rather tired. It was not until the next morning when I was rummaging through my bag that I remembered the package. The name and address were written clearly on it and, what's more, a phone number had also been included. That's a stroke of luck, I thought, as I wasn't really sure where the address was. I could ask over the phone before I went there.

When I rang the number the phone was answered by a woman with a very soft voice.

'Mrs Nana?' I asked.

'That's right. And you are...?'

'My name is Amin. I've just come from J. I've a package here for you'.

'Who from?'

'From Colonel Tanto'.

'Oh I see. Thank you. I'll come and get it later. What's your address?'

'No that won't be necessary. The colonel asked me to deliver it to you personally if that's alright'.

'You must be tired from carrying it so far and you want to bring it all the way to my house? I think I'm the one who should come to collect it'.

'It's no trouble, really, I'd like to come to your place if it's no inconvenience'.

'Not at all'.

'Good. Could you tell me how to get there. I'll come by later on'.

The woman gave me directions to her house over the phone. Now I was able to work out where she lived. It was in the southern part of the city.

That afternoon I went to the woman's house. As it turned out she was a warm, friendly and attractive woman, with a striking appearance. She was around forty-five years old, no longer young, but traces of her beauty were still clearly evident. She was happy to receive the package.

'Do you know who this package is from?' she asked me after I'd sat down.

'The name of the sender is mentioned there', I said.

'That's right. She's my daughter'.

'Oh. What's your daughter's connection with Colonel Tanto?'

'She's married to the colonel's son. The eldest boy'.

'So you and the colonel are in-laws?'

'Hmm, yes. She's my second child. My first is in B. My eldest's a girl too'.

'Are there any Grandchildren?'

'Two little girls from my second daughter. They're so sweet and adorable!'

Then she opened the letter which was stuck to the package and gazed at it for several moments, trying to read it.

'I've forgotten much of this language. If it's not too much trouble, would you mind reading my daughter's letter and translating it?'

I took the letter and translated it to her. She was very happy listening to the letter, smiling.

'How long has it been since you've seen your daughter?'

'A dozen years or more', she said, 'since she was small'.

'So you must have lived in J once'.

'Yes, for about seven years. I don't know, after a while I just didn't feel at home there. I always remembered my home and my parents. I asked to come home, here, but my husband wouldn't give me permission. Finally I asked for a divorce and came home alone myself. The children stayed with their father in J'.

'Oh', I said, without passing comment.

This woman must have certainly been through some tough times I thought. I watched as she sat quietly for a few moments, her eyes blinking as if holding back tears. Then she quickly glanced up at me and smiled.

'Have you met my daughter too?'

'Oh no. I only just bumped into Colonel Tanto several minutes before leaving'.

'What did he tell you?'

'Nothing. He just gave me that package'.

'He didn't mention me?'

'As I said, he only told me to deliver that package to you personally'.

The woman smiled.

'He's a good fellow'.

'You know him?'

'We've met, the time he came here several years ago to visit his child'.

'Bambang?'

'Hmm, yes that's him'.

'I'm his best friend'.

'Oh. Where is he now?'

'He's still here'.

'Give my regards to him. I've also met him once'.

So Bambang and his father have already been here, I thought. But Bambang had never told me about the relationship between this woman and his father. He usually tells me about all the people he knows. Maybe he forgot or maybe it wasn't important, who knows?

'Bambang doesn't come here anymore?'

'Only the once, with his father'.

'Oh, maybe he's been busy'.

'Perhaps. Actually, every now and then I could really do with his help'.

'Hm, perhaps I could help you. What's the problem?'

'Oh it's nothing really. Occasionally I feel like writing to my child. I can't write in your language anymore, but my child can't read any other'.

'I can help you with that'.

'Would you?'

'Of course'.

'Oh thank you. How about now?'

'Sure'.

So she dictated it to me and I wrote down the translation. It seemed she yearned to be with her daughter. The letter was full of emotion and rather long.

'You know', she said when I wanted to ask her permission to leave, 'there's something that I haven't told you yet, about my third child. My one and only son. At the time I left he had just turned three. After several years here, I was shocked to receive some very disturbing news. My son had died. Apparently he had fallen whilst climbing a jambu tree in the front yard. Since that moment I've just been so sad. Perhaps that's been my punishment for leaving my children. Do you think I was wrong to leave?'

I was silent, unable to answer. She was probably very distressed about it all. I noticed that her eyes had filled with tears. With a heavy heart I took my leave, and headed home.

Two days later I went to Bambang's, Colonel Tanto's son. After chatting about nothing in particular I told him about the package for the woman entrusted to me by his father.

'You've already met her?' he asked, surprised.

'Yes', I said, 'I even thought I should take the package to her house personally'.

'To her house?'

'Yes. It was your father himself who told me to take it. She also sends her regards to you and hopes that you'll pay a visit. You've been there once with your father?'

'Yes, only once, and never again'.

'Why? Your brother's married to her daughter. Although it's indirect, you're still family'.

'Maybe so', he said listlessly. 'But maybe you don't know anything about this woman yet'.

'About what?'

'Well, it's like this', he said continuing. Then, as if forced, he slowly began to tell the story. Apparently his brother's mother-in-law had been unfaithful. He hadn't realised it initially. He wasn't aware of it when he went to visit her with his father. Afterwards, when he found out from a friend, at first he couldn't believe it. It was only after he had looked into it himself, that he was sure it was true. From this friend he had found out that she had been divorced by her husband because she had been playing around with other men in J.

He hadn't a clue whether his father had heard of all this or not, but apparently she used to be a dancer in a night club.

'But she told me it was because she never really felt at home in J', I protested.

'Well, that's a lie!' he said, 'and her first daughter, she was also divorced by her husband because she was playing around with other men. The news in B now is that she has a bit of a reputation and operates as a high-class lady. Just like her mother, who has operated here for years as well'.

I almost couldn't believe it. But I couldn't refute it either. What I saw when I met the woman at her house was quite normal, I thought. Her appearance and her style of dress were rather striking, but at the time this didn't imply anything out of the ordinary. By all appearances she was warm and friendly. That's how I recalled our first meeting several years ago.

I didn't meet the woman for some years after this. Nor did I ever go to her house again, in order to avoid any discomfort, I thought. I only ever saw her a few times, once in a car with some man, and another time getting out of someone's car in the city. On another occasion I saw her, standing at a city bus stop in an unusual state. Her clothes and hair were rather messed up, and she looked a lot older than she actually was. I've no idea what had happened.

I only saw her from the top of a passing bus. She was probably waiting for another bus, not the one I was on.

When Bambang came to my house one afternoon a while ago he told me that this woman's daughter, who had been living in B, was here now too.

'Do you know Riska?' he asked me.

'No', I said, 'who's she?'

'That woman's daughter. She lived in B'.

'So? What's up?'

'She's here now. You know that B has been caught up in the fighting'.

'How long has she been here?'

'Who knows? Yesterday I met her and her mother in the city. She came over and flirted a bit. She invited me to her house. So did her mother. I said that I'd drop in later if I had the time. Then I quickly excused myself. I told them there were some important things that I needed to take care of'.

'Speaking of which, the other day I saw her, the mother I mean. She looked rather unkempt and sad'.

'You're right. She did look rather pale and thin, like she was sick'.

Sometime after that Bambang came to my house in quite a state. Hello! Something's going on, I thought. He'd not even sat down before he began spitting out fire and brimstone.

'I was right, I was right to be worried!' he said.

'What's happened?' I asked.

'My brother!' he added.

'What about him?'

'He's divorced his wife! That bloody whore!'

'Settle down', I said, 'just tell me, calmly, what happened. It's no use getting all worked up'.

He sat in a chair, staring up at the sky. It was a few moments before he spoke. He was probably trying to get a grip on his emotions. After he had calmed down a little he began to explain:

'I knew that she'd eventually deceive my brother', he said. 'I was worried this would happen from the outset. My poor brother and his poor kids, they're still so young, my poor nieces and nephews'.

'Has your brother already divorced her?'

'Yes', he said, 'apparently she had been playing up behind his back for ages. He only caught her at it recently. I reckon he'd been hearing rumours about her for a long time, but he didn't want to believe them unless he saw it with his own eyes. He's shattered. Can't do a thing. She'd apparently been fooling around with someone from the army. He was so stung he divorced her and threw her out of the house'.

'Is she still over there?'

'I think so. I expect eventually she'll come here to be with her mother and sister'.

As it turned out my friend was right. Several days afterwards, without any hint of warning, the woman, Mrs Nana, suddenly came to my house. Presumably she'd kept the address that I had given her before. When I opened the door she was standing there looking exhausted. Her face was drawn and thin, her movements nervous.

'Excuse me Amin', she said rather hoarsely, 'I hope I'm not disturbing you, dropping in like this'.

'Oh no', I said, inviting her to come in.

'I was forced to come. I need your help'.

'Please, go on', I added.

She hurriedly felt around in her bag, gingerly pulled out a packet of cigarettes and lit one.

'You don't smoke?' she asked as she offered me the pack.

'No. Thank you', I said

'It's like this', she said and then coughed, 'I must write a letter to my daughter in J immediately. She's just divorced from her husband and intends to follow me here'.

'How do you know?' I asked.

'She wrote a letter to my daughter Riska, and she told me'.

'And you want your daughter to come immediately?'

'No!' she shouted abruptly, 'I don't want her to come here at all! She must stay with her children and try to get back together with her husband!'

I was quiet as I sank into my chair. She appeared increasingly nervous. Her breathing was anxious and staccato. I quickly went to the kitchen to fetch a glass of water. After several mouthfuls she seemed to calm down.

'I don't want my daughter to be like me', she said, 'I don't want her to follow in my footsteps. I've told Riska this but she won't listen to what I have to say. Instead, she's really keen for her sister to come'.

Now the woman's eyes began to cloud over.

'Why can't I be the only one to mess things up. There's no point in my children making the same mistakes. Is it my fault if they follow in my footsteps, even if I've already warned them against it?'

I was silent and did not reply.

'I'm sick, Amin. My body is already riddled with cancer, my skin and bones. The doctor's told me. Pretty soon I'll die. I'm afraid but I can't do anything', she said as her voice became low and shaky.

'You're right. It's better if your daughter doesn't come. She should stay close to her children', I said.

'Yes, but all I can do before I die is tell her that. I'm scared. I want to make up for the things I've done but I can't'.

'Yes you can', I said, trying to encourage her.

Then I fetched a pen and paper and I wrote down all she wanted. Afterwards she seemed very relieved.

Several weeks later I heard that the woman had died, just as she had predicted. Together with Bambang I felt the need to visit her house and pay my last respects. As it turned out, Riska was there with her younger sister, who'd arrived precisely on the day her mother died.

'Your ex-sister-in-law is here', I whispered to Bambang.

'The only ones I'm concerned about are my nieces and nephews', he said to me.

As we were going home he said the mother's behaviour was far more dangerous than the cancer from which she suffered. Her poor example for her children was the cancer of all cancers. I was silent and offered no comment.

(originally published as 'Kanker', *Horison*, 1984, XIX(7), July, pp.290–293.)

Pop Dreaming

Y. B. Mangunwijaya

---

translated by Tom Plummer

Early one December morning—well not too early really, I suppose—at 9.12 am, suddenly the phone rang! As if I'd been stung by a bee, I awoke with a start.

'Since when have I had a telephone?' I thought, still groggy. It turns out Lilian, the girl of my dreams, the Vice-Chancellor's daughter, was there sitting on the edge of my bed. Wearing a colourful *batik* gown and spreading the sweet fragrance of *Joie de Paris*. Her smile, as bright as Ancol Fun Park, would tempt even Pangabean or Sudomo. And then, as melodious and touching as Iin from Trio Bimbo, she cooes, 'Bongki darling...'

'Eh, what kind of apparition is this?' I thought in infinite confusion, because just last night I saw her stuck fast, arm in arm, with the Asean Campus weightlifting champ, the spiteful Rhino.

'There's a phone call for you'.

This is crazy. Tell me if I'm dreaming? I pinched my arm, as thin as the neck of a guitar. Then I pinched my scrawny, xylophone rib cage. I'm not dreaming. In my confusion Lilian leant over and kissed me softly, gently, in the tradition of the East yet as modern as the biological sciences. Still dazed because my mental computer had not yet warmed up, I reached for the carved antique silver telephone.

(=) 'Hallooo!' I yawned, 'Bongki. What's up?'

(+) 'Good morning sir. Is this Mr Bongki, the Menak Jingga University lecturer? (Suddenly it dawned on me!) This is Colonel Full-Alert, Gidion Full-Alert. From Kodalihura (the Law and Order Corps). You're not teaching today, are you Sir?'

(=) ‘Hang on, there’s no need to call me ‘sir’. I’m not even a lecturer. I’m just an under-graduate student, and I haven’t even passed Concrete Construction yet’.

(+) ‘Oh, never mind, Sir. We’ve been given instructions, effective from yesterday, to use the term ‘Sir’ to address all young people of the next generation. In the revolution, Slamet Riyadi and the others became regiment commanders even though they were only twenty two or twenty three. We have a strong desire, well, ever since the decision yesterday, to return to the spirit of 1945, Sir’.

(=) ‘Eh? I don’t quite understand?’

(+) ‘There’s no need to understand. All revolutions happen in a flash and generally aren’t understood. But Sir, we don’t mean to waste your time; you’re probably busy with study and other university commitments. Let me put it this way: As head of the student council, you’ll be leading the upcoming demonstration, won’t you? Make sure it doesn’t get cancelled, will you’.

(=) ‘What the...? What demonstration? Look, I’m not the head of the student council, or anything like it. I just write reviews for the student literary magazine, *SITTER UNIVERSITER*. And that’s only because I’m forced to, to pay the rent’.

(+) ‘Where’s your apartment? In New Kebayoran?’

(=) Come off it! You’ve got to be joking! It’s in Tanjung Priok! The malaria’s endemic! It’s behind the piles of confiscated containers from the embassy, between the sewage drain and the State Electricity Commission scrapyard! It’s a killer!’

(+) ‘Ahh, that’s an embarrassment to the state and country. Just one moment, sir. Hey, Major Markundang! Call the Hilton! Book me a luxury suite for one of the great hopes of our nation. At our expense! Make sure it’s in a part of the hotel that’s quiet because a student’s workload these days is extremely demanding. Nothing like us in the old days. Graduates from any old institution could become liberal ministers. Hallo sir, are you there? Everything’s been fixed up. Now, as I said, last night we received a telegram from the highest echelon, stating that before the 1 January all power will be delegated to the New Generation. That’s if they want it’.

(=) 'If not?'

(+) 'If not, what can we do? It doesn't really matter. That's logical isn't it. Oh by the way, this is meant to be a national secret, but somehow everyone on the street is already aware of it: you, sir, are going to become the Minister for Social Affairs'.

(=) 'What the...? This is insane, Gidion! You must have dialled the wrong number! Check it again will you?'

(+) 'There's no need to worry, sir. In the security forces we always check the number by computer before dialling. One other thing, your flatmate, Mr Kingki, is to become Communications Minister'.

(=) 'That's crazy! That speed demon Kingki as Communications Minister?? That'd be a disaster! He's never even paid his radio tax. Hello, Gidion Un-Alert! You can't be serious! You must have the wrong number!'

(+) 'Hahaahaa, there's no way it's wrong. You're already too well known, Sir. After all, you're the youngest son of His Royal Highness Wiridiguno-guno LLB, aren't you? Import-Export Director for The Longstreet Tobacco Company. isn't he?'

(=) 'True, true! My dad's the head of the 'Along the Street' Cigarette Butt Collection Syndicate, making black-market cigarettes'.

(+) 'Ah, that's right! Precisely. It's creative people like that who're needed by their country these days. Don't just imitate the West with all its luxuries and wasted inertia'.

(=) 'Ah, excuse me, isn't that supposed to be 'enerGY'? 'Inertia' means laziness'.

(+) 'Right. Thank you for the constructive criticism. We've received government orders to remain open to all criticism and correction. There's no need for alibis any more. It's okay to criticise. It's all right if it's not constructive, provided that it's logical. You see, we've been waiting ages for student demonstrations, even cigarette-butt collectors' demonstrations. In fact, we're experiencing a definite shortage of demonstrations. Our troops are just hanging around playing chess or dominoes, or sitting around chatting because there's nothing happening. It's frustrating'.

(=) 'Really. They tell us that demonstrations are forbidden, that we must maintain our Eastern etiquette and everything that goes with it. But hang on! I'm *not* the leader of the Student Council, and not one of the nation's great hopes. I'm not one of the new generation or some strapping hope for the future—even if my sandals are strapped. I'm just an ordinary student who plays chess and fronts up to his tutors, lecturers and even the landlady. My only hobby is having my girlfriend stolen from me. (Lilian kissed my left ear, ahh how embarrassing, before I'd even showered, whilst whispering proudly: 'My Hero!') To hell with demonstrations!'

(+) 'What! You can't say that, you've already agreed. If the students don't demonstrate who else will? The pedicab drivers? That wouldn't be fair, they'd lose a day's pay. Us from the Kodalihura and Kodali-demons? That'd be pretty odd. Besides, how would that be viewed internationally!'

(=) 'Well, what do you expect me to do? So you're in a tough spot!'

(+) 'No, please try to understand, you students are the only voice the poor have these days'.

(=) 'Really?'

(+) 'Truly. Believe me!'

(=) 'Come off it!'

(+) 'Look, don't be so apathetic. Why are you so hesitant? We need a generation that doesn't know what it means to be unsure'.

(=) 'But they say that it's a normal, human response to feel a bit unsure; you can't be always on top of things'.

(+) 'Ah, that's typical Western thinking, and you know it! It's incompatible with a revolutionary spirit. In politics, we must always feel we're perfect. Right or wrong, I'm always perfect. That's how it is'.

(=) 'Geez, I reckon you're a bit odd. Us stubborn students are supposed to ask permission to hold demonstrations. Then you slick dudes are supposed to automatically ban them. So what are you doing trying to put me up to demonstrating? As it just so happens, I feel like going for a wander, shooting squirrels for dinner tonight. Besides, I reckon there might be more to this than meets the eye!'

(+) 'Oh, not at all! It's really quite simple. We understand now, we know what's going on. As proof, our anti-riot troops have been given instructions not to carry rifles or pistols; we realise that old-fashioned weapons are no longer up-to-date; gifts of food, Fanta and Sarsparilla are what's needed. If there's even the slightest indication of anything suspicious, straight away, without mercy, we'll begin serving food and Fanta'.

(=) 'Yeh, all right then, whatever you reckon', I answered impatiently.

So as it happened, in the Hilton Hotel I washed European style like a albino duck in a porcelain bath filled with Freisland cow's milk, a squirt of Max Factor, and a lather of a thousand roses. This I followed with some anti-dandruff shampoo and Brylcreem, as befits my status as a ministerial candidate. With a determined stride I moved toward my Rolls Royce, chauffeured by the 'killer' Professor Dr Ms Tuminah (Construction Chemistry) who had once cut me down to size right in front of Lilian, saying I didn't know the difference between concrete and jackfruit seeds. Off to the 'Blue Campus'. In my black diplomat-style Samsonite case, neatly arranged by the Intelligence Bureau, were the files for my exams, complete with the correct answers. Divulged to me by the 'killer' professor from Concrete Construction's cute young niece, because after the demonstration I'd still have to sit those bloody exams. Once inside the campus I was greeted with cheers of relief by my student comrades awaiting my commands. Though I couldn't fathom why (maybe as a psychological strategy) they had all dressed up smartly, tidy and well-groomed, no-one with long hair, and all wearing ties. The girls were wearing traditional dress, as if they were attending the wedding of Queen Sirikit of Thailand. Banners made from the finest silk decorated with hair-raising slogans: 'We demand clean government! But if we don't get it, no problem!' There were ones with modern slogans: 'OLD ORDER: Political rats in command, NEW ORDER: Incompetent spies in command, SUPERNEW ORDER: Girlfriends in command'. Another slogan scrawled across the windscreen of one of the demonstrator's Mercedes Benz: 'They're the drumband of the Director-General 'YOUNG AND TOO LATE'. We're the drumband of the Corporal 'OLD AND TOO EARLY'.' A group of four slender students dressed in traditional costume from Sumatra, Sulawesi, Sumba and Bali carried a huge marble gravestone above their heads. It had an almost illegible inscription, written in an old mystical Javanese script. Following them, a huge puppet made from paper mache in the form of a young man, clutching a young man, clutching a pistol, with the title: 'Study Club. The Art of Self Defence'. I couldn't understand what it meant.

In front of the Regional Special Operations headquarters, with a self-contented smile, stood Major General Susdayuddha with his wife and eldest daughter. His daughter, who had recently been crowned Riot Queen, greeted me with a kiss on the cheek. From his wife I got a necklace of orchids and from the Major himself, a bright orange pennant with shiny gold lettering: '*Bhinneka Reka Wasana Shama Aja*'. (Whatever you try to do, it makes no difference in the end), a slogan that I consider extremely progressive and realistic. Because my colleagues had been such good models of proper orderly discipline, I suggested that the packages of food, Fanta and Sarsparilla be taken home as gifts for the families of the riot troops, a suggestion greeted by the troop's unanimous approval: 'Thannnnnk...You!'.

Along the road we witnessed the overwhelming enthusiasm of the masses, especially the not-so-bright ones, as they embraced us for giving voice to their true feelings. Clearly, thanks to our fieldwork in the village, an intimate rapport had developed between elite students such as us and the silent grassroots majority. I myself was amazed that my achievements had become so prestigious. I'd never dreamt of becoming Student Leader, let alone such a successful one. Usually office-bearers in student and youth groups have already completed their Masters degree, or are at least party representatives from the upper classes with seven kids and preferably three grandkids. Where do I fit in then? It's simple: provided we are given an opportunity anything is possible! That's the key. The most important thing is: don't dream. And it's now crystal clear, I've already checked my guitar-neck arm and my xylophone-rib chest a number of times. I'm NOT dreaming. The Vice-Chancellor of Menak Jingga University and all the senate members greeted my arrival in front of the petrol bowsers on Campus Street. In the midst of the thronging masses, the Vice-Chancellor (beside him, Lilian) handed me an exemption certificate whilst stating that I didn't have to sit the Concrete Construction exam. (What's more, they'd fired the professor that day too.) To top it off, he presented me with an honorary Masters degree in Political Science and Performing Arts. Unable to contain herself, Lilian burst through the police lines, then in front of everyone hugged and kissed me with overwhelming enthusiasm. Indescribable in aspect, prospect and suspect. The Tarakanita Drumband and the harmonies of the Fire Fighting Brigade struck up, whilst forming lines in the shape of large letters: B-O-N-G-K-I. Happy Christmas. Congratulations.

Hordes of journalists, both local and international, clicked away at me and their cassette recorders asked questions. What programme would I implement after becoming minister, what was my opinion on the banning of the film 'Wasdri', whether or not the judge from Batu Road was wise or not, and so on. There was even one crazy journalist, probably from the Communist Party, who asked if I had decided on where I was going to be buried. But I was already very slick at handling journalists, and answered as calmly as an OPEC diplomat whilst heading coolly to my Rolls Royce: 'Wait and see'. Or 'We must be objective as well as being subjective. To show emotion is okay provided we keep a cool head'. Or 'An answer must be constitutional. To answer in the street like this is impolite'. Or the one that's always a knock out: 'My personal opinion isn't important. What is important is the opinion of the government's Legislative Assembly'. The opposition will love that!

My driver for the return trip turned out to be Harold Untahurug (the weight-lifting Rhino, Lilian's boyfriend last night). He stooped down to bow to me, as though he was a servant in the Cirebon palace, but awkwardly and clumsily. I pretended not to notice him. And whilst lighting up a

Ministerial-size Marlboro with a gold Cardin lighter I instructed, terse and businesslike: 'Priok!'

(+) 'Where, Sir: the Hilton Hotel?'

(=) ' Are your eardrums made of steel, Rhino? Priok, OK? Priok!'

(+) 'Sorry Sir, which street?'

(=) 'Uh, you crass Jakartan Rhino! Behind the piles of confiscated containers from the embassy! Between the sewage drain and the State Electricity Commission's scrap yard! Make it snappy! Time is Science! Understand?'

(+) 'Yes Sir!' (Once inside the car I hummed a few verses from the pop song 'Tanjung Priuk'.)

The next morning, I came across a faded envelope sitting on the flimsy table in the boarding house. It contained a newspaper clipping: 'Recently happily married: Lilian Kampusiawati and Harold Untahurug'. There was a scribbled ballpoint note along the edge: 'If you mess around with my wife, I'll beat the shit out of that computer at the end of your neck! Signed, Harold'.

Suddenly I was overcome by joy. Maybe the Christmas spirit. A melodious voice singing sweetly in my heart: it was Harold and my killers, no mistake, my most amiable companions. And the Kodalihura troops, full of wisdom, my much loved brothers. I began to see poetry, smiling, in the composition of greenery and water hyacinths contrasted with the fragrant black chemical sludge with its aroma of *Joie de Paris*. And weren't the Electricity Commission's heaps of scrap steel and old tar drums a transparent expression of aesthetic structuralism, trembling with the offer of a new dawn? Adieu Lilian! Have fun Harold! I offer you this bunch of orchids, my beloved killers. Enjoy the picket, my comrade Gidion Full-Alert! Enjoy polluting the newspaper pages, Mangunwijaya. I'm young and I will always bounce back fresh and rejuvenated. I'm the one who's going to take possession of my life and determine my own future. Not you. Happy Christmas!

(originally published as 'Renungan Pop', *Horison*, 1985, XIX, February, pp.62–64)

The Governor's Cats

A. A. Navis

translated by Meta Mulia

If the Convenors had any brains, there is no way they would have scheduled Banda's paper for the session after lunch. His droning voice was as monotonous as a trapped bee buzzing round and round. To make matters worse, his topic was passe, and his attempt at analysis was simply a garbled compilation of quotations from official speeches and legislation, complete with full reference details, file numbers, and year of promulgation. It was no surprise the audience grew drowsy. So, to shake their lethargy, they started drifting out of the room to wash their faces, go to the toilet, or find a friend for a chat. I wandered out too. Despite going out and drenching my face, drowsiness descended again as soon as I returned to my chair. Irritated by such unbearable boredom, I was grumbling about the Convenors, complaining to a friend beside me that they shouldn't have invited a bureaucrat like Banda even if his office had helped fund the seminar.

In an attempt to suppress my sleepiness, I flicked through the pages of my notebook. I was drawn to the comments of Professor Alatas, a scholar working on the sociology of corruption. In my pad I'd written:

'The relationship between mice and development: The 1963 census in Indonesia stated that 30% of the rice crop had been devoured by mice. That would have been enough to feed the population of Singaporean for 16 years. If the government wants to maximise development, it needs to develop a strategy to exterminate mice. If mice are allowed to run rampant, they'll gradually influence human nature. Therefore, exterminate the mice so humans don't start immitating them'.

Suddenly, tapping me on the shoulder my friend said, 'Look at Mangku. What on earth is he writing down so busily?'

'Perhaps it's his way of staying awake', I said. 'It is more polite than chatting'.

With my attention caught by Mr Mangku, in my struggle with drowsiness I remembered his period as governor. By association I thought, too, of several other former governors, who'd come and gone, occupying the large building known as the *Gubernuran*, where the seminar was being held. The *Gubernuran* was both the offices and the residence of the governor. When the governorship was relocated to another city, it became the house of the colonial Resident. When Indonesia gained her independence, the position of governor was restored, and the building again became the governor's residence. During the Japanese occupation, it had been occupied by the military commander. Ever since then, mice had started to breed there. Various attempts were made to eliminate the mice after the Japanese left, using mousetraps, for instance, or spreading poison, but in the end, as the story goes, keeping cats proved the most effective.

The first effort at eradication using mousetraps had minimal results. Apparently, after initial success, the remaining mice avoided the traps. So poison was spread throughout, but this created a new problem. After eating the poison, the mice died everywhere, some even in the governor's bedroom or study. Gradually, a putrid odour spread throughout the residence. Initially, the odour was nauseating, but, after a while, all the residents became immune to it. This olfactory immunity spread to all the governor's office staff, especially to those who frequently appeared before him. Even the noses of the people who only came occasionally became immune, too. Nobody held their noses in the precincts of the governor.

When there was a change of governor, the new appointee immediately smelt the putrid odour. His first action was to try to eliminate the stench completely: washing and rinsing the entire building with carbolic acid, replacing existing office equipment, and occasionally spraying perfumed room de-odouriser around to conceal the reek, especially when there were guests from the central government.

'No matter what you do to conceal it, I'm afraid that odour lingers on', said the Minister as he departed for Jakarta, after a night in the residence.

The governor then assembled his staff to eradicate the incessant stink. But no-one could suggest a strategy for, as far as they could see, though the stench remained, it couldn't possibly be caused by rotting mice carcasses any longer. The residence had long been cleaned out, and even if one or two carcasses remained, they would have dried out long ago and wouldn't smell any more. But, the minister had spoken!

So, Professor Alatas was invited to solve the problem. Although an expert in the field of corruption, the professor knew exactly what was happening in the Governor's facility as soon as he arrived.

'You've got too many mice, Governor. It would be preferable to eliminate them naturally by keeping some cats', said the professor, stroking his thick black beard. 'Mousetraps are not effective. Once a mousetrap has caught something, other mice avoid it, even if the baits seem attractive. You see the mouse's IQ is extremely high'.

So, five cats were acquired; they consisted of one male and four females. Nobody knew why such a composition was selected. The professor, in fact, never suggested it. Perhaps, psychologists could fathom it.

Fertility in cats is high, even if not as high as in mice, so the constantly increasing number of cats in the area did cause the mice to flee. They moved into neighbouring buildings, leaving the Governor's residence completely free. Their urine stench, which had disturbed guests' noses for so long, had gone. Room de-odouriser was no longer needed when guests came.

But keeping cats required special funds. Not only for their food, but also for employing special personnel, including a veterinarian to monitor the cats' health, as neglected cats could spread fleas, or catch rabies, threatening the lives of the governor and his senior staff! The government might even be imperiled. The costs were quite steep but fortunately funds didn't need authorisation from the regional parliament, and could be obtained from other legal allocations. After all, it would be no joke if the budget for cat maintenance had to be debated by provincial parliament which was generally very critical!

The presence of the cats turned out to be very effective, despite the fact that none of the mice were actually caught by the growing number of cats, for the rodents simply evacuated to neighbouring houses or found safe hideaways. In fact, the cats never actually did much to exterminate the mice. With their spoilt treatment and highly nutritious diet, the cat population multiplied by the month. Their bodies grew fat, their footsteps heavy, and every lounge or chair became a place to curl up for a relaxing snooze. When guests arrived, it was difficult to chase the cats away. If you wanted to get rid of them, they had to be carried off.

The time was ripe to rationalise the number of cats required to prevent the mice's infiltration from outside. However, the governor had become used to the large number of cats, and the kittens' behaviour proved an enjoyable entertainment, especially for the governor's children. The cats had become an inseparable part of the governor's circle.

Of all the animals, cats have one of the lowest IQs, certainly lower than that of mice, and having been spoilt rotten by the governor, their manners towards the governor's guests were appalling. Besides refusing to vacate chairs meant for guests, the cats also urinated on visitors' trousers and jumped on ladies' laps as they were in audience with the governor. But still, no one felt daunted about visiting the governor.

When the ambassador of a friendly country stayed overnight, the cats caused a commotion. The governor's wife looked hysterical. She flushed with shame while the guests were around, but was furious after they'd gone. The problem was that the cats had mewed in passion all night long, so that the ambassador and his wife couldn't get a wink of sleep.

'Just get the hell out of here!' she screamed at the cats, after the guests had departed. But the problem couldn't be solved by simply getting rid of the cats, as they'd done good service in freeing the governor from the mice plague.

An entrepreneur, who had made a fortune clear-felling all the forests of a particular island so that from the air it looked yellow, heard about the incident. He came, bringing a cat in a box.

'We've got too many cats here already', responded the governor's wife rather spitefully, contrary to her usual gentility.

'But this isn't a local cat, ma'am. Local cats like to stir up trouble. They eat huge amounts yet do nothing except sleep. They're ugly, too. This is a Persian cat, ma'am, that I bought in Hong Kong. Before I went to Hong Kong, I had a male Persian which I'd brought from Paris. But when I got back from Hong Kong yesterday, it'd died. Been hit by a car. So I thought I'd bring you this one now and next time I go abroad, I'll find a mate for it, so that you can have a pair of multinational cats'.

The governor's wife was attracted to the cat's thick fur and beautiful eyes. 'How would it mix with the cats here?', she asked after stroking it for a while on her lap.

The businessman, who didn't know the history of the governor's cats, replied abruptly, 'Best get rid of them, ma'am'.

However, the governor's wife did not have the heart to get rid of all her house cats, and neither did the governor who said, 'I'd happily oust thieves in my office, but exterminating the cats would be inhumane'.

'Ah, don't worry about that, Governor', said the entrepreneur.

And when the governor and his wife returned home from overseas, having fulfilled an invitation from the ambassador who'd once stayed with them, they found the house unusually quiet. The governor sensed something was missing. For a while he was confused, wondering what could have happened while he'd been away. But it was only when a pair of Persian cats came out of his children's bedroom mewing that he realised that the dozens of cats that had lived with him for so long had vanished.

The governor didn't ask anyone how they'd disappeared. In fact, to be honest, he was relieved. When he'd been in Rome, he'd been a bit horrified when he saw vast numbers of felines nesting under the gloomy niches of that ancient ruined antiquity, the Colosseum, in the twilight.

A rumour had it the governor's cats had been loaded into a truck, then discarded in the middle of some faraway jungle (fortunate enough to have escaped logging by the entrepreneur!). And, just as often happens with humans, having previously been spoilt so badly many of the cats died within days of landing in the wild. But as the law of the jungle dictates, the strong survived and turned feral. Eventually the survivors made their way home, and found the governor lying beside his wife, having a snooze. 'Governor, what have we done wrong to be cast out like this? Was it because we are only native cats? Didn't we do you a service by getting rid of the mice?'

The governor was shaken awake by his wife as he moaned in his sleep. Over and over he recited a prayer for God's forgiveness. But, since then, he began to deteriorate physically and mentally. The government was soon forced to replace him with a younger appointee. But the mice started to nest in the governor's residence again.

When I lifted my head, Mr Mangku was still scribbling in his notebook. But his fingers kept massaging the bridge of his nose. Only a few people were still in their seats, as Banda pressed on with his conference paper at the podium. And drowsiness came over me again.

Padang, 5 October 1984

(originally published as 'Kucing Gubernuran', *Horison*, 1986, XXI(7), July, pp.239–41.)

On the Dark Side of the Moon

Moes Loindong

---

translated by Simone Robinson

When Marno and his wife returned home after many months stationed abroad, he was posted to a large port town. They were provided with a staff house in the large housing complex for officers in the Department in which Marno worked. Two days after they'd moved in, Marno's wife got an invitation from some of the local wives to come to their regular get-together. She showed the invitation to her husband.

'Do you think I should accept?'

'Of course, we've got to start mixing. We're not overseas any longer. We're back home, so you'd better watch how you behave'.

'Don't worry, Marno. I won't embarrass you. You didn't marry me for nothing, you know!' said Marno's wife, boasting just a little.

Marno beamed.

As evening approached, his wife returned.

'How did it go? What was it like?' Marno asked.

'A pretentious display of ostentation and extravagance!' she answered.

'So how did you react? Did it appeal to you?' asked Marno.

'I felt really repulsed. I just couldn't bear to look. All of a sudden, all I wanted was to expose their arrogance and self-importance for what it was. I don't know whether I was just being envious, or jealous, just spiteful, seeing them behave like that, but, basically, I just feel absolutely disgusted'.

Marno listened quietly, allowing his wife to vent her feelings.

'I'm amazed. Overseas we met people who had been spoilt by affluence, but somehow it didn't affect me quite like this. I didn't feel anything. So, why do I feel so different about these women? I don't understand'.

'It's only natural. You're confronted by your own people. You also know that there're so many people here who are still struggling and destitute. So you're not prepared to stand by and put up with such blatant social inequality in front of your own eyes. You want things to be fair and just, like it was abroad. But that's impossible. Because people are free to make what they will of their freedom, and those women are too. It all comes down to people themselves, and whether they want to show self-restraint or not'.

'Yeh, maybe you're right'.

'In fact, the situation overseas is even more complicated. But because we were foreigners, it seemed like things were equitable and fair. It was more that we didn't care much, because we didn't feel we had any real stake in it. In our own country, you want to fight it', said Marno looking tenderly at his wife. 'But you should be proud of how you feel', he continued, 'because it shows how much you care about what is happening here, how devoted you are to your own community, even those women. Don't you reckon?'

'I don't know. Maybe you're right. I suppose, if I think about it for a while, basically I feel sorry for them. Actually they're kind of sick-at-heart; don't know where they're heading. They need some purpose, some peace of mind. And they seem to find it by flaunting their wealth and extravagance. As if they need a stage, and these social occasions present a stage. Maybe that's how it is', said Marno's wife.

She paused, then continued. 'They want a platform on which to vie and compete, searching for something to be proud of, some peace of mind, some self-worth. But the ones who can't maintain the competition become more chronic. They're sick, obsessed with the search for their own identity. A cultural transformation creating moral crises and seducing with its materialism. Maybe it's a disease of people in developing countries. But then I ask myself, what are their husbands like? Maybe it's their husbands who've pushed them into this? I don't know. Do you have any idea?

'I don't reckon there's any point worrying about it. The only thing I'm curious about is how deeply troubled by all this you are. That's all, nothing else bothers me', said Marno.

'Of course I was upset!'

'So you reacted against them, and started wanting to compete?'

'Not at all! I know you and there's no way you'd be drawn into all that. Do you really think I'd be so easily influenced?' asked Marno's wife.

Marno felt proud at her response. 'Who knows?' he said with a grin.

'I'm not in the slightest! I understand what's going on. This country has already invested at great deal in training you to help develop the country. Educating you overseas. Sending you on training programs abroad. Of course you don't want to let the country down. No. I've no desire to make my husband a victim of my vanity and arrogance. I'm no Eve seducing you to eat my apple. Not at all!' said Marno's wife.

'Do you think you can resist it all? Can you overcome the temptations?'

'What makes you think I'm being tempted by a demon?'

'Our eyes are the devil's route to tempt us. You wouldn't be human if you could resist. The devil's been in our hearts since the beginning of time. The problem now is whether we are prepared to resist or not. I'm not sure you're up to it', said Marno baiting his wife a little.

'I'm not saying I am. But I'll certainly try. After all, this life's a constant struggle, isn't it? When we were both growing up neither of our families were wealthy. Why shouldn't we live within our means? We did it abroad. Why shouldn't we be able to cope at home? I'll make the effort. I can't promise, but I reckon I'm up to it'.

'You're sounding philosophical, but aren't you too idealistic? Like we're somewhere up above all of this, looking down and playing some verbal game with everyone here on earth? But that's fine. It's quite cute. Makes me fall in love with you all over again!'

'What do you mean? Have you been having second thoughts lately?' asked Marno's wife, suspiciously.

'No, that's not what I meant! What I mean is being in love always seems new and fresh. And that constant newness is itself a potent magic. I want to love you like that, always'. His wife smiled. Marno beamed too. They continued their conversation in bed, then fell asleep.

The next day in the office, one of the field staff came in to see Marno, carrying a portfolio of import documents and a box containing samples of imported goods. He handed them all over to Marno, who studied them closely. It was evident that there was a discrepancy between the product samples and the names of the goods which were included in the import documents. For someone with an untrained eye, such a slight administrative deception would have been difficult to recognise. But Marno was a committed specialist in recognising such product types. That was exactly what he had been studying overseas. So he said to the field-worker, 'Leave it here. I'll have to process them first'.

'Can't you do it now, sir. I'll wait'.

'Does it really have to be completed now?'

'Yes, sir. That's been the procedure in the past', said the field-worker.

Marno nodded, pretending to understand.

'It's just that, I'm still new here. So I have to make sure I check everything out properly first. It's impossible for me to finish it now. You head back to the field. But keep your eye on the goods'.

The staffer left. Marno realised the subtle and clever attempt at smuggling. It must be dealt with appropriately and reported. He began to compile a smuggling report. He wanted to demonstrate just what he was capable of. Now is my chance, he thought. He imagined tomorrow, when he submitted the report to his boss, the gleam of admiration that was sure to cross his boss' face. He became engrossed in his report on the smuggling attempt, spurred on by a sense of pride in his achievement.

The next day, before Marno finished the report, his boss' pretty secretary called. The boss wanted Marno immediately. He went straight in.

Before his boss could come to the point, Marno tried to pre-empt him by reporting the results of his findings. He described clearly and completely the details of the smuggling attempt.

But his boss advised him that the importer was one of the largest most reliable commodity exporting companies in the region, and the highest tax payer. It employed tens of thousands, soaking up the largest labour force in the state. And the goods it was importing were the main raw materials for their export items. The company's current stock of raw materials would only last another two days, which meant it was facing a production crisis. The situation was critical and they needed help.

'That's why I called you in so early. Because, apparently yesterday the proprietor complained to some senior government officials that his imports were being held up. So, last night, they rang straight through to me'.

Marno kept quiet, waiting to see how his boss would continue.

'The Governor asked me to ensure that our department didn't stand in the way of the development in our region. We were asked to provide facilities and opportunities for entrepreneurs showing the major potential to contribute to that development. The military commander asked me to assist in maintaining national stability. And from the Department of Labour, I was asked to avoid unwittingly causing workplace unrest, and to aid the social stability in the region. I was backed into a corner; there was nothing I could do. So, I called you in to help me analyse the problem and find the best solution'.

Marno remained silent, trying to think of a way out.

'Our dilemma now is, do we absolutely insist on enforcing the regulations, or do we actively contribute to the success of national development in our region. It's a difficult choice', said Marno's boss.

'It is indeed. Because we couldn't possibly contravene the requirements and regulations set in the capital. If we break those, we'd be aiding and abetting in smuggling. But, couldn't we urge the proprietor to negotiate a special exemption from the capital government. That may be the best tack to take, sir', said Marno showing something of his determination.

'I've already thought of that too, but we don't have enough time. What chance would we have of getting all that through in the next couple of days? There's absolutely no possibility. Why, the bureaucratic ins-and-outs would take months. By the time we wait for an exemption, the company'll have gone broke, starved of raw materials. Then what'll happened to their tens of thousands of employees? I'm worried they'd really take it hard, and that'll snowball right through the community, and end up triggering wider social unrest. It can happen so easily in a society like ours, so fragile and susceptible to turmoil', said the boss, staring at Marno, waiting to see how he responded. But Marno was poker-faced, thinking through the options.

'What worries me even more, Marno, is that such disturbances could escalate nationally, through various other regions. And all because of our pigheaded adherence to regulation'.

Marno didn't say a word. He slumped down, transfixed. In his mind's eye, he conjured up tens of thousands of sacked employees running amuck in the streets. That'd doubtless escalate into broader community unrest. Then there'd be the agitators who'd try to take advantage of any opportunity to make trouble. And what about those political operators with an axe to grind, always exploiting any situation for the sake of their own political interests? There could be hundreds of thousands, maybe even millions, of people all caught up in the chaos. The idea of everyone running amuck swept over Marno like a tremour, terrifying him. A violent riot could sweep the countryside. In which case, the company's owner could simply wash his hands of it, and blame the whole thing on the department. They might even be detained, charged with subversion. There'd be no chance subsequent investigation would identify the underlying reason for the incident; it'd only point to what caused the unrest. This is really dangerous, thought Marno, as he remembered his wife, and worried about her getting drawn into all this. He drew a long, deep breath, trying to relax himself, but it took all his strength to stay calm.

‘Apart from special exemption from the capital sir, I can’t see what else we can do. Now, it’s really a matter for your judgement’, said Marno beginning to give up. Gone was his pride in his ability. All he’d studied abroad meant nothing.

‘Don’t be like that. I want us to come to a mutual agreement on this, based on consensus and discussion, so that whatever action we take, we both agree and support it. I don’t want to put pressure on you. But, if you like, I’ll tell you want I think and, who knows, maybe that will help us make a decision more confidently’, said the boss, taking a gulp from his drink from the desk.

‘It’s our duty to uphold guidelines and regulations set by the government in the capital. We have to. But if that becomes an obstacle to national development and becomes the cause of social instability here, should we remain idle?’ the boss asked rhetorically.

‘Of course not! And we shouldn’t be surprised if government regulations and policies often change too quickly. The problem is, we are a developing country in the very process of taking shape. Those very changes demonstrate how rapidly we’re developing. Consequently, regulations and requirements are often out of pace with changing demands’, said the boss directing Marno’s train of thought.

‘I agree, sir’, said Marno.

‘Now then, getting back to the regulations and guidelines which underpin our work here, perhaps it’s time that they were revised if they can’t respond to the speed of economic development. But because of the bureaucracy and the inability of the people who determine the regulations to anticipate changes, such regulations seem immutable, like some heroic statue, which we all look to, but which is oblivious to its surroundings. And it’s here we’ve got to exercise our judgement. Otherwise we’d just be robots, waiting to be programmed. Hopefully you take my point’.

Marno nodded, listlessly.

‘And we’ve got a taxing job here in the regions. It demands considerable judgement, extensive insight, innovation, creativity, and skill in handling matters, considering all aspects and angles. We're expected to be innovators, pioneers, taking the initiative to support the government's determination to implement development, to improve the community's standard of living. The fundamental question now is, do we have the conviction to carry out that initiative? Can we admit the company's imports? That's the challenge we face'.

The boss' elaborate opinion and very persuasive tone reminded Marno of when his father used to give him advice. That was the way he did it. At great length, never tiring, somewhat overstated. Maybe all parents have the gift, thought Marno. Just then he remembered his father's advice when he first began working.

'We're Christians, and Christ teaches us to respect your mother and father. In your office, you'll work under the authority of your boss. Respect him, because he's your father-figure in the office. He'll guide you, accompany you, educate you, protect you and equip you for your future', his father counselled. Well, this seems an appropriate time to follow Dad's advice, thought Marno with resignation, as his boss started up again.

'So, what are we going to do? Should we reject the imports for the sake of the current regulations and requirements, or do we take care of it judiciously for the sake of national development in our region? What do you choose?' asked Marno's boss.

'I can't choose, sir. But I do understand what you mean. I appreciate your opinion. It'll be very helpful for my future career. With regard to the imports, can I ask you for a dispensation, sir?'

'You don't need any dispensation from me. You can handle it satisfactorily yourself'.

'What I meant was, it is more accurate, sir', said Marno a little more forcefully.

'If I have to give a dispensation that would mean that these products required special attention because they couldn't be taken care of properly at a lower level. This may later attract the attention of the verification team from the capital to undertake subsequent corrections. We've got to avoid this. If you can, arrange for the things to get through the customs legitimately under regulations in effect, so that it doesn't raise any eyebrows. I'm confident you can take care of it. In the meantime I'll prepare a report for the capital requesting further consideration of all the regulations and guidelines which are no longer relevant. What do you think of that?' asked Marno's boss with a warm smile.

'I suppose so, sir. The important thing is that you know how the goods are being imported, and that you agree they can come in legally'. His boss nodded in agreement. Marno returned to his work room. And the boss daydreamed. He recalled the unexpected visit to his house last night by the entrepreneur who was trying to import the materials.

'You've really made an error putting someone like him in that position', said the businesman last night.

'There's nothing I can do. It's a decision from the capital'.

'You should've suggested someone more malleable'.

'If I did that, the department would be suspicious. That's precisely what I'm trying to avoid. But don't worry, tomorrow I'll bring him around'.

And it appeared the boss was able to win over Marno convincingly. And there was no possibility that Marno would check with the Governor, or the military commander, or the Department of Labour, whether they actually did telephone me last night. I'm positive Marno has high morals and ethics, thought the boss placating his conscience. The boss drew a deep breath, proud of his achievement.

Around the middle of the day, a prominent entrepreneur, owner of the imported articles, dropped in on Marno at work. Just wanting to get acquainted, he said, and to express his gratitude. He left a large envelope on Marno's desk.

After he'd gone, Marno opened the envelope. Quite a large sum of money, by Marno's standards, was inside the envelope. He was shocked. But the businessman had already gone. This isn't right! Methods like this must be wiped out. It ruins morals. It's got to be reported to the boss, so that the businessman can be strongly reprimanded, thought Marno. He went back to see his boss.

'Did he give it to you before or after you'd processed his products?' asked the boss.

'After, sir', said Marno.

'If it'd been before, it could have meant that you were extorting him. But if it was after, it just means that he was expressing his gratitude financially. That's natural. Just accept it. A bonus like that would please your wife, wouldn't it?'

'I think I should hand it in to you, sir. I have no right to accept it'.

'Just take it. That amount's chicken-feed to a man like that! He's already made a packet out of this country. What's so wrong about us benefiting a bit?'

'What I am worried about, sir, is that he may attempt to influence me, to put pressure on me'.

'That depends. On whether you cave in to the pressure or not. On whether you allow yourself to be influenced or not. If not, don't worry about it. The important thing is that we have principles', continued the boss. 'It's funny that sometimes we feel a bit offended if we're given something, because we've been brought up in a culture where gratitude is sufficient if expressed verbally. So if we're thanked in the form of money, we feel bribed or bought off. That's what a lot of people think. But we don't realise that many other ethnic groups feel they have to express their gratitude in money or goods'.

'I realise that, sir. But I'm worried that he might tell someone. This could undermine my reputation and credibility, even the good standing of the department. It may even reflect upon your own authority, sir' said Marno.

'There's no possibility of that. I've known this fellow for a long time. He's been brought up in an ethnic community where the philosophy of life is see no evil, hear no evil, speak no evil. Christianity, your religion, is even clearer. I'm not a Christian, but I know there's a verse in the Bible which says, never let the right hand know what the left is doing. Isn't that right?'

Marno nodded in agreement.

'My own ancestral culture states, we shouldn't gossip. So as far as I'm concerned, you don't need to worry in the slightest about accepting the gift. Just take it. Look, you're new here. Just regard it my personal expression of welcome'.

In an instant it dawned on Marno. If the businessman had known my boss for a long time, he thought, and I don't accept the money, he's likely to get offended. That could influence my promotion report, achievement record, career and my entire future in the office. After all, my boss directly determines my fate in the department. I'll just accept the money, so that he is satisfied. Shouldn't subordinates know how to get on the good side of their bosses? Besides, I can sense that close working ties have begun to be cultivated. These need to be maintained well. Finally Marno said, 'Alright sir. Thank you very much'.

The boss laughed. Marno was surprised: why did his boss laugh?

'That's the way. We were indeed brought up in a culture where a verbal expression of gratitude is sufficient', said the boss.

Now Marno also laughed.

Marno left. And the boss thought, how very straightforward this person is. An incorruptible person who is just beginning to be affected by the way his society does things.

That afternoon at home, after Marno returned from the office, he gave the envelope of money to his wife. Then he related his conversation about the envelope with his boss in the office. Marno's wife understood. Then they agreed to use the money to finish furnishing their house, to make a donation to the church, to help the orphanage and some close relatives whom they considered needy.

Two years later, Marno was transferred to another region, and became regional head of the department. He continued to work well, honestly, incorruptibly, with discipline and with complete dedication to the state. Likewise Marno's wife continued to maintain a way of life appropriate to the level of her husband's income.

This continued until Marno was summoned to the capital and never returned again. He was detained because of his involvement in a smuggling incident where he'd been posted several years ago. Marno's wife's heart sank when she heard the news. She didn't believe that Marno could have been involved in smuggling.

But then, gradually she began to get suspicious. Perhaps it was really true that Marno was involved in smuggling. Then where have the profits from the smuggling been going all this time? Maybe Marno has a secret wife? Maybe he'd given the money to her? It's possible that Marno had been deceiving me all this time. Men everywhere are the same. Liar!, she thought, resentfully. Her loyalty was tested. Doubt gnawed her heart. Feeling as she did, Marno's wife sought out her husband who was being detained at the capital.

But after Marno related all that had actually happened several years ago, his wife felt guilty for having distrusted her husband.

'That's all that happened'.

'Have you told the attorney all of this?'

'Yes'.

'Was your old boss also detained?'

'He's already dead'.

'And the wealthy businessman?'

'He's already fled the country taking everything with him'.

At that instant Marno's wife fell limply into a chair. Now she was really distressed. But she tried to pull herself together. She realised what had happened. She didn't want to show her weakness in front of her husband.

'We'll just surrender it all to God. We'll just trust in Him. God won't neglect his people if they're innocent', she said trying to reassure her husband as well as herself.

'The moment we're in trouble, we always run to God. Perhaps because we hope for a miracle', said Marno as if giving up hope.

'Don't talk like that! It makes it seem like we don't believe!' she said holding her husband's hands intimately. She concentrated all her love, her loyalty, all her resignation there. Marno could feel it. Without realising it, their tears fell together.

Surabaya, February 1989

(originally published as 'Di Balik Matahari', *Horison*, 1992, 12, December, pp.423–27.)

Dialogue

Safron Rasyidi Sidal

translated by Bishi Leathem

Dasimo's face furrowed as he surveyed the headstones he'd engraved, now scattered around the yard. They were strewn all over the place, completely taking up the narrow and obviously disorganised garden. They took up his whole life. It was because of these headstones that he was often called Mr 'Simo Headstone'. Simo's professional reputation had ensured his wares were in great demand. But despite this he felt deeply troubled, for he profited from those who were devastated by grief as they made their funderal arrangements. Occasionally he would feel a small trembling welling up within him. But he had no idea how to free himself of such concerns. Once he told his wife about these strange occurrences, but she simply said it was his own fault, since it was he who had chosen the profession in the first place: becoming a headstone engraver in the hope that those in mourning would take a moment to appreciate his work.

'Do you seriously think you have any other skill besides sculpting headstones? Why don't you just forget all this nonsense, and be grateful you lead a better life than the homeless', his wife would say without giving him any way out. Attitudes like this made him increasingly jittery. He had to be self-sufficient; he had to bear it all alone. He had no one to complain to, no one to confer with, to exchange ideas with, to help free him of this weariness that had weighed him down for years. When faced with these difficulties the silence would become his mediator as he persevered engraving the headstones that had been ordered. Alone, with his feelings of confusion.

Tak...tek...tak...tek...tek...tak...tak...tak...tek...tek.

The special feature of Simo's headstones was the crown, where he sculpted the image of the deceased's face. The headstones displayed fine workmanship; they seemed alive. So realistic were they that the family left behind could easily identify their loved one from the carved headstone planted on the grave.

Because of his expertise Simo was able to carve the facial features of the deceased faithfully. Sometimes the gleaming of the carved eyes radiated from the statue, causing those that saw them to shudder. Sometimes Simo himself trembled in awe as he witnessed the result of his own work, which increasingly came to overshadow every aspect of his life, often carrying over into his sleep.

With so many faces etched into his memory, he would occasionally wake in fright in the dead of night. It was as if the many faces he had carved had come alive and were inviting him to chat, inviting him to hear their tales of experiences beyond the grave. Sometimes he felt moved to pity by these requests, but other times he was just frightened.

Then he could only shiver in fear, silently screaming, as he plunged into the emptiness. He felt caught in space, alone in a crowd. Often he felt he had become a living corpse, already buried beneath the graveyard soil even though he could still walk and breathe...He felt alone, only able to converse with his isolation and confusion. He was bewildered by his powerlessness. Simo had lost his bearings. He coughed and started to engrave again. Tak...tek...tek...tak...tak...tak... tak!

***

For some reason, for the past several months, many headstone orders, complete with the engraved image of a loved one's face, had not been collected by the various families that had ordered them. Now Simo was working on a headstone ordered by the family of a senior official from the colonial era. His heart pounded and he felt a little shiver, as he counted the ghoulish faces scattered around the yard. Much to his surprise, there were forty nine in all! Including the half-finished one he was still working on, they totalled fifty!

Sometimes the fifty faces would line up together, each confronting him with a myriad of problems. The fifty faces, supernatural and terrifying, would trigger a torturous wail from the grave, causing Simo to freeze in bewilderment. He was muzzled by silence. He did not know who to talk to. Most people didn't care or believe him. Simo was afraid, shrinking back from the fifty faces which began to visit him more and more frequently. His mouth was locked tight. His eyes, too, were tightly closed but, even so, the faces still trampled on his grasp of reality, making many people wonder at his bizarre behaviour.

Simo didn't care. After all, he had always been in command of his own life. He had been diligent and loyal to his profession as a headstone mason: the chips that fell as he carved the stones were his sustenance.

His eldest child suggested that he seek treatment from a psychologist, or look for comfort in the brothels (I beg your pardon!) so some new experience might re-ignite his passion for work.

'You bastard!' cursed Simo. His child recoiled from the tongue-lashing, not brave enough to look his furious father in the face. Simo was deeply insulted.

'Who do you think I am? I may only be your father, but I still have my dignity. Just you remember that! Do you think I'm crazy, sending me to a shrink, sending me off whoring! What the hell! Is that the kind of thing you've been getting up to all this time, eh?' snapped Simo getting louder. When she heard Simo and his son arguing, Simo's wife raced in to break up the fight.

'For crying out loud, you're behaving just like your son!' Grabbing hold of his arm Mrs Simo urged her husband into the small inner room of the house and quickly whipped up a cup of tea for them both. Usually after a cup of tea all would be quickly forgotten and Simo would return to his former self. He would begin carving again, and tidying up the engravings that had been ordered so that they matched the photo provided by a member of the deceased's family. Tak...tak... tek...tek...

The longer he worked on the carvings, the more perfect they became. When the task was nearly completed he was already well acquainted with the face that confronted him. Eerily, the more he studied the fiftieth face, the more his heart pounded. Cold sweat poured from his whole body. Then suddenly it struck him as his hand followed the line of his own face 'Why on earth does it look so much like me?' he mumbled. Meanwhile his heartbeat was becoming painful, as if it wanted to surge from his chest cavity. He felt faint. Alone.

Simo could make no sense of it, as he inspected the fiftieth carving, comparing it to his own face in the mirror.

'It's crazy. That's me! Am I close to my own death? Why does it look so much like me?' Simo wondered. He was in turmoil. His heart sank further as he inspected the face on the grave stone. He pinched himself. He was awake; it did hurt. He wasn't dreaming. Only trapped by his fear. Increasingly Simo felt there was something strange taking place before his eyes. There was something not right; another life had risen up to greet him.

Sweat soaked him. With wobbly steps, he tried to distance himself from the face that looked so strikingly like his own. His vision became dazed. Frightening images continued to descend upon him. Unsteady on his feet, he was forced to hold himself up lest he faint. He hurled away all his engraving tools. He lashed out at the face that was so similar to his own with whatever he could throw at it to smash it and end his terror. But nothing struck the mark! He was beside himself with rage, his breath increasingly erratic.

Simo became more and more insensed, his actions chaotic and wild. He was puffing. His hair was tossed about. Some covered his brow; some blocked his vision. Simo went berserk. He was shouting and cursing himself.

Everyone around was startled, and began careering around, running hither and thither, then trying to approach Simo who was running amuck in his work room. Someone clamped his mouth shut from behind while someone else tried to bring him to his senses by poking him in the arse. Others tried to lift him on to a bamboo bed. But Simo broke loose. He struggled, writhing in the hands of the panicking crowd. He was shaken around, a prisoner in the hands of those who held him. He was faint and powerless. The fainter he became the more feeble his voice. His breathing became shallow and difficult, coming out in puffs. He slumped down, exhausted.

People lifted him back onto the bamboo bed. His wife busily applied compresses to him. Some people burnt incense as an offering to the spirits. But Simo fainted, as the smoke swirled forth and filled his work room. The atmosphere was hushed. Everyone held back from speaking, not knowing what next to do. With the smoke from the incense billowing forth asphyxiatingly, many coughed. More began to feel dizzy, some falling unconscious. People became more flustered and panicked. Many fainted, and the confusion, no longer kept in check, spread. Feet staggered across the floor. Bodies began to sway. Blood-curdling screams echoed into the darkening evening.

The villagers were in turmoil. Someone headed off to find the doctor who was at a practice elsewhere. The sky above became blacker. Suddenly thunder exploded with a roar. Disaster loomed. Confusion mounted. The doctor started to throw up his hands. Several of the villagers were beyond help, dying, accompanied by the screams of their wives and children. The grating screech of a crow added to the eerie atmosphere. The night arrived carrying millions of His secrets...A chant echoed from the loudspeakers in the minarets of the mosque. A sacred hymn echoed, spreading like a thick gloom. Jangling nerves. Meanwhile, the sound of a person engraving headstones could be heard coming from Simo's workroom. Tak tek...tak tek...tek...tek...tak...tak... taktek.

Sometimes the sound was just the occasional chinking of stone. Sometimes it was rhythmical, noisy. Terrifying. No one could shut it up. The sound of the engraving became more rhythmical. Mouths clenched in fear. The villagers fell silent. Dumb. Then all the secrets and all else that nightfall brings with it rolled in. Owls and insects called back and forth adding to the eeriness. Simo remained powerless.

Approaching midnight he came to again, although he still continued to slip in and out of consciousness. His lips were moving. Then quiet again. The night was well advanced. He closed his eyes and slept, lapsing again into confusion.

***

Lost in thought Simo gazed at the ceiling. He was still seeing flashes in front of his eyes. He rolled to the right and to the left. He noticed his wife who had fallen asleep on the edge of the bed still holding the cold compress. Simo had the desire to get up, to hold his wife close to his chest—like when they were newlyweds and the flame of passion still burned. He struggled to rise, but couldn't. Even deeper in thought he stared at the ceiling. The clinking of his steel engraving tools cutting into the stone as it was carved, as it did when he was working, still rang dully in his eardrums. And suddenly there was a throbbing, constricting his chest which was already struggling with a nervous shudder...

Simo wanted to scream. But he had no strength. Tears began to stream from his eyes. Cold. He was delirious. His body felt very light, floating in the air. It was as if his whole body was flying, but he could see his body was still in a fever on the bed.

He tried again for the umpteenth time to scream. But he still could not, his voice catching in his throat, congealing in his chest. His body felt like it was shooting up into the air, flying above the faces which he had engraved with such patience and devotion.

The trembling within him intensified. The eyes he had carved gleamed, penetrating into the recesses of his soul. Completely filling his whole body so that it felt weightless and unconstrained. The statues seemed to be alive, their mouths smiling, very sweetly, as if demanding the life of their maker. Simo was terrified. He clenched his eyes tightly shut, but it made no difference. The statues' gaze continued to penetrate the lids of his eyes, though tightly shut. Most penetrating were the eyes of the carving that resembled his own face. He wasn't able to look at them.

Simo gave up, submitting to his fear.

The fifty faces which he knew so well started up a dialogue with each other. They held up their trembling hands, as if about to pounce on something. They closed ranks, lead by the carving whose face was so incredibly similar to Simo's.

Simo became even more horrified. He shuddered, trying to support his powerless soul, as it was attacked by fifty figures, who had formerly seemed intimately involved in his struggle. Faces which seemed so familiar to his: faces that had helped create his charismatic life and his extraordinary career. So much so, that now there was no one who could replace him, because he felt he had achieved it all, attained everything worthy of owning. Now it was as if Simo was coming face to face with his old friends, whom he had once fought alongside. Simo was cornered, because the faces knew of all his deceit, and were prepared to disclose this to everyone. He had behaved dishonestly, in taking from the river the stones that were there to hold back the current. Then he had sold them for his own profit, with no concern for the interests of others. He had not even replaced them with any substitute rocks to hold back the river's flow, so that the water would not break through the banks and flood. He had behaved greedily, said the fifty faces.

Nature would now judge him! The rocks had became the witness to all his greed and corruption.

Simo wanted to scream in protest. He wanted to find someone to defend him, who would speak highly of his services and so take the sting out of their case. But he could not make a sound. The fifty faces had now carved a relief all across his body. He accused them of subversive activities, of activities which aimed to topple his authority and power, without any hard evidence, based only on spite and jealousy. It wasn't fair! It was looking like an attempt to subvert his personal authority.

The strange thing was all the reliefs, now decorating his entire body, were in the form of writing. They exposed his thoughts—which until now had been suppressed by Simo's strength and power and so had had no voice. At least, he had been able to suppress them, in the hope that one day he would become unassailable.

All the statues engraved his body. Simo could not prevent them. He was powerlessness. He couldn't stop the writing going berserk all over his body. Then Simo's body was planted in the graveyard: like some ancient stone inscription! Then they signed his body with ink of blood and hate.

'Hey, what the hell do you want?', asked Simo defiantly of the leader of the faces, after he had regained his voice.

'Tak… tek… tak… tek… tak. La… la… la… li… li', they answered in chorus, their voices harmonious and sensitive.

'Whatever you might think of my current condition, there is no point in you pretending you're all so pure and holy. Fancy you, trying to judge me! I reckon you're all just plotting to attack me. Wanting to seize my power, as your maker and the one who holds sway over gravestones. My honourable headstones, come to your senses and do as I say. Reconcile yourselves to our agreement and the rules which we have determined together, and which have almost been promulgated', said Simo diplomatically.

'Tak… la… la… tek… li… li… tak… tak… tak!' answered the engravings inlaid onto his body, their voices echoing in unison. Various headstones endeavoured to speak loudest, wanting to compete with their leader, vying for the chance to speak directly with Simo whose body was covered in wild graffiti. The atmosphere was chaotic. The carved face that resembled Simo intervened. He carved into Simo even harder, on behalf of the fifty comrades.

'Dug… deg… deg… la… li… lo… lo… tak… tek… tek… tak!'

'I know you mean well. But look at how you're going about it! There is a right way to do this, so don't make all the other headstones suspicious. Or they'll all end up jumping on the bandwagon and suspecting me', said Simo displaying his oratory skill. He was diplomatic and composed, his thunderous voice even audible over the chorus coming from the fifty headstones.

'I respect what you're trying to do. But you are attacking what is your destiny. It was me who made you happy, helped you with my skills. It was me who created you all. So, it's me who should have the power over where you are placed and over everything to do with you, in whatever way I deem appropriate. You think about it, and don't create a fuss. Look at all the people who have no idea what you're on about, but who have already become the victims of your ambition', said Simo getting worked up.

'If a flood or some other natural disaster occurred, it was meant to happen. There was someone setting it up. Don't accuse me of causing floods and disasters, just because I took some stones from the river. After all, if I hadn't taken them none of you would be anything. You wouldn't have risen above the water-level and would have never been seen up here with human-beings. All you could ever have been were stones people squatted on when they are having a shit!' added Simo in annoyance. He could clearly see that the headstones were intending to carry out a coup d'etat by publicising his mistakes, forgetting his meritorious service and deeming him to be authoritarian and intent on selfish victory, while refusing to step aside for anyone else. This made him furious... so he accused them of subversion!

'Laaaaaaaaalaaaaaalaaaaaa' answered the headstones together. They appeared ill at ease. Determined, whatever the risks, to proclaim their signatures on other headstones. The tension neared breaking point. Simo twisted and stretched. His wife was nervous. Quickly a cloth compress was placed on her husband's brow. Simo took the medicine that the doctor had given him. He fell again into deep sleep. Simo's wife looked relieved; her husband appeared to be on the mend.

Meanwhile as Simo slept soundly the dialogue with the headstones became more heated, and their disagreement more pronounced.

The headstones were determined to spread the news to all the other headstones in all the other graveyards. So thousands of headstones demonstrated, creating a scene in all the cemeteries. People started to loose their nerve, hearing the rowdy noises coming from the graveyards. The headstones seemed to be swaying from side to side, as if the corpses that were under them were rebelling and trying to escape from the confines of their coffins. A hair-raising din arose from the headstones. It seemed they had forgotten to make offerings to the graves and their occupants!

Simo fell into deeper sleep. His wife was feeling happier—but had no idea of what was raging under his quiet composure as he slept.

Their dialogue was not reaching any agreement. The headstones accused Simo of being too greedy.

Simo's position as headstone maker was under increasing threat. Half conscious he shouted 'All of you headstones, especially the group of fifty—from today on, you are not allowed out of my house. As humans say, you're black-listed! As of this moment, you are under my surveillance. Look, I've already made new loyal headstones to supervise you all. Don't think that any of you can escape'. The fifty headstones fell silent. Their faces returned to their former state. Quiet. Dead, just like ordinary statues, not insinuating a thing. Returned to dumb stone. Only fit to be engraved and sold.

But suddenly it was as if the headstones were alive again. They began to attack the headstone whose face resembled Simo's. The forty nine headstones went berserk, smashing to pieces the entire headstone whose face was like Simo's.

The headstone that was similar to Simo screamed. He was now smashed into tiny pieces. His body scattered around. His face no longer recognisable. The forty nine headstones grinned smugly as they witnessed the destruction of their leader. Then they fell silent. The graves also returned to their former silence.

Simo blinked his eyes. His body felt well again. He was freed from the forty-nine frenzied headstones. Slowly he got up.

Simo looked startled and confused. Rubbing his eyes he saw dozens of local villagers carrying various weapons, used to destroy the headstone that resembled him. And they were lead by a young man well known to him: his own son!

Simo looked intently into his son's eyes. A rough groan ushered forth from his lips, like he was delirious. It was unclear.

The wailing siren screeched as it neared Simo's home. The huge convoy arrived in procession. They were there to pick up the ordered headstone of the official, so that it could be put in the soil above the official's corpse.

The sirens came nearer. The procession could now be seen quite clearly; they were in uniform. The headstone ordered by the official's family needed to be finished today, so that it could be placed on the grave immediately during the huge and extravagant ceremony.

Simo's trembling increased, as he witnessed the group, which had come to pick up the carving ordered by the official's family, approach his house. He was scared; the ordered headstone had already been smashed to pieces by the villagers. His own son had led them. He looked at his son who was smiling proudly. The procession arrived: Simo fainted again!

Everyone began to make a fuss. Someone called the doctor while another busily applied cold compresses. Simo came to.

The leader of the procession informed Simo that he wanted to pick up the headstone of the official. Simo was silent. Dumb. Before fainting again he informed them that the headstone they had ordered had been smashed to pieces. He became conscious again and asked for a drink of water. But when he saw the leader of the group, he fainted again! He was terrified of having to face everyone.

People began to whisper. They began to accuse each other of destroying the headstone ordered by the official's family. Fear spread across their faces. The weapons they had gripped firmly earlier, now began to drop from their grasp. Their faces paled; it seemed disaster was looming.

Then silence fell.

The locals who had been accused of smashing the headstone where herded down towards the road. They did not know where they were being taken!

They were accused of ruining the glorious ceremony, at which the headstone of the former colonial official was to be placed on his grave. The official had apparently been a very influential and respected man. This was proven by the willingness of the crowd to be herded along in an orderly and smooth manner. There was no force, let alone cruel treatment...(but who knows if they were pressured!). Sometimes cruelty is required to achieve a balance!

The people were escorted out of sight, later to face charges. Their charge: undermining the respect for a long deceased official. They had to take the consequences of their actions, in accordance with the current regulations governing insult to a corpse!!

Simo began to come to. He looked fresher. He noticed his house was quiet once more.

'Where is Wawan? He said he was off to university but it's been a while and he still hasn't come home, has he? Has he already gone off to do his fieldwork? I'm proud to have a son who can get a degree, even if I have to sell headstones to pay for his university and all the other things he needs. Where has Wawan gone? I miss him'. Haltingly Simo tried to speak. He still remembered his son, who had once suggested he look for a 'breath of fresh air' and go whoring! He would have to scold his son for having such thoughts, so that the boy did not poison the minds of his peers: because nowadays AIDS was everywhere.

Mrs Simo was quiet, ashen. She left her husband's questions hanging in mid air. Then it was quiet. Tears dropped from his eyes as he looked at the forty nine headstones scattered around; not yet taken by the people who had ordered them. He didn't know what the future held in store. What was the use of headstones that could not be drawn into conversation? The poor things were rained on and suffered in the heat. They couldn't be used for anything else; people were afraid to display them as house decorations because of the ill-fortune deep within!

(originally published as 'Dialog', in *Horison*, 1993, 1(27), January, pp.12–17.)

Support Our Troops

Amri Marzali

translated by Kenneth Eu Tuck Wah

America began its saturation bombing of Iraq on 15 January 1991, but it was more than a month before it felt confident that victory was definitely within its grasp. It demonstrated all manner of murder and bombardment despite the absence of any resistance: there were carpet bombs, napalm bombs, laser bombs, friendly bombs, smart bombs, the whole gamut. Shells landed on Saddam Hussein's War Command Headquarters, the radio broadcasting station, suspension bridges, date plantations, goat pens, and every other conceivable location.

Only after that did Bush instruct his people to gather at the Square of the state capital in Washington D.C. to witness his important announcement. 'Let us join together in a prayer for peace, and to support our troops'.

After that, the anti-war demonstrations, which initially seemed to be gaining strength, began to ebb, all across America. Anti-war groups became the declining minority, shrinking away like a snail from salt. On the other hand, demonstrations of 'Long Live America', 'Smash Iraq', or 'Support our Troops', spread like the falling winter snow. Those seeking to annihilate Iraq were less reluctant to take action than they had been before the war broke out. They were proud to be Americans. Giving support to our kids in the Gulf War. Such was the common theme of all demonstrations and the symbol used was a yellow ribbon.

The yellow ribbon was tied to the ends of car radio antennae, pinned on coat lapels, nailed to front doors. When I was returning from Salem in Rachmat's car, after visiting my mates

Teddy (as Sutedjo Harimurti was known) and Darmono, I even saw a huge yellow ribbon spread out across the front wall of an old church, making it look more like a political assembly hall rather than a place for holy worship. 'The Americans are starting to get a bit carried away with their victory', commented Rachmat.

The religious propaganda of Saddam Hussein had backfired against him. It wasn't clear whether he'd won the sympathy of the Muslims, but the anger of the Christians had become crystal clear.

I was still thinking about our visit to Teddy at his laundry business in Salem. He felt Saddam Hussein was going to lose. 'I feel sorry for the Muslims', he'd said. Everything had been completely wiped out by the American bombs.

Teddy was a warm, down-to-earth fellow. He had been living in America for 16 years after jumping ship from a freighter on which he had been working. Fortunately for him he had the common sense to complete his schooling, even though it meant some pretty hard times, eventually getting a Bachelor of Arts degree from Salem City College. After that, Teddy worked for a few years in a computer factory in Lynn, but it never quite suited him. He felt more contented working for himself. Now he owned a laundry and had the newspaper distribution agency for the whole city of Salem.

Teddy's life style was pretty comfortable now. He'd bought a house on instalment, where he lived with his Caucasian wife and two kids. The longer he lived in America, the more he knew about the West and the more devoted he became to Islam. Now his wife had even become a Muslim and was learning how to pray, he said.

Nevertheless, towards the end of our visit, I recall Teddy voicing his doubts as to whether the war against Saddam Hussein was really a war against Islam. After all, Egypt, Syria, Saudi Arabia and Kuwait, which were fighting against Saddam Hussein, were Muslim countries too. 'It's not clear who we should be supporting', he said looking puzzled.

From Teddy's place, we dropped in at Darmono's home in Lynn. Darmono was an old work-mate of Teddy's on the freighter. Like Teddy, Darmono too jumped ship and married a Caucasian girl and now had a 14 year old son. Like Teddy, Darmono was Javanese and, even more coincidentally, was also from Cilacap.

But unlike Teddy, Darmono had been baptised a Catholic before marrying his wife who was of Greek descent. Another difference between the two was that Darmono was very pro-America and hated Saddam Hussein. On the door of his son's room I noticed a 'Support Our Troops' sticker and a yellow ribbon.

We were offered lunch at Darmono's and while eating we chatted about his good prospects at his job in an electronics factory, the progress of my dissertation at Boston University, and about Rachmat's laboratory experiments at MIT.

'When are you going to finish your dissertations and head off home to Indonesia?' Darmono asked us.

'No idea!', we both answered in almost the same breath. We laughed. It was a bit of a joke, both answering at the same time, but it was because we were both facing the same challenge. Both Rachmat Nainggolan and I were struggling to complete our doctoral theses, which didn't seem to be heading anywhere. I was in the Composition Department of the School of Music and Rachmat Nainggolan was in the Physics Department.

This was my fifth year living and suffering in America, and for Rachmat it was his seventh, far from family, from Dad and Mum, brothers and sisters. I was close to Rachmat because we were both bachelors. We went everywhere together.

We didn't discuss the Gulf War which had become daily headline news in the paper and on television. I reckon Darmono would have guessed that the two of us hated the war, so he restrained himself out of concern for his guests' feelings, as one would expect given his Javanese ancestry. Although a Catholic and married to a Caucasian, he was still a Javanese. 'If you return to Indonesia, we'll really miss you. There'd be no Indonesian friends in Boston to visit us any more', said Darmono as he bid us goodbye at the front door. We took around 30 minutes to get home to Boston from Lynn.

Before Rachmat drove me to my place in Somerville, and then returned home to Arlington, we drove around down town. He liked just cruising around to fill up the weekend.

Suddenly at Prudence Road, we caught sight of an extraordinary scene. The eastern wall of the John Hancock Building, the tallest in Boston with 125 storeys (from the top, visitors can see the whole of Boston city!) was now covered by a huge American flag.

The entire eastern wall, from top to bottom, left to right, was covered by the famous Stars and Stripes. It was a huge flag! In the middle, there was a massive yellow ribbon. Below the ribbon great plastic letters spelling out 'Support Our Troops' were pasted onto the flag, which was tied at one metre intervals to the edge of the building. The middle section of the flag was also fixed to the wall every meter, stitched like a mattress, so as not to be easily blown away by the wind.

'What do you make of that, Mat?' I said to Rachmat. Actually I wasn't asking, only confirming the opinion of the Gulf War and the attitudes of the Americans that we both shared. Rachmat knew what I meant.

'Yeh…What do you reckon?', Rachmat sighed, dismayed but not unnerved. 'They're welcome to make a fuss and glory in their victory. But wouldn't you think one of the world's technological giants like America would be a bit embarrassed to celebrate a victory snatched from a tiny country like Iraq?' asked Rachmat, knowing I needn't answer because he already knew where I stood.

'You'd think they'd be ashamed, not proud! But… well…that's the way it is in America'. Rachmat Nainggolan seldom swore or got carried away. He rarely expressed hatred for anyone. He always tried to accept the way things were. Rachmat had experienced a lot about America through contact with his classmates at MIT, with flat mates, people he'd got to know in the library, in the pizza parlour, and elsewhere around the place. From all of this, he'd learned that America was a multi-ethnic society with great achievements, but precisely because of this, Americans often behaved really arrogantly.

From the John Hancock building we drove around to Newbury Road. At the third intersection we turned right into Exter Street, then left into Boylston Street, passing in front of the Boston Public Library (which is as huge as the Sate Building in Bandung!) then headed back towards the John Hancock building but from the back.

Beyond the library, there should have been a huge open space in front of the old Trinity Church built in 1733. The church was built of brick and a large portion of it was carved like the Borobudur temple. Even the roof was made from brick slate. The church looked black, brown, green and eerie. It gave a unique appearance to the modern centre of Boston. The square in front of the church covered an area of about 400 square metres. It was quite large. Here and there, around the square were steel benches for people to sit around.

Normally during the summer, there were lots of people here, taking a break after window shopping or visiting the art gallery down Boylston Street, resting their eyes after long hours in the Public Library, or adding to the plaque in their teeth by eating a whopper and french fries from Burger King across the road, or just hanging around. Besides this, there were normally homeless down-and-out Whites sitting or sleeping it off on one or two of the benches, always with an empty bottle of alcohol lying beneath the bench.

During the winter like now, the steel benches would normally be unoccupied. Who wants to sit outside and turn into an ice berg (like Malin Kundang who turned to salt)? All the trees in amongst the benches shed their leaves in autumn. Even the pigeons, which flock in their hundreds during summer to flit about and caprice for left over food or titbits tossed to them by the public, don't bother to drop in now.

In Jakarta I reckon all the open spaces like this have long since disappeared, exploited by officials from the Town Hall. The land would be sold off to someone who was just as hungry for profit as the bureaucrat, some entrepreneur who would turn the space into a shopping complex. Some bureaucrats in Jakarta can't sit still. It's like they've got some allergy; they're just itching to get their hands on any vacant land in the city centre.

Their entrepreneurial talents immediately emerge. The aesthetics of space and architecture in the city are beyond the breadth of their vision, for when they grew up, it was amongst the village paddy fields and rubber plantations.

When we reached the edge of the Public Library the scene on the square had changed dramatically. It was extraordinary! There was no open ground left. White tents had been erected. In several places fake date palms made from plywood had been stood up. Beneath them, were tied fake plywood camels. The palms and camels were painted to resemble the real thing. Wandering in and out of the tents were several Whites in blue denim jackets with *kaffiyeh* on their heads, like Yaser Arafat.

On each of the four corners of the area was a tall pole, tied with a yellow ribbon and flying an American flag. In front of several of the tents, were fixed signs saying 'Support Our Troops', as part of this extraordinary victory celebration.

Under normal circumstances, all this would contravene town-planning regulations, but these were special days. The City Council was exercising tolerance. This is usually how it works. Anywhere in the world, the Government will always treat breaches of the law sympathetically so long as any violation supports Government policies. Whether in super-democratic America, in *Pancasila*-ist Indonesia, or in Communist Cuba, it's all the same.

After passing the 'Support Our Troops' tent complex, we followed the huge city park called Boston Garden. From here, Rachmat headed for North 93rd Street, one of his favourite routes. We continued home, starting to feel fed up at the sight of yellow ribbons and 'Support Our Troops' labels.

After the massive land operation was launched against Saddam's troops for four consecutive days and nights, on 27 February at 9.00pm Bush announced from the White House that Iraq had been defeated. The Iraqis had been forced out of Kuwait and more, for even the southern part of Iraq had been occupied by American and Coalition forces. Such was the outstanding military strategy used by American General Norman Schwarzkopf.

At 24.00 (Eastern American Time) the American and Coalition troops were to cease their operations. Whether this postponement was to be followed by an armistice depended on the cessation of Iraqi hostilities against the American and Coalition troops, and scud missile launches against Saudi Arabia and primarily against Israel, plus a variety of other conditions. If Saddam Hussein remained intractable, the Americans were ready to occupy Baghdad and take Saddam to an international court, as had been the fate of the luckless Noriega of Panama.

Three cheers! Everyone in America was delighted. It was a great victory against Iraq, and it needed to be celebrated. America could be proud of its great achievement. It turned out Iraq was no more than a paper tiger when faced with the might of America.

Next morning I woke up at 6am as usual and switched on the television to get more news about the easy American and Coalition victory over Saddam's troops. The female newscaster was more spirited than usual, and yellow ribbon bubbled from her mouth whenever she uttered the words 'Support Our Troops'.

At 8.00am after breakfast, I left home for my office at Boston University. At first I walked along Holland Street heading for the underground train station (what people in Boston call the 'T station') in Davis Square.

The scenes on the left and right of the road were not the usual. More houses were hoisting the Stars and Stripes. As I crossed the road in front of Au Bon Pain coffee shop, I was nearly knocked over by a car happily speeding past. On the side window I noticed a new sticker with a picture of an American flag and the words 'Proud To Be American'.

Exactly six minutes walk from home, I reached Davis Square's T Station. After entering, I jumped on to the escalator heading towards the lower ground floor. While standing on the escalator I usually searched for the train pass in my pocket in order to save time, imitating the Americans who are supposed to be so efficient and culturally sophisticated.

At the toll entrance which is near the ticketing counter, I inserted my train pass into the 'shit hole' (that's what Boston students call the machine, in pretty poor taste for those with civilised sensibilities!). I pushed the toll gate open and walked down the stairs to the lower platform where passengers wait for the train.

A short while later, the T came from the direction of Alewife. From a distance I could see a huge yellow ribbon sticker pasted on front of the train's windscreen. It was apparently today's new addition. I said to myself, now even the T's joining America's celebration of victory over Iraq.

As usual in Harvard Square Station, lots of passengers got on the train, including a decrepid old lady helped by a young girl, who may have been her granddaughter. Plugged into the old lady's ears was a walkman, so her ears couldn't have been as senile as her legs. More impressive was the yellow ribbon pinned on her overcoat pocket as a sign of the victory. Thankfully, the old lady was still able to rejoice in American pride before departing for the Hereafter.

At Park Street Station, I changed from the red T to the green T heading for Boston University. The green T wasn't packed to overflowing this time; there were even a few vacant seats still left in the back.

Farther off at the front, a young White girl was seated facing the back of the train, that is, in my direction. She looked neat and pretty with her hair cut like Lady Diana, but her eyes looked tired as if she'd not had enough sleep. She may have quarrelled last night with the man she lives with. In Boston, especially among the students, living together and quarrelling are normal.

She didn't look like a student though. She was made up too neatly. She must have been an office worker, most of whom alight at Copley Square, the business district in the city centre.

The custom when sitting on the T in Boston is not to look anyone in the eye. If it does happen unintentionally or by accident, don't stare for long. Ogling at someone, looking stupid and confused like some Jakarta bumpkin, is considered insulting. You'd end up getting abused.

My eyes are 'made in Indonesia', and after all these years staring in Jakarta, they just can't stumble onto something stunningly attractive, without sticking to them like a leech to your calf. To adjust to the conventions required when sitting on the Boston T, I forced myself to pretend I was covering my face with my hands as if I was deep in thought. Every now and then I pretended to adjust my glasses, but the single motive was to sneak a glance at Lady Di sitting way off in front of me.

Suddenly, I saw her give a wide yawn, exposing her entire oral cavity. In Boston, unlike Indonesia, when yawning widely, there's no need to cover your mouth, because it's regarded as natural.

Such differences aren't surprising. As the Indonesian saying goes, 'Other places, other customs'. What surprised me about Lady Di's yawn was the inner cavity of her round mouth. Deep inside her throat was a shiny yellow ribbon and on its top, a sticker declaring 'Support Our Troops'.

I alighted at Boston University Central Station and went straight to the library instead of to my office, to read the free newspapers in the reading room. I wanted to know exactly how Iraq lost to America and the Coalition. In the newspaper such things are normally explained more clearly complete with a battle diagram and a map of the Middle East.

As I was flipping through the newspaper to read the important bits, a young White student pulled out a chair on the right in front of where I was sitting. While skimming the books he'd brought, his feet went up on the table top. It is an automatic response. His winter boots were directly opposite my forehead, as if offering me something to reflect upon.

A public notice, saying 'Please be courteous, considerate, and quiet. Thank you' that I'd noticed ages ago stuck up beside the reading room entrance door had had about as much impact as a Coca Cola poster on this student. You could chose to buy it, or not. Either that, or what was meant by 'Be Courteous' on the notice did not include sticking your feet up on the desk in front of other people.

But since everyone else in the reading room, front and back, left and right, said nothing, and simply busied themselves with their reading, I concluded that the student's behaviour was normal. I quickly tried to lower my blood pressure and calm the throbbing in my head. I returned to the newspaper in front of me, although not with much success.

After reading the newspaper, I left feeling peeved, and headed off towards my office in the School of Music. The experiences that I'd had these past few days had disoriented me. At times I'd felt revolted, bored and confused. Especially with the behaviour of the young student. I was not used to being insulted like that, at least not by a young student. Although I was now a student here, in Indonesia I was a well-respected academic. I, Herman Onesimus Manoppo from Bolaang Mangondow, felt like I'd been farted on!

But even on top of all of this, there was one thing that kept haunting me about the student's boot. I could still see before me the sole of the shoe, filthy from walking through the muddy snow, poking up in my face. Stuck on its sole was a yellow ribbon and a sticker: 'Support Our Troops'.

Boston University, 1 March 1991

(originally published as 'Beri Semangat kepada Pasukan Kita', *Horison*, 1993, XXVII(3), March, pp.99–103.)

A Banana in the Corpse's Stomach

M. Shoim Anwar

---

translated by Amanda Miller

The corpse's litter was slowly put down. The mourners who had come to pay their respects, formed a circle around the grave. Inside it were three people ready to receive the corpse which had been taken out of the bier. The smell of perfume from the body wafted quickly by as the mat wrapping was opened. White. White. White. The stillness was broken as people bowed in sorrow.

'Closer', I said to Kusmo, pulling his arm.

'This is far enough', he said looking at me intently.

Because there were so many mourners wanting to get close to the grave, I had to drag Kusmo by his arm slowly but surely to the front. Finally Kusmo stood there beside me. I knew he was unhappy that I made him come up close.

The shroud was slowly removed from the corpse's head. Idam's profile was visible, pale and frozen. After that the corpse's body was angled to the west, propped up by three fistfuls of earth. The call to prayer was heard echoing with a rhythm that trembled. The mourners were motionless. There was a woman standing near the grave, crying. Just then, a frangipani flower fell onto the heap of earth, then rolled into the grave and landed on the corpse's cheek.

'Allah…', sounded a voice at the grave's edge.

Suddenly Kusmo sighed, turning his head right around to the rear. For an instant I glared at him. He seemed to be holding something back. He looked around briefly, his eyes darting here and there. He was behaving so badly, especially for a time like this, when we were so visible up the front.

All of a sudden, completely unexpectedly, Kusmo turned around and took off, leaving the ceremony and forging his exit through the mourners. Immediately, their attention was drawn to him. Kusmo could be heard muttering something under his breath. The procession was really disrupted.

After the interment, a member of the deceased's family gave a word of welcome. The mourners were asked to draw near.

'On *Kliwon** Tuesday 30 June 1992, Idam departed this life for eternity. On behalf of the deceased's family, may we beg your forgiveness if Idam did anything wrong to any of you, during his life, either intended or otherwise. We also invite you to contact the family if Idam still had any loan or debts which his family may not know about'.

Rather than listen to the end of speech, Kusmo, already quite far from the graveside, quickly moved further away. How rude he was being! I felt he was being disrespectful towards the whole affair. I noticed him hanging around the front of the graveyard. The mourners were sure to have been offended by his behaviour. I felt personally insulted, since it was me who had urged him to pay his condolences and accompany me to the grave. What's more, Idam was a friend of ours, and these were the final respects for him.

I felt shocked at the news of Idam's death. It had only been two days since he last met me at Suripan's house.

'I want to collect writings of mine which were published a few years ago', said Idam leafing through some clippings.

'Do you want to publish them?'

'Maybe later when I'm dead someone may want to. That often happens, doesn't it?'

A few moments later, Idam's conversation turned to the paintings mounted on the wall.

'This Amang Rahman painting radiates a spirit of death', he said.

'You've been talking quite a bit about death today', I interrupted.

---

* Kilwon is the fifth day in the five-day Javanese week.

'Just take a look. This painting takes as its subject an old person with arms folded, painted in a greenish blue. While in their chest is depicted a small girl carrying a single flower as a symbol of the soul and the spirit that will soon be plucked'.

It was this which had now come to pass. The issue of death that Idam had spoken of over the last few days turned out to be so close. Maybe Idam began to feel that the door of death was beginning to open. He died suddenly after he had bathed, allegedly of a heart attack. But, I had been friends with him for several years and there were absolutely no indications that he suffered from a heart problem. People, maybe the doctor too, just wanted to take the easy way out, as no other cause for death was found. In such cases, it is said that so-and-so had a heart attack. Maybe people, or the doctors, really did look for some logical reason. But the existence of humankind is like an iceberg on the surface of the ocean. Logical things are like the ice which the eye can see. Whereas it is the invisible ice underneath the surface that is larger. It's a mystery that cannot be explained.

It's true that Idam's death really shocked a lot of people. He was taken away at a time when everyone was sure that his death could not possibly be so imminent. Yet despite this, Kusmo was willing to trample on the feelings of so many people. How could he be so very blatant in front of everyone?

'Kusmo, why did you act like an idiot when Idam was buried earlier?' I pounded on the door of his house. Kusmo was a little startled. He looked straight into my eyes.

'I'm sorry. I had to come home early', he said, without any regard.

'That was very hurtful!'

'I had already said I wasn't coming to pay respects, but you made me'.

'That's stupid, Kusmo. We had an obligation!'

'What obligation?' he said, his tone rising.

'To go to the bathing of the body, to pray and to accompany him to the grave. It's a community obligation'.

'There were already lots of mourners, weren't there?'

'What would happen if everybody thought like that?'

Kusmo didn't answer. He looked towards the ground. I felt a little happier in myself after broaching these sentiments. Kusmo still didn't feel he had done anything wrong. The atmosphere was still for a few moments. For an instant the room froze.

'Now', I said breaking the silence, 'why did you act that way?'

Kusmo gave a wry smile, nodding his head. Outside a dry wind was beating, carrying clouds of dust. I waited and waited for Kusmo's answer, yet his mouth remained locked tight. Suddenly I could no longer suppress my unease.

'You must have a reason!' I raised my voice a little.

'I saw a banana in the stomach of Idam's corpse', answered Kusmo lifting his head.

'A banana?'

'Yeh'.

'You're not still thinking about that banana of yours that Idam took at the reception?'

Kusmo nodded. I couldn't fathom how come Kusmo couldn't forget some old banana. Athough remnants were embedded deep within Kusmo, the incident had actually happened three years ago.

'You're so stingy, Kusmo'.

'I'm not stingy. This is a matter of honour and integrity. He swiped a banana which should have been mine by right. At a time when I really needed it. He may have only stolen a single banana, but he still took it without any regard for anybody else. What would it be like if he was some big official who had the chance to be corrupt every day?'

'What kind of comparison is that, Kusmo?'

'The point is, honesty has to start with trivialities. It is impossible for people to have integrity if they can't even be honest about small things. We can't belittle other people's rights'.

'I understand, Kusmo, but you must forgive. He won't be coming back'.

'How can I possibly forgive him; he wouldn't apologise while he was still alive. I hinted to him about it a couple of times, but he just roared with laughter like some boozy drunk. When he was being buried earlier, all the mourners were bowing and scraping, as if they were honouring someone holy. In fact, he was a bastard, gobbling down other people's bananas just as he pleased. Just at that precise moment I remembered my banana in his stomach'.

'Everyone has their faults, Kusmo, that's true. But his family have asked forgiveness. We have to show a little wisdom. You've been making an issue out of that banana for ages. You've never looked at the good as well as the bad in Idam. You keep going over and over the negatives, as if he has nothing but bad points. It's unbelievable that your own self-respect only adds up to a banana'.

'Stop!' said Kusmo butting in. 'You should be saying this to Idam. I'll bet that all the food he has ever consumed will appear before God in one great throng. One by one, He will question them. And it will be my banana, that he stole, which will protest to God. That banana will drag Kusmo to hell'.

'God is on the side of those who forgive, Kusmo', I said, feeling drained. 'God loves people who are sincere'.

'But God also hates dishonesty. He is on my side for sure! God won't allow people to steal bananas'.

'What kind of Satan has taken you over, Kusmo?'

'Satan will never side with those who uphold honesty'.

Suddenly I felt unsteady, up against Kusmo. This big-bellied huge bloke was now bringing God's name into this. He reckoned it was through small issues that we had to get close to God. It is impossible to get close to God, he went on, if you only counted the large events, and ignored the smaller ones.

Kusmo was never hesitant about forming his opinions. He would make his mind up very quickly. Kusmo used to be in the military, but he got out while still a corporal.

'If you're a corporal you're always ordered around', he once said. 'There's no opportunity to produce ideas'.

'You're too idealistic, Kusmo', I replied.

This deliberation about a banana seemed to stray right off the track. Kusmo was as steadfast as steel, holding firmly to his convictions. A few times he defended his position with what seemed like excessive enthusiasm. At one point he poked his finger at my face while he was talking. He would lift his rear-end from the chair, and walk around me as if acting in some dramatic play. At moments like this, I was sure his blood was boiling. His face was the colour of a rose. His eyes darted around out of control.

'Now, how about this, Kusmo', I took a stance. 'Let me take you to Idam's family to request they replace the banana'.

'Ask his family for a replacement?'

'Yes!'

'If I do that it'll mean my self-respect is only worth a banana!' Kusmo replied resolutely while jabbing his index finger at me. He looked at me mockingly.

'But that's the most sensible solution'.

'The problem now is not just a banana. It has developed into a certain state of mind. We can't deny that. We can be run over and our heads crushed by a truck, just because a speck of dust has lodged in our eye. I felt my self-worth had been rubbished, trampled upon when, in total disregard, Idam stole that banana right in front of me and ate it. After he'd gulped it down, he reshaped the banana skin and placed it back right in front of me. I really felt like an idiot when I went to eat it. Everyone laughed'.

'How do you know it was Idam who stole the banana?'

'Everyone pointed straight to him. They even said outright that Idam had swiped it. But he was putting on airs, pretending he didn't know anything. Spiteful bastard!'

Kusmo unexpectedly jumped onto the chair, squatting down like somebody wanting to defecate. His vision was piercing. His teeth chattered. It felt like the room would lunge out. There was a picture of a lion mounted on the wall, its mouth like a trap getting wider and wider. Kusmo's body gave the impression that it was about to explode. Beads of sweat seemed to be steaming. The beat of his heart pounded beneath his shirt.

'I was really offended'. Kusmo opened his mouth again. 'After the reception was finished, I went straight up to Idam. I wanted to pulverise him but he kept avoiding me, the queer bastard. For an instant, Hitler's soul entered my body. I took off after Idam. In the dimness I lunged out and grabbed him. The bloody bastard, he broke away and tried to run, spilling some food from the reception that I was carrying in my left hand. I was getting madder and madder. Idam poked the left side of my chest. Then he spilled the food he was carrying too. I stopped him just as he was about to run off. I brought him down, sprawling to the ground. Just then Bandi came along to break up the fight. A few blokes grabbed hold of me. Idam took the chance to make a break. But I couldn't keep still. Napoleon Bonaparte pulsed through my veins. Then I remembered, as a ex-cop, I had to remain always alert and able. I quickly flung aside the people holding me. They all tumbled over, head over heels. I took off after Idam in the darkness. As an old military man, I didn't want to be beaten'.

'Kusmo, you should have felt ashamed of yourself. Fancy an ex-cop making such a fuss over a banana not worth Rp.100'.

'That's precisely what is so special about the police. Even one hundred rupiah has to be investigated and dealt with. After all, it's still somebody's livelihood. But I haven't finished speaking. Don't cut in!'

Kusmo jumped down off the chair. Now he stood haughtily, hands on hips in front of me. Straightaway, he began complaining again.

'That night people began making a fuss. I continued to chase Idam. He ran home. I broke down the door of his house which he had closed. His wife and kids were scared. Idam ran off again, breaking through the back door. I made a dash for him. Meanwhile his wife was shouting for help. But, bloody hell! He had disappeared into the darkness. I lost his trail. For several days after that, I lay in wait for him but he didn't come out in the open. At that stage I wanted to slaughter him. I carried a knife wherever I went. I knew lots of people were whispering and gossiping about me but I didn't care! People are really unable to differentiate between rights and obligations. As a police officer I had been trained to make that distinction. Hitler's spirit continued to well up inside my body'.

'You keep mentioning that god-forsaken Hitler, Kusmo'.

'What do you mean, 'god-forsaken'? History is made up of the interests of a myriad of people. The facts are always turned upside down. You judge Hitler a demonic figure because your interests are different from his. Hitler emerged when the world was possessed by imperialism, when every nation was offered two choices: colonise or be colonised, attack or be attacked, dominate or be dominated. Hitler made an exacting decision. In a short space of time he was capable of knocking down his opponents. He was a star. Many large nations felt thwarted by the defeat they suffered. So, after Hitler fell, these crushed nations endeavoured to fashion world opinion about Hitler. But in point of fact, when the moment had come, they had failed to seize the upper hand. Hitler had been the victor. So whether one is a hero or a bastard is only a matter of perspective and interests. In his day, Hitler was a hero for his nation, and the Allies were the bastards! Get it!'

'That is going too far, Kusmo', I said.

'Too far?' his eyes opened wide. 'You want an example that's closer to home? In Indonesian history for example, we're acquainted with what is called the 'Dutch Aggression', but the Dutch use the term 'Police Action'. Now, do you reckon that our people were all such scoundrels and thieves that the Dutch had to install themselves as a policing force? And beautiful, gentle Cleopatra, who is admired by the Egyptians as a great alluring hero, who managed to subjugate her enemies with only flowers as weapons. Well, Westerners paint Cleopatra as a cruel scheming woman'.

'Let's get back to that banana now, Kusmo. You've talked for too long. You have been calling Idam a thief over one lousy banana. I'm afraid this is only a difference in opinion, like when you were judging Hitler earlier on'.

'No! No! At that reception we were not faced with a decision to dominate or be dominated. I had no interest in dominating Idam's banana, so our moral positions were neutral. What was at issue were our respective rights. Suddenly Idam stole my banana, which unbalanced the scales. This is where moral values say a lot. The relationship was corrupting and so became unbalanced. I am not hiding any facts. The question of perspective, as in those historical references earlier, is not valid. Morally and essentially, Idam is still a thief. Once a thief, always a thief.

Kusmo stamped his feet to the ground. It seemed the room would collapse. He patted his pot-belly. I felt at a loss. How on earth could the problems to do with a single banana be compared with global issues? Whether Kusmo was being stupid or smart was becoming increasingly unclear. Or maybe it was actually me who was not clever enough to understand the problem. If I was to think like Kusmo, then who could fittingly have been regarded the hero, Japan or America, when the Americans dropped atom bombs on Japan, annihilating innocent masses?

'So what do you want to do now, Kusmo?'

'Just let me stick to my own views!'

'But it could stop Idam's journey to face God for his final judgement'.

'Let him reap what he has sown, and account for all his deeds on earth'.

'Forgive him, Kusmo'.

'It isn't instructive. Forgiving tends to make people undisciplined. Because once forgiven, people usually aren't reluctant to repeat their deed again'.

'But God is all-forgiving, Kusmo'.

'That's precisely it. I don't feel like God does. I cannot be like God'.

'Kusmo, God's characteristics are examples for us'.

'God isn't as finicky as you!'

Suddenly my head broke open. Its debris flew into the air, scattering into the sky. With great difficulty I pulled myself together again. Kusmo quickly took off his shirt and hung it on a nail embedded in the wall. I looked at Mount Merapi perched on his body. Who knows what could be inside a stomach as big as that. This man as big as an elephant.

After I recovered I began to speak.

'Kusmo, you're so obstinate'.

'Get out of here. *Hell is the other*!'

'What did you say, Kusmo?' I was startled once again.

'Hell is other people. That's what Sartre said'.

'Sartre? That's what some frustrated madman would say!'

'Stop! I am my own responsibility!'

'You prick!'

Since then my relationship with Kusmo hasn't been very close. Maybe he thought that I had interfered too much in his affairs. He was a tough nut. At least I felt relieved I'd got everything off my chest about him. For days Kusmo disappeared from circulation. He could enjoy his life more without the burden of all the whispers. In the end I was really shocked when news spread that Kusmo had passed away. The motor cycle he was driving ran over a banana, skidded and fell. Kusmo was flung off and was run over by a truck which happened to be speeding along behind him. Kusmo's body was crushed beyond recognition. Silently I regretted what had happened.

For an instant I thought maybe the banana which caused his death, came from the stomach of Idam's corpse!

Surabaya, Jombang, July 1992

(originally published as 'Sebiji Pisang dalam Perut Jenazah', *Horison*, 1993, 4, April, pp.129–33; then an extended version was included in M. Shoim Anwar, 1993, *Musyawarah Para Bajingan*, Gaya Masa, Surabaya, pp.55–65.)

Publication Details

'Swaying' by Gerson Poyk was originally published as 'Oleng-kemoleng', 1968, *Horison*, 7(3), pp.200–1, 223.

'Applause on a Journey', by Gerson Poyk was originally published as 'Tepuk Tangan Perjalanan', 1970, *Horison*, 6(5), pp.170–72, 175.

'A Letter' by Putu Wijaya was originally published as 'Ini Sebuah Surat', 1970, *Horison,* 5, pp.132–34, and reprinted in Ajip Rosidi (ed.), 1977, *Laut Biru Langit Biru*, Pustaka Jaya, Jakarta, pp.595–600.

'Jakarta' by Totilawati Tjitrawasita was originally appeared in Indonesian in *Mimbar*, 1972, 21(2), pp.39–41 and then in *Sebuah Cinta Sekolah Rakyat*, 1976, Pustaka Jaya, Jakarta, pp.38–45.

'Matias Akankari' by Gerson Poyk was originally published in Gerson Poyk, 1972, *Matias Akankari: Kumpulan Cerita Pendek*, Balai Pustaka, Jakarta (2nd ed., 1975).

'Coming Home' by Wildan Yatim was originally published as 'Pulang' in *Budaya Jaya*, 1973, 63(6), pp.491–512.

'Drought' by M. Fudoli Zaini was originally published in *Dari Jodoh Sampai Supiyah*, 1976, Radio Nederland Wereldomroep & Djambatan, Jakarta, pp 70-76

'Telephone' by Chairul Harun was originally published as 'Telepon', *Horison*, 1976, 10–11(XI), October-November, pp.332–35.

'The Lebaran Prayers of a Group of Political Prisoners in a Concentration Camp' by Sides Sudyarto DS was originally published as 'Sholat Lebaran Kawanan Tahanan Politik dalam Sebuah Kamp Konsentrasi', *Horison*, 1977, XII(8), pp.249–51.

'The Critic' by Pamusuk Eneste, was originally published as 'Sang Kritikus', *Horison*, 1980, p.125.

'Generals' by Pamusuk Eneste was originally published as 'Jenderal-jenderal', *Horison*, 1980, p.130.

'The Debt' by Jasso Winarto was originally published as 'Utang', *Horison*, 1980, 5(15), pp.160–61, 165.

'Long Life for Mr Joyokoyoroyo and his Cronies' by Hamsad Rangkuti, was originally published as 'Umur panjang untuk Tuan Joyokoyoroyo CS', *Horison*, 1980, 8(15), pp.267–70.

'The General Smiles on 17th August' by Hamsad Rangkuti was originally published as 'Senyum seorang jenderal pada 17 Agustus', *Horison*, 1980, 9(15), pp.303–05.

'The Factory' by Nh. Dini, was originally published as 'Pabrik' in Nh. Dini, *Tuileries*, Sinar Harapan, 1982, Jakarta, pp.37–48.

'Cancer' by M. Fudoli Zaini, was originally published as 'Kanker', *Horison*, XIX(7), 1984, pp.290–93.

'Pop dreaming' by Y. B Mangunwijaya was originally published as 'Renungan Pop', *Horison*, 1985, XIX, pp.62–64.

'The Governor's Cats' by A.A. Navis was originally published as 'Kucing Gubernuran', *Horison*, 7(XXI), 1986, pp.239–41.

'On the Dark Side of the Moon' by Moes Loindong was originally published as 'Di Balik Matahari', *Horison*, 1992, 12, pp. 423–27.

'Dialogue' by Safron Rasyidi Sidal was originally published as 'Dialog', *Horison*, 1993, 1(27), pp.12–17.

'Support Our Troops' by Amri Marzali was originally published as 'Beri Semangat kepada Pasukan Kita', *Horison*, 1993, 3(XXVII), pp.99–103.

'A Banana in the Corpse's Stomach', by M. Shoim Anwar was originally published as 'Sebiji Pisang dalam Perut Jenazah', *Horison*, 1993, 4, pp.129–33; then included in M. Shoim Anwar (1993) *Musyawarah Para Bajingan*, Gaya Masa, Surabaya, pp.55–65.

Further Reading

The following books may be helpful to readers of English with a desire to become more familiar with Indonesian fiction in translation.

Select Discussions of Indonesian Literature

Foulcher, Keith 1986, *Social Commitment in Literature and the Arts: The Indonesian Institute of People's Culture 1950–1965*, Centre of Southeast Asian Studies, Monash University, Clayton.

Roskies, D.M. (ed.) 1993, *Text/Politics in Island Southeast Asia: Essays in Interpretation*, Ohio University Monographs in International Studies, Southeast Asia Series No. 19, Athens, Ohio.

Teeuw, A. 1967, 1979, *Modern Indonesian Literature*, (Volumes 1 & 2), Martinus Nijhoff, The Hague.

English Translations of Indonesian Fiction

Ajidarma, Seno Gumira, 1995, *Eyewitness*, (trans. Jan Lingard with Bibi Langker and Suzan Piper), Imprint, Sydney.

Allen, Pamela (trans.) 1995, *Women's Voices: An Anthology of Short Stories by Indonesian Women Writers*, Longman, Melbourne.

Aveling, Harry (ed. & trans) 1975, *Gestapu: Indonesian Short Stories on the Abortive Communist Coup of 30th September 1965*, Southeast Asian Studies Program, University of Hawaii.

—— (ed. & trans) 1976, *From Surabaya to Armageddon: Indonesian Short Stories*, Heinemann, Singapore.

—— (trans.) 1986, *Crossing the Border: Five Indonesian Short Stories* (by Danarto and Pramoedya Ananta Toer) Centre of

Southeast Asian Studies, Working Paper No.38, Monash University, Clayton.

Chudori, Leila S., 1989a, 'Thumps of Gumboot Dance on Water', *Solidarity*, 122, April-June, pp.140–45.

—— 1989b, 'The Purification of Sita', (trans. by Claire Siverson), *Solidarity*, 123, July-Sept, pp.126–29.

Danarto 1978, *Abracadabra* (trans. Harry Aveling), Heinemann, Singapore.

Hendon, Rufus S., 1968, *Six Indonesian Short Stories*, Yale University SEA Studies Translation Series.

Hoerip, Satyagraha (ed.) 1991, *New York After Midnight: 11 Indonesian Short Stories*, Executive Committee, Festival of Indonesia USA 1990–1991, Jakarta.

Idrus 1982, 'Another Road to Rome', (trans M. Cammack), *Indonesia*, 34, October, pp.41–54.

—— 1986, 'The New Java', (trans. by T.J. Hudak), *Indonesia*, 41, April, pp.131–34

—— 1988, 'Kota harmoni' (trans. by T.J. Hudak), *Indonesia* 45, April, pp.105–8.

Kartodikromo, Mas Marco 1981, *Three Early Indonesian Short Stories*, (trans. Paul Tickell), Centre for Southeast Asian Studies, Working Paper No.23, Monash University, Clayton.

Lubis, Mochtar 1982, *A Road with no End*, (trans. Anthony Johns) Graham Brash, Singapore.

—— 1983, *Twilight in Jakarta*, (trans. Claire Holt), Oxford University Press, Kuala Lumpur

—— 1987, *The Outlaw and Other Stories*, (trans. Jeanette Lingard), Oxford University Press, Singapore.

—— 1991, *Tiger!,* (trans. Florence Lamoureux), Select Books, Singapore.

Mangunwijaya, Y.B., 1991, *The Weaverbirds* (trans. Thomas M. Hunter), Yayasan Lontar, Jakarta.

McGlynn, John H., (ed.) 1992, *Menagerie 1*, Lontar Foundation, Jakarta.

Mihardja, Achdiat K., 1972, *Atheis* (trans. by R.J. Maguire), UQP, St Lucia.

—— 1990 'A Twist of Fate' (Belitan Nasib) (trans. D.M. Roskies), *Indonesia*, 49, April, pp.117–26.

Navis, A.A., 1991, 'The Helmet' (intro. and trans. by D.M. Roskies) *RIMA*, 25, pp.53–63.

Pane, Armijn 1988, *Shackles: A Novel*, (trans. by J. H. McGlynn), Lontar Foundation, Jakarta.

Poyk, Gerson 1987, 'The Love Letters of Alexander Rajagukguk' (trans. M. L. Wang), *Indonesia,* 43, April, pp.30–42.

Rafferty, Ellen & Laurie J. Sears (eds), 1988, *Bomb: Indonesian short stories by Putu Wijaya*, CSEAS, University of Wisconsin, Madison.

Simatupang, Iwan 1975, *The Pilgrim* (trans. H. Aveling), Heinemann, Hong Kong.

—— 1978, *Drought* (trans. H. Aveling), Heinemann, Singapore.

—— 1986, *Kooong: The Story of a Pigeon* (trans. Swami Anand Haridas (H. Aveling)), Writers Workshop, Calcutta.

Toer, Pramoedya Ananta 1975a, *The Fugitive*, (trans. H. Aveling) Heinemann, Hong Kong.

—— 1975b, *A Heap of Ashes*, (trans. H. Aveling) UQP, St Lucia.

—— 1982, 'Mrs Veterinary Doctor Suharko', (trans. B. Anderson), *Indonesia,* 34, October, pp.65–74.

—— 1989, 'Times' (trans. D.T. Sicular), *Indonesia*, 47, April, pp.19–24

—— 1990a, *Awakenings*, (trans. M. Lane) Penguin, Harmondsworth. (This volume is a re-issuing of two novels, previously published by Penguin as *This Earth of Mankind* and *Child of all nations*.)

—— 1990b, *Footsteps*, (trans by M. Lane), Penguin, Ringwood.

—— 1991, *The Girl from the Coast*, (trans by H. Aveling), Select Books, Singapore.

—— 1992, *House of Glass*, (trans by M. Lane), Penguin, Ringwood.

